Better Luck Next Time

ALSO BY JULIA CLAIBORNE JOHNSON

Be Frank with Me

Better Luck Next Time

A Novel

Julia Claiborne Johnson

HARPER LARGE PRINT
An Imprint of HarperCollins*Publishers*

This is a work of fiction. Names, characters, places, and incidents are products of the author's imagination or are used fictitiously and are not to be construed as real. Any resemblance to actual events, locales, organizations, or persons, living or dead, is entirely coincidental.

 For information, address HarperCollins Publishers, 195 Broadway, New York, NY 10007.

HarperCollins books may be purchased for educational, business, or sales promotional use. For information, please e-mail the Special Markets Department at SPsales@harpercollins.com.

FIRST HARPER LARGE PRINT EDITION

ISBN: 978-0-06-306296-2

Library of Congress Cataloging-in-Publication Data is available upon request.

21 22 23 24 25 LSC 10 9 8 7 6 5 4 3 2 1

FOR

MY FATHER,

briefly the cowboy;

AND

MY MOTHER,

always the doctor.

A girl must marry for love, and keep marrying until she finds it.

—Zsa Zsa Gabor

Marriage is a wonderful institution. But who wants to live in an institution?

—Groucho Marx

Prologue

Tennessee, 1988

Yes, you have come to the right place. Dr. Howard Stovall Bennett III at your service.

Hand me that magnifying glass, will you, and I'll have a look at what you've got there. That's me, all right, the tall one in the beat-up Stetson, surrounded by all the ladies. When I first got that hat I had to run it over with the ranch's station wagon so it didn't look too new. I must have been, let me see now, twenty-four, twenty-five years old. Hard to believe I was ever that young. I was flat broke, but I was pretty then, and jobs were hard to come by during the Depression. If somebody offered me one, I took it. Working on a dude ranch outside Reno that catered to the divorce trade beat the heck out of digging ditches, I can tell you that.

Some men are born gigolos; others have it thrust upon them. That's a little joke I always told myself in later years when a nurse or one of my fellow doctors noted the excellence of my bedside manner. Some knuckleheads seem to think bedside manner can't be taught. Hogwash. Anybody with a lick of sense and a little compassion can pick up the essentials. Make eye contact, let the person hurting tell you what pains them, and for heaven's sake, if you have cold hands, run them under hot water or rub your palms together before you start examining a patient.

Of course I'm joking when I say that. A gigolo? Far from it. The cowboys at the Flying Leap were there to look at, not to touch. Fraternization with our guests was in fact grounds for getting yourself fired. We were on hand to do chores around the ranch, of course, but mostly we were hired to squire rich, brokenhearted ladies around Reno, hold their purses while they shopped, and lead them on trail rides through the high desert. We chatted with them about the weather, offered a sympathetic ear when they wanted to talk about their troubles, told them they looked good when they needed to hear it most. All excellent training for a career in medicine, if you ask me.

So, sure, pull up a chair. I'd be happy to tell you what I know. No, I don't mind if you record our conversation. This will be a treat for me, particularly after all these years. I learned long ago not to talk about my cowboy past because people have such lurid tabloid sensibilities that it was hard to make anybody understand what that job was like. I'm as bad as anybody, I guess, making light of something I have no business making jokes about. It was serious work, taking care of our ladies during such a painful time in their lives. I think I learned more about the subtleties of suffering and the milk of human kindness working on the ranch than I did in all the years that came after. I wouldn't take anything for that experience.

Let's see if I can identify the other characters in this photograph for you. First and last names? Well, I'll try. Here's the other cowboy who worked alongside me. Sam. He favors Gary Cooper in *High Noon,* don't you think? What? You've never seen it? Well, you're missing out. It's a good one. Was on the late show just last week. I stayed up half the night watching it. An upside of retirement, knowing nobody needs you to be anywhere that matters in the morning. Nobody cares anymore.

Sam's last name was Vittori, that I know. Now, this gentleman in the sharp-looking suit, that's Max.

Maxwell Gregory. Used to be some kind of businessman in Chicago. Came to Reno looking for fresh air and investment opportunities and a way out of the big bad city. Margaret, here, with the curly black hair and Shirley Temple dimples, his partner in business and in life, ran the house, kept the books, dispensed wisdom. She'd read about divorce ranches in a movie magazine, as I remember, and convinced Max to buy a washed-up cattle ranch and set up shop. The idea of busting out of failed marriages and starting fresh was more or less a new idea then, you see, and Reno was the place to do it. After six weeks hand-running of residency there our guests were legally unhitched by the great state of Nevada. Free to roll the dice again, if they so desired. Many a second marriage I know of has outperformed the first. Yes. Exactly. Not going in with blinders on. It's when you get up into the third and fourth and seventh ones that people may start to wonder, but who's to say? It might take that many tries to pick a winner.

Anyway. Max hired a Hollywood set designer to make the place over into the movie-magazine version of the Old West—boulders, sagebrush, a corral, what have you. Margaret renamed the ranch The Flying Leap and got it outfitted with the modern amenities the clientele they were after wouldn't want to do without—electricity, indoor plumbing, a telephone. The two of them were such delightful hosts that the well-heeled and often-married set came back there for all their divorces, or tried to.

This blonde on my left who's as tall as I am, for example, was one of our repeat customers, Nina O'Malley. Max and Margaret loved her. So did Sam. So did I, eventually. Her partner in crime that go-round was this one, Emily Sommer. Nina and Emily must be old women now, or dead. Imagine that. These other half a dozen ladies, give me some time and maybe their names will come to me.

You know, I used to have a copy of this very photograph. Funny, isn't it, how you're sure you'll never want to see a thing again but after it's lost to you, you wish you had it back again. How much time you got? I believe I could fill your whole book with the shenanigans from that single six-week cycle. It came right at the tail end of my time there, as it happens, so I remember it better than I might otherwise. Something like fifty years ago now. Hard to believe.

Chapter One

Nevada, June 1938

I drove the stagecoach to the airport to pick up Nina.

Back when Max and the Hollywood set designer had been shopping for frontier paraphernalia for the ranch, they'd stumbled onto it rotting under a tarp in a shed over in Virginia City. Max bought the stagecoach on the spot, figuring it would be a smart promotional gimmick, the ideal vehicle for picking up ladies at the train. He got that creaky old gut-juggler refurbished and painted a Pegasus on its doors. The winged horse, yes, jumping through a hoop of words that read *The Flying Leap Dude Ranch.* Max wanted to add a slogan, a line a Reno judge used every time he gaveled a woman from wife to divorcée: *Better luck next time.* But

Margaret, always the voice of reason, put the kibosh on that.

I don't know how much Max paid for our antediluvian taxi, but it was worth every penny. It was all but guaranteed a guest's face would light up when she realized the coach had come for her. You could see her thinking that her once-upon-a-time might not be over and done with yet if such a good-looking cowboy awaited her, ready to relieve her of her baggage and hand her inside that carriage. Max called that old rattletrap conveyance the Mixmaster because he swore an hour of being shaken half to death inside it could make friends of women with little in common other than great wealth and marital distress. Friends, if not for life, at least for their stretch with us, which was what we cared about.

The day Nina arrived I'd shucked off my shirt while I hitched four of our six horses to the coach. My mother would have had the vapors if she'd caught me working shirtless anyplace where a lady might lay eyes on me. Max, however, instructed us to strip to the waist whenever we did chores, weather permitting. A little perk for the clientele, honest labor and rippling muscles being two things our affluent ladies might not have seen very much of lately, or at all.

But that afternoon was hotter than the hinges of hell, so I had no qualms about going around half-naked. There was no one around to see, anyway, Sam having volunteered to drive all our other guests into town in the wood-paneled Chevrolet. Margaret was busy with the endless chores inside the house that came of taking care of the eight ladies, give or take, we had in residence at any one time. Max had gone to the courthouse to stand witness for a departing guest, swearing on a Bible that Suzy had not set foot outside Nevada for the past six weeks. As soon as the judge proclaimed Suzy Nevada's newest legal resident and Reno's freshest grass widow, she'd board a train for her real home, Chicago.

Emily, as it turned out, had stayed behind while the others went into town. She'd arrived at the ranch a few evenings earlier behind the wheel of a Pierce-Arrow she'd driven solo the two hundred or so miles from San Francisco, sitting on top of a big square pillow to make her tall enough to see over the steering wheel without getting a crick in her neck. She'd pulled into the barnyard just before dusk, the top of her convertible lowered for the breeze, her uncovered hair whipped into a rat's nest. Darkness fell around 9:00 P.M. that time of year, so Emily's arrival had raised quite a ruckus among our guests and also the chickens, both groups just starting to make noises about settling in for the night. By the time her luggage was unloaded and the cooling engine had stopped ticking, some of the poultry had roosted on the Pierce-Arrow's windshield and the barn cats were sharpening their claws on its upholstery. I shooed the critters off and put the sedan in an outbuilding next to the stagecoach, then covered it with the Mixmaster's antique tarp.

The other women congratulated Emily on her bravery for undertaking such an epic voyage alone. "Not brave," she said. "Desperate. If I hadn't left when I did, I wouldn't have left at all." She had the plummy accent of women who cycled through the Seven Sisters colleges back East, but her voice was surprisingly deep and gravelly for such a little thing.

"My dear, your voice," one of our older ladies said. "You sound absolutely exhausted."

"Oh, I always sound like this," Emily said. "I'm sure it was cute when I was five years old, but now—" She shrugged and shook her head. "Fingernails on a chalkboard. According to my darling husband, anyway. But yes, I am very, very tired."

A couple of days in Margaret's care, however, had perked Emily up considerably. Just as I was hitching up the last of the horses to head over to the airport, she appeared at my elbow saying, "Well, if it isn't Cary Grant in cowboy boots."

She had on a pair of cowboy boots herself, with a loose summer dress, a look I'd never seen back then that I've noticed some of the young girls go for now. Emily always put her own spin on the rich-lady uniforms our guests wore at the ranch: the tight-legged, baggy-seated jodhpur pants and tall English boots they all brought along for horseback riding, for example, that they'd replace with cookie-cutter fancy western wear bought in Reno, which they'd abandon as soon as they were home again. There was a sameness about our guests' coiffures, too, lacquered into submission usually and blond more often than could be natural from a statistical standpoint. What Sam used to call "suicide blondes," as in "dyed by their own hands." Emily's hair, however, was an untamable mass of dark ringlets, the bedspring kind that begged to be pulled straight and released back into coiled spirals. She had huge, wide-set brown eyes and a Kewpie doll's little curved mouth, which, along with her small stature, gave her the appearance of an unusually wise and solemn child. Until she spoke, that is, in a rasp that suggested her vocal cords had been freshly tuned up on a cheese grater.

As I'd thought Emily had gone into town with the others, I like to have jumped out of my skin when I heard her voice. "I'm sorry," she said. "I didn't mean to startle you."

"I confess you got the drop on me, ma'am," I said. While I was hitching up the team I'd fallen to brooding about a departed lacquered blonde just a year older than I was who I'd risked my job to be with the summer before. Now, what was her name? Rachel? Mitzi? Laura or, perhaps, Laurie? Funny, there was a time I believed I'd never forget that woman. Go figure. I do remember she always wore door-knocker-sized emerald earrings, day and night, that matched her green eyes. I know that because I remember thinking she must have paid as much for those earrings as my parents' house was worth before the Crash.

From the way Emily had her eyes fastened on the bandana I had knotted at my neck, I suspected my naked chest was making her uncomfortable. I untied my shirt from around my waist, wiped my face on the sleeve, and pulled it on. "What can I do for you, ma'am?"

"So this is the stagecoach I've heard so much about," Emily said. "Where are you taking it?"

"To pick up a guest."

"Can I come, too?"

"I'm not going to the train depot, if that's what you're thinking," I said. "The airport is in the opposite direction. If you wanted to go into Reno you should have gone in with Sam and the others when you had the chance."

"I've been into town already. Yesterday. I bought these boots." Her boots were red, intricately embroidered, and possibly cost more than a semester of Ivy League tuition. Emily seemed surprised to see them on her feet. "I didn't think I needed cowboy boots, but the salesman said I had to have them if I was staying on a ranch. He told me they were the best insurance there was against rattlesnakes and other varmints. He used 'varmint' in a sentence. How could I resist that? My daughter's feet are as big as mine are already, so I thought there was a chance she'd insist on taking these boots from me when I get home. I've already sent her a postcard telling her all about them. I figured she'd read a postcard whether she wanted to or not before tearing it up and throwing it in the trash, which is what she said she'd do with my letters so I shouldn't waste my time writing any."

She cleared her throat, then cleared it again and swallowed hard, all signs I'd come to recognize by then as precursors of a come-apart. "The other ladies said they were either going in to shop or gamble this afternoon," she added with forced cheerfulness. "I decided not to go with them because I don't like shopping much and I really don't like gambling."

And yet you got married, I thought but did not say. By the summer of 1938 I'd seen plenty of evidence that matrimony was about the biggest crapshoot going. There's nothing like working a divorce ranch to make a person question the likelihood of happily ever after. I dug a bandana from my pocket and offered it to Emily just as her brimming eyes spilled over. Max equipped each of his ranch hands with an endless supply of these brightly patterned cowboy hankies for moments just like this. "What's your daughter's name?" I asked.

"Portia. I tried to get her to come with me, but—" She shook her head and looked away. "She's thirteen. You know how that is."

I didn't, not then, but I nodded anyway. "Portia," I said. "The pound-of-flesh girl in Shakespeare."

"Oh. You know that play?" Emily asked, surprised. "It's one of my favorites. All the characters get what's coming to them. It almost makes a person believe there could be justice in the real world. What's your name, cowboy?"

"Ward," I said.

"How old are you, Ward? If you don't mind me asking."

"I'm twenty-five, ma'am. Almost."

She smiled. "I remember being twenty-five, almost. Just barely. Portia was three years old. I don't think I'd slept through the night once between then and the day she was born. I know Portia hadn't. Do you know, I almost miss that time? She used to start crying if I left the room, and now she wants nothing to do with me. Before I left, my daughter told me I'm the dullest, most predictable person she's ever met. That she can't believe I waste my breath talking when she always knows exactly what I'm going to say. Can you imagine saying something so hurtful to your mother?"

"No, ma'am, I cannot," I said. My mother, Pamela, and I were close, as close as people could be when one lived in Tennessee and the other in Nevada, back when nobody made long-distance phone calls unless somebody had died.

Emily gave me a watery smile. "Oh, well," she said. "Would it be all right if I came along to the airport? The other women keep talking about riding in the stagecoach. I feel left out."

I'd been looking forward to my solo journey out, me all by my lonesome up in the driver's box, a double fistful of reins in my hands, parched sepia fields scrolling past, a Sam-rolled cigarette I'd never smoke tucked behind an ear. Somewhere some tattered scraps of poetry I wrote about such a day might still exist, but I sure hope not. "Maybe another time," I said. "It's hot as blazes inside the coach this time of day." I stepped on the front carriage wheel and hoisted myself up top. "If you'll pardon me, ma'am, I really have to get going now. I don't want to keep our guest waiting."

"If it's so hot inside I could ride up there with you," Emily said. "I promise I won't say a word. You won't even know I exist."

I couldn't have it getting back to Margaret that I was refusing such an innocent request. "All right. Put your foot on the spoke of the wheel there, like I did, and hop on up." I leaned over and offered her my hand. Thanks to the looseness of her dress I guess I hadn't realized how slight she was, because when she hopped and I pulled I almost threw her clear over the stagecoach instead of into the driver's box. She landed more or less on top of me.

"Sorry about that," I said after I scraped her off and settled her on the seat beside me. "You're lighter than I thought you'd be considering how big your head is."

"I have a lot of hair," she said. "Also I've lost weight lately. Not on purpose."

Ah. The Heartbreak Diet. Food on the table, but no appetite for it. Lots of our ladies came to us looking famished from it. In my early days on the ranch I confess I begrudged them the luxury of pushing a full plate away when so many people were going hungry. But it didn't take me so very long to come to understand that our ladies' brand of anguish counted, too. No fair saying their suffering wasn't genuine just because they had money in the bank and a bed to sleep in. Pain is pain.

I dug around in my pocket and handed Emily another bandana.

"I won't need that. I'm done with crying," she said.

"It's to keep dust out of your nose and mouth," I said. "Come to think of it, you need a hat. Did the salesman talk you into one to go with those boots?" I wasn't excited about handing over mine once the sun started scrambling her brains. Also, once she went inside to fetch her own hat she might decide she didn't want to come along after all. Then she would be Margaret's problem.

"No," she said. "How far are we going?"

"About four miles."

"Is that all? I won't need a hat for that."

"The sun is fierce this time of day," I said. "Tell you what. You wear my hat. It should fit. I've got an awful big head, too."

"I couldn't take your hat," she said. "What will happen to you?"

"Me? I'm like an old piece of leather already. Please, take it. Margaret will have my hide if I let you get sunburned on my watch."

"Well, in that case."

My hat was a little sweaty, so I tucked yet another bandana inside before I put it on her head. It fit nicely. Then I showed her how to tie the other bandana over her nose and mouth, bandit-style, against the dust the horses were about to kick up.

"Thanks," she said, knotting it in place. "So the new guest is coming in an airplane? How exciting! I've never been on an airplane. Have you?"

"About as often as you've ridden a stagecoach, ma'am." I picked up the reins and squinted off toward the road. The sun was so bright that I could still see the afterimage of the ranch house projected on the back of my eyelids when I closed my eyes against the glare. While I had them shut Emily touched my elbow and I jumped.

"I didn't mean to startle you again," she said. "I should have said your name instead. Ward. Like an orphan in a Victorian novel. Taken in by a relative."

"Yes," I said. "Like that."

Chapter Two

I believe Emily had a crush on Nina from the beginning. I could hardly blame her. I was pretty dazzled by Nina, too.

"Is she some kind of gold digger?" Emily asked before either of us laid eyes on her. "I've heard of women burying three husbands over the course of a lifetime, but a woman anywhere close to my age who's *divorced* three! None of my friends have gotten divorced even once."

As promised, Emily hadn't said a mumbling word on the way out, just raked the surroundings with those eyes of hers and furrowed her brow a few times. The stagecoach traveled at a blistering speed of six miles an hour, tops, so she had plenty of time to take everything in. Once we arrived and I had the horses settled, she turned her headlamps on me and let loose with, "So who's this Nina?"

When I'd asked Sam more or less the same question, he'd resettled his cowboy hat on his head, squinted, and said, "Nina? She's a stem-winder." Nina had been just shy of twenty when she arrived with the first octet of pre-divorcées come to wait out their six weeks at the Flying Leap, and had repeated some years later. I gathered Max and Margaret were fond of her or she wouldn't have been welcomed back. Let me tell you, it was a job of work, juggling the comings and goings of our guests. My hat goes off to Margaret there. It was easier for everybody involved if our guests arrived more or less in batches. Over the years, however, between choreographing all the comings and goings and not-going-through-with-its and managing a wait list about as long as your arm, our ladies' six weeks spent with us weren't always in perfect sync.

To help herself keep things straight when she did the booking and, eventually, to thin the herd, Margaret kept score on past guests in a secret ledger locked in her desk drawer. *Fight-picker, drunk by lunchtime, mean to staff, loudmouth, idiot,* or, worst of all, *bore.* I once passed Margaret on the telephone at her desk as she finished recommending alternate accommodations to someone so memorably unpleasant she hadn't had to check her notes. "Nancy Casper from Denver," she'd said when I raised an eyebrow. "Life is too short to put up with that piece again."

"I haven't met Nina yet," I said. "Sam says she's a stem-winder."

"What's a stem-winder?" Emily asked.

"That's what I asked Sam," I said. "He couldn't really explain it to me very well, aside from saying, 'That's what Nina is. A stem-winder.' I gather it's some fancy modern watch that keeps better time than most. Or something."

Emily nodded. After some consideration, she added, "Maybe she's an actress. Some Hollywood people marry four or five times and nobody bats an eyelash. They say pretending to be in love when you're making a movie can make two people fall in love for real. I'm not so sure I believe that's possible. But then, of course, I'm not an actress."

I parked the stagecoach a fair distance from the runway so the horses wouldn't spook, set the brake and looped the reins around the driver's knob, then went to the stagecoach boot for the nosebags I'd stocked with grain back at the stable.

A gangly kid I'd noticed sitting on an upturned bucket outside one of the hangars trotted over to offer his assistance. Boys like him were thick on the ground around the train station and the big hotels in town, angling for tips for helping wealthy tourists with their luggage. I admired the kid's initiative for seeking out new markets and gave him a nickel for his efforts, a considerable percentage of what I kept back for myself from the pay I sent home to Tennessee.

"What's this?" he asked.

"It's a tip."

He pointed to the buffalo on the coin. "What I mean is, what do you think this is?"

"Oh, that," I said. "That's a buffalo."

"I know what a buffalo is," he said. "This is a nickel."

"So?"

"So, I guess that bellowing I just heard came from your pocket when you pinched this nickel so hard it woke the buffalo up."

"That's about the size of it," I said.

The kid sighed, but helped me with the nosebags anyway.

Emily, who'd waved me away when I offered to hand her down from the stagecoach roof, had managed to descend on her own without breaking her neck or exposing her drawers to God and everybody. She returned my hat to me and arranged herself in the stagecoach's shadow.

I put my hat on and scanned the horizon for some sign of Nina's plane.

"It must be fun to pretend you're something you're not and get paid to do it," Emily said. I must have looked baffled, so she added, "Actresses."

"Ah." I nodded and turned in a slow circle, searching the sky in every direction. Guests came to us from all over, and I realized I didn't have the least idea where Nina was heading in from. We'd had a maharaja all the way from India once, one of our infrequent male visitors. We weren't really set up for male guests, but he said he'd always dreamed of being a cowboy and so was happy enough to be quartered in one side of the bunkhouse while Sam and I doubled up temporarily in the other. A courtly, dapper man, our maharaja, who'd called himself Mr. Smith when he'd engaged his accommodations. Once he'd relaxed enough to reveal his true identity, I said I thought a maharaja could have as many wives as he wanted so I didn't see the point in divorcing one he didn't get along with. He answered in an accent that would have done our friend Shakespeare proud: "And I thought everyone where you come from went barefoot and played that shrunken version of a sitar you hillbillies call a banjo." Still, a nice man. As fellow southerners—him of Asia and Sam and me of the United States—he made us promise we'd drop by for a visit if either of us ever found ourselves in his neck of the woods.

"How about you?" Emily asked abruptly.

"How about me?"

"Are you an actor?"

"An actor? Me?"

"I thought you might be. Since you're familiar with Shakespeare's plays."

"No, ma'am."

"Also every hero in the Western serials looks more or less like you. Men who are too handsome to get hired for real jobs seem to gravitate to the motion pictures." That hung in the air between us for a bit before she said, "That came out wrong."

"You don't have to explain," I said. "There are worse things on earth than being told you're too handsome." At least she hadn't suggested I was too pretty to be smart.

A tiny dot in the blue-white distance gradually got bigger as its horsefly buzz grew into a puttering roar.

"Look!" I said, happy for the opportunity to change the subject. "That must be Nina's plane."

A double-cockpit biplane with an orange undercarriage and silver wings swept past, touched down, and taxied to a hangar at the opposite end of the runway, the jouncing figure of the pilot in back and his smaller passenger bobbling along up front. I gave the gangly boy another of my precious nickels to mind the horses while we went over to collect Nina. He pulled a face and said, "Oh, goody. Maybe the buffalo on this one will fall in love with the other one and they'll start minting nickels. Before you know it I'll be rich."

As Emily and I approached we saw the pilot grab the airplane's upper wing, cantilever himself to standing and step out onto the lower one. He bent over Nina briefly, then looked to have grabbed her by the scruff of her neck and pitched her out on the far side of the plane. He jumped down after. I broke into a run.

By the time I was within a hundred yards of the plane the pilot had come around the airplane's nose, spotted me, grinned boyishly, and waved. He was a slim drink of water, jaunty, six feet if he was an inch, with a pale, smooth face teetering between impish and angelic. The kind of pretty young man Miss Pam called "a fine-looking boy" until he was fifty. Or so I thought until he removed his goggles and aviator's cap, shook out silvery-blond hair, and resolved himself into a grimy-faced female with a figure eight of clean white flesh around her eyes. "Ahoy there, cowboy!" she shouted, though I was hardly more than an arm's length away from her by then. "Are you here for me?"

"Yes!" I shouted back, the way you catch yourself whispering responses to somebody who's lost their voice. I decided it was her packaging that had made me mistake Nina for a boy at first. She wore a roomy white shirt, none too clean, with a man's necktie loosely knotted at her throat. A parachutist's backpack strapped between her trouser legs and over the shoulders of her leather jacket, and a gun belt canted across her hips.

She shed the parachute and jacket as she shouted, "Where's my buddy Sam? Don't break my heart and say he's left the ranch."

"He took a carload of ladies into town," I said.

"What's that?" she asked, cupping a hand behind her ear. I found out later it always took a while for her hearing to recover after hours of wind roaring past in the open cockpit.

"Reno!" I hollered. "Carload of ladies! Back later!"

"Carload of ladies? Sam's made of sterner stuff than I am! Do you have anything to drink?"

"I have water in the stagecoach!"

"Say again?"

"I have water!"

"Water! That's what I thought you said! I didn't ask for a bath, cowboy, I asked for a drink! Though God knows I could use both! Give me a hand with this duffel, would you? It weighs more than I do!"

"Oh," Emily scraped, when she caught up to me and got a load of Nina. "If that's what a stem-winder is, I want to be one, too."

Chapter Three

By the time Nina and Emily exited the Mixmaster, heads together, they were giggling like schoolgirls. "Oh, no," Emily said. "I really couldn't. Not in a million years."

"Of course you could," Nina said, tucking Emily's hand into the crook of her elbow as they started for the house. "You drove here by yourself, all the way from San Francisco, didn't you? You're very brave, I think."

"More like very desperate," Emily said.

"There's nothing like a nip of desperation to make a person brave," Nina said. "Alcohol also helps."

"Oh, I don't drink."

Nina patted Emily's hand. "You don't drink *yet.*"

Margaret emerged on the ranch house porch. Nina let go of her new friend to run up the steps and throw herself into Margaret's arms as if she were a soldier just home from the wars.

Yes, the ranch house had a porch. Oh, I see, you don't have a photograph of it and you were picturing something low-slung and adobe. No, no, the main house at the Flying Leap was a gabled clapboard Victorian with gingerbread trim and a porch that wrapped around three sides. The dream house of some miner born poor back East who'd suddenly found himself flush with cash. A six-bedroom, high-desert white elephant, picturesque but not the best match for Reno's extremes of climate. You saw a lot of this sort of thing around Nevada back then, the residue of the newly and briefly rich, rambling mansions dropped into a landscape that looked like the surface of the moon. It was a good fit for our transient customers, though, who cared about picturesque and weren't around long enough to be ground down by the impracticalities of the place. Max and Margaret had oil heat installed for winter and ceiling fans for summer. They lived in a first-floor bedroom behind the kitchen and so didn't suffer so much from the fluctuations in temperature. Sam and I slept in a detached two-room bunkhouse by the barn the set designer had built for us out of gray-weathered wood he'd scavenged from some collapsing miners' shacks over in Spanish Springs.

Nina had asked to be put up in Scorpion, the little bedroom tucked under the attic eaves. That room was tiny, hot in summer and drafty in winter; the stairs to it were many; and it was quite a hike from the bathroom facilities on the second floor. But it was a single, the only one inside the ranch house, and it had the best views of the distant mountains, the Sierra Nevada range. The room stood empty much of the year, called into service only when the Flying Leap was overfull or a beloved repeat customer asked to have it. Margaret believed privacy was the last thing our ladies needed, you see. Too easy when sleeping solo to spiral into a funk when the lights went out and the bad thoughts crowded in. "It's like stabling a goat with a thoroughbred to keep the horse from kicking its stall to pieces," Margaret explained.

"How do you tell the thoroughbred from the goat?" I asked.

"Easy," she said. "Everybody's both."

Nina's choice of bedroom meant I had to lug her enormous duffel up three flights of stairs. That bag was impressively heavy. When I'd first hefted it at the airport I'd exclaimed, "What do you have in here? Bricks?"

"The canned remains of every man who's ever underestimated me," she'd said, and winked. "So watch yourself, Handsome." As I manhandled that duffel up those flights of stairs, I decided the shifting lumps inside it must in fact be books. In the 1930s, calling novels the canned remains of men really wasn't far off base as metaphors went.

By the time I was back downstairs, Emily had vanished. Nina and Margaret were still entangled in their reunion, so I lingered, taking my time about hanging Nina's jacket up in the closet under the stairs. In the daylight hours the back of the hallway was dim enough to make it hard to notice anybody standing there, and the acoustics were excellent if you left the closet door open and stood in front of it. My mother, God rest her soul, always said you never really knew another person until you'd walked a mile in their shoes or overheard a fair amount of their conversations without them knowing. So in the interest of providing better client service, I chose to listen in.

"You know, you don't have to keep getting married just to visit me," Margaret said.

"That's not the only reason," Nina replied. "I want to see Sam, too. That other cowboy said he'd gone to Reno for the afternoon."

"Yes. He should be back soon."

"Reno, ugh. Sodom for amateurs. Gomorrah for photographers." From the shadows I watched Nina standing in the bright frame of the doorway, loosening the knot in her necktie and slipping it over her head, exposing the strand of gumball-sized pearls she wore underneath. Her pearls were like Doorknockers' emeralds. Even when wearing nothing else, a pricey piece of jewelry kept those rich girls from feeling absolutely naked when they absolutely were. But I'm getting ahead of my story.

"Listen, Margaret, I know I asked for Scorpion, but I've decided I want Coyote, same as last time."

"Coyote is a double."

"Yes. I remember that."

"And I remember you saying hell would have to freeze over before you would agree to have a roommate again."

Nina teased apart the necktie's noose and studiously wrapped its length around her wrist. Then she tucked her chin and shot a glance at Margaret from under her lashes. "When I said that, I hadn't met Emily. She's not one of those old bags you always stuck me with. They kept giving me tips on marriage. I know how to get married. I've done it three times already."

"Those old bags?" Margaret asked. "Look who you're talking to, Nina. I'm as old as any of them were."

"You? You're ageless, Margaret. Also more of a valise."

Margaret snorted, but didn't budge.

"Emily said her roommate left this morning," Nina said. "The next one won't be here until next week. She's afraid she'll cry all night if she's not sharing a room with somebody. Please? Think of all the fun Emily and I could have together."

Margaret's face softened. "All right," she said, "as long as Emily agrees."

"I know she will," Nina said. "It was her idea."

That would have been news to Emily since, of course, it wasn't.

By the end of the week Nina and Emily had become inseparable. Bent over a jigsaw puzzle in the library for hours, whispering. Sprawled on the porch roof underneath their bedroom window early in the morning before it was hot or along toward evening after the day cooled down, reading books from Nina's duffel of canned remains. Carrying between them from barn to house a pail of milk I'd relieved our cow Katie of, like Marie Antoinette's ladies-in-waiting playing milkmaid, sloshing out so much in transit that half the milk was gone by the time they handed Margaret the bucket.

I will not lie to you. There were times when I liked being around people who still had so much money that a half-spilled bucket of milk was nothing to cry about. Such carelessness almost made me feel like I had money, too. I'd only ever been small-town rich, of course, but small-town rich makes you the equal of a Vanderbilt as long as you stick close to home. If nothing else, working at the ranch gave me some perspective. A few years of fetching and carrying there taught me I wasn't near as fancy as my mother had led me to believe.

I was shelling peas on the porch late one afternoon when I heard footsteps on its roof, followed by Nina's voice. "The way they fixed the crossbars on the posts to hold up the roses makes it easy. Just don't look down." The climbing rose that perfumed the entryway started to rustle and shake as first Nina's riding boots, then her britches and gun belt, and finally Nina herself appeared. Once she made it to the ground she stepped back and looked up expectantly.

"Shouldn't you take your gun belt off before you do that?" I asked.

She didn't seem as surprised to see me on the porch as she was surprised to be questioned about anything she did. "The bullets are in my pocket, if that's what you're worried about," she said. "The gun is just for show. To scare off wolves."

"How do you scare wolves if the gun isn't loaded?" I asked.

"Two-legged wolves are pretty easy to scare."

The rosebush started shaking again and Emily's voice tumbled down. "Ow," she said. "It's thorny."

"Don't grab the branches. Hold the trellis."

"I'll fall."

"You won't."

"What are you doing?" I asked.

"Teaching Emily how to leave a house by the bedroom window."

"Why?"

"Because she's never done it." It was clear from Nina's tone of voice that she considered my query idiotic.

The next day I was in the kitchen, wearing one of Margaret's aprons while I dried cutlery on a towel, when Emily and Nina drifted through. They had the pinked skin and wet hair of children just out of the bath and were so sunk in conversation that neither seemed to notice me.

As they disappeared out the back door Margaret came into the kitchen carrying a basket of laundry she'd harvested from the clothesline. She put her basket on the counter and stood at the kitchen window, watching Nina and Emily climb into the hammock strung between shade trees at the side of the house. Margaret shook her head and tsked. "I like to think people come to us because they haven't given up on finding their other half," she said. "But that one says she's not marrying again. Not ever."

"Who? Emily?" I asked.

"Emily? No. The Emilys of this earth are always married."

"Nina?"

Margaret tapped her nose and winked at me. "You could get work as a detective," she said, then sighed. "That poor kid can't catch a break." She took a stack of folded kitchen towels from the basket, opened a drawer, and tucked in all but one. "You know, Ward, if I've learned anything in the last few years it's that marriage depends on luck as much as anything. First of all you have to be in the right place at the right time to meet the person you're meant for. What are the chances of that happening for anybody the first time? But everybody—*almost* everybody—goes in with such high hopes, sold on the best selves the person they're marrying has shown them up until then. Some hit the jackpot, but others are just letting themselves in for a world of hurt. In my mother's day the only way out of a bad match was feet first. Poor Mama." She handed the towel she'd saved back to me. "I think the saddest thing of all is when two people who honestly believe they're in love marry and then find out they can't live with each other."

"Don't most people who marry believe they're in love?" I asked.

She took my chin between her thumb and forefinger. She had a special fondness for the cleft in it. God's thumbprint, she called it. "When you were fresh out of the oven up in heaven," she'd explained to me once, fitting her thumb into that declivity, "He took hold of your chin and turned your face side to side like this." She demonstrated. "Then He said, 'This one's perfect. Send him down the chute.' Off you went, born to your mother. Because you hadn't cooled off yet when He touched you, His thumb left its imprint there. It proves you're special. That's what the nuns used to tell us in Catholic school, anyway. That, and how you'll fry in hell if you get divorced. So take that for what it's worth."

That day in the kitchen she repeated my question before she let my chin go. "Don't most people who marry believe they're in love? Oh, Ward. Sometimes I forget how young you are."

I seem to remember Max was supposed to pick up the woman meant to be Emily's new roommate at the train the following week when he drove a carload of glum-faced guests, Nina and Emily among them, into town to meet with their lawyers. That intended roommate never showed. Every now and then that happened. The threat of the packed suitcase by the front door would make an errant husband mend his ways. Particularly, as Margaret was fond of remarking, if the wife was the one with all the cash. Sometimes I wonder if everything might have worked out differently if Emily had ended up with that other roommate, some nice middle-aged lady who didn't lie awake at night trying to think of fresh new ways to shake up the world.

That morning I was in Dumpling's stall, going over his withers with a currycomb, when Nina came looking for me. Good old Dumpling. He was a short-legged, potbellied gelding with a wide, serrated blaze jagging down his forehead and white stockings on all four legs that rose above his knees, markings that hinted at some piebald mustang forebear. Dumpling may not have had a fancy pedigree or, heck, any pedigree at all, but he was a true gentleman, the most tractable and empathetic animal I've ever known. When I first came to the Flying Leap he went by Lightning, the name he'd been given as a colt based on that blaze or his speed or possibly both. By the time I joined the staff, though, that old boy could have been outrun by a turtle. However, he was a perfect love and we developed such a bond that I'd taken to calling him "Dumpling," same as my mother had called me when I was a chubby-cheeked little boy. Soon I had everybody on the ranch calling him that.

While I was grooming my old friend that morning he took to swiveling his ears the way a dog lifts his head and sniffs when he realizes company's coming. I straightened up and there was Nina on Dumpling's other side, a folded note in one hand and Emily's automobile keys in the other. She had on a ladylike dove-gray dress, her pearls of course, no gun belt. I'll say this for Nina: she cleaned up good. She had her hair up in a French twist and looked as innocent as a Sunday school teacher back home in Tennessee, if that Sunday school teacher had more money than God to spend on clothes. You know who she reminds me of, come to think of it? That actress who became Princess of Monaco. Grace Kelly. Grace Kelly, if she'd been stretched on a rack until she was almost as tall as Gary Cooper, who her character is married to in *High Noon*. There's another reason to watch that movie. You could probably rent it on videocassette, if you have a player. Anyway. Nina's ensemble was just the right amount of prim for visiting a divorce lawyer in Reno. Which is what I thought she was doing, so I was surprised to see her standing there with Emily's keys.

"I've been looking all over for you," Nina said. "I thought Sam would work just as well, but Emily said no. She wanted you. I don't see what the difference is."

"Sam's three inches taller," I said. "Ten years older. Blond. Aside from that our own mothers couldn't tell us apart."

"It doesn't matter what you look like," Nina said. "What matters is whether or not you know how to drive a car."

"I know how to drive, ma'am. I started driving when I was eleven years old."

"Last year, then," she said.

She couldn't have been more than a handful of years older than I was. "I'm twenty-five, almost," I said, then felt like a four-year-old telling a five-year-old that I was four and a *half.* "Is Max back from town with all the other ladies?"

"No," she said. "The two of us came back early in a taxi. Max said we could take a cowboy and Emily's car and clear out until the crisis passes, as long as we're home in time for dinner."

"I'm glad to oblige, ma'am, but why do you need me?" I ducked under Dumpling's neck to come around to her side. "I know Emily doesn't like to drive much, but can't you do it?" I confess I was more excited at the prospect of driving the Pierce-Arrow than I ought to have let myself been. They don't make those cars anymore, and even in those days they didn't make a lot of them. Only the cream of the elite drove them. Presidents. Princes. John D. Rockefeller. Orville Wright, Babe Ruth. You get the picture.

"I never learned to drive," Nina said.

"You can fly an airplane, but you don't know how to drive a car?"

"Any imbecile can drive a car," she said, and handed me the keys. "Here you go."

Dumpling twisted his head around to see who I was talking to and Nina suddenly brightened. "Why, it's Lightning, isn't it?" she asked.

"That's right," I said. "Except now we call him Dumpling."

"I've known this horse since we were both hardly more than babies." Nina took the gelding's face between her hands and nuzzled his forehead with her nose. "Hello, old friend," she said. "How's my favorite boy and why are these silly cowboys calling you Dumpling?"

"He isn't as fast on his feet as he used to be," I said. "Calling him Lightning had started seeming disrespectful."

Nina stepped back and looked the gelding over. "Well, I guess time is hanging a little heavy on him around the middle. Happens to the best of us. It hurts to think my sweetheart here is an old man already. He'll always be my favorite."

"Dumpling still has plenty of good years left in him, knock wood." I rapped the stable wall with my knuckles. "He's my favorite, too," I said as I tucked Emily's keys into my pocket. "Worth all the others put together, even if he's getting on in years."

"How about that," Nina said, nodding and eyeing me speculatively. "You have good taste. Emily told me you weren't as stupid as you look."

"I hope not, ma'am," I said. "By the way, my name is Ward." I extended a hand for her to shake. She put the folded note in it. Maybe I was as stupid as I looked, after all. "What's the big crisis?" I asked as I unfolded it.

"Emily is having second thoughts. Only made it as far as the front door of the lawyer's building. Couldn't bear to go inside. Some of those old biddies told her cold feet were a sign she's still in love with Archer. As if being in love with anybody was ever enough. What a lot of idiotic Hollywood rubbish."

Of course, I owed my job to idiotic Hollywood rubbish. Margaret had been hot to hire me because I reminded her of that young actor playing the beefcake innocent in her favorite movie, a Mae West comedy called *She Done Him Wrong.* Cary Grant, yes. The very one. "He has that twinkle, Max," Margaret had said of me as I put my shirt back on and buttoned it after my interview was finished. "Twinkle's hard to come by in a boy as muscled-up as this young man is. It's hard to come by, period." I think of Margaret every time I pass a pet shop and see a puppy twinkling beseechingly at me through the window, every wiggling inch of dog assuring me that he's worth the money, that he'll never let me down if I'll just give him a chance. When I watch an old gangster movie on the late show—*Scarface, Public Enemy, White Heat*—I remember Max. "Such beautiful suits," he always said after seeing one of those films over in Reno at the Majestic. "The artistry in the tailoring, only to be shot full of holes in the end. It makes a person think." Of what, I never asked.

Do what this woman says, Max's note read, *and nobody will get hurt.*

Chapter Four

When we got to the shed where the Pierce-Arrow was stored, the car was still under the tarp and Emily was nowhere to be seen.

"I told her to wait right here," Nina said. "I should have known she'd chicken out."

"I didn't chicken out!" It was Emily's unmistakable croak, but so muffled it sounded as if it were coming from underneath a pile of blankets. "I'm here!"

When Nina snatched the tarp off the car I realized it had been a mistake not to roll up the windows and close the roof before I'd covered it. I'd been so mesmerized by the beauty of its insides—the dimpled fawn upholstery, the sinuous silver knobs on the burled wood dashboard, the ebonized circle of steering wheel—

that I hadn't thought that business through. Now a tortoiseshell cat was nursing a litter of newborn kittens on its back seat.

Other than the cats, the car was empty.

"Where are you?" Nina called. "For Pete's sake, Emily. We're in a hurry."

The stagecoach door popped open and Emily emerged, a moth-eaten white boa draped over her shoulder. "How could you think I'd chicken out?" she asked. "Not half an hour ago you were telling me what a hero I am."

Right away I noticed a long scratch on her left cheek I hadn't seen before. Then I realized the boa was the giant, scruffy tom who'd appointed himself king of our barnyard cats.

"Isn't it a little hot out to be wearing fur?" Nina asked.

"Please. I'm wearing purr," Emily replied, strumming the animal's length, producing a pretty faithful imitation of a locomotive engine going full blast. Emily sniffled and rubbed her eyes. "My friend here was fighting with a gray cat under the coach, so I broke it up and shut this one in here with me. We've done a wonderful job of calming each other down but I think I may be allergic to it. The cat, I mean, not calming down."

"That's Caterwaul," I said, relieving her of the beast and shooing him outside. "He's one for wailing when he's riled. Or whenever he feels like crying."

"No wonder we like each other," Emily said, and sneezed.

I fished out a bandana and handed it to her. "We call him Wally, mostly. He's the resident ladies' man. I expect he was trying to romance the cat you caught him fighting with. More than likely he's responsible for those kittens in the back seat of your car, too."

Emily stopped dabbing her nose with the bandana. "There are kittens in the back seat of my car?"

"See for yourself," I said. While she looked I rested my left hand on the seat back, then rubbed a thumb over the upholstery. It reminded me of a sweater my mother had given me when I left for college in the East. "Is this cashmere?" I asked.

Nina had been lounging against the stagecoach, trying not to look impatient. "Cashmere!" she hooted. "Listen to you, cowboy."

Emily ignored this. "Yes. Archer—my husband—chose it. First he insisted on buying a Pierce-Arrow because the hood ornament is a little man with a bow and arrow. Then he said we couldn't have it unless it was upholstered in cashmere. I said leather was more practical. Then he said, 'Practical? That's rich, coming from you.'"

"Sorry about the mess," I said. "Cats like to kitten in dark places."

"It's all right," she said. "When I get back to San Francisco I'll buy another."

Huh. Until this very moment it had slipped my mind how easily Emily tossed that off when I brought up the damage to her upholstery. Not, "It will take a lot of elbow grease and prayer to get those stains out." Or, "When I get back to San Francisco I'll have the back seat reupholstered." At the time I just thought I couldn't have heard her right. "Buy another what?" I asked.

"Another car," she said. "Nina, come and see the kittens. Aren't they the cutest things?"

"If you like cats," Nina said, not looking. She'd been shifting her weight from one foot to the other for a while by then and couldn't take it anymore. "Emily, please. You have to change before we leave."

Emily looked down at her funereal black visiting-the-lawyer outfit, now tinseled with silvery filaments of Wally. "It's just cat hair," she said.

"It's not the cat hair, it's the dress. I'm changing, too. Pants. Come on. We need to hurry."

The variable in their escape plan, the “flaw in the ointment,” as a beloved malapropism-prone guest of yore had been fond of saying, was the imminent return of Max and the other ladies. While Emily and Nina changed I busied myself with the kittens. Soon I was sunk in a battle of wills with Taffy, née Catastrophe, over the relocation of her brood.

There wasn’t time to hunt up a box, so I’d opened the stagecoach boot, spread a saddle blanket over the bottom, and eased a couple of her babies in. They’d be safe there for the time being. Taffy hadn’t pretended to be happy about this, but I’d put on a pair of the gloves we wore to stretch barbed wire before I started so her protests were for naught. When I came back for more kittens she’d abandoned the field of battle. This made it easier to help myself to her progeny, but it worried me a little. Sometimes when you move newborns the mama cat will abandon the litter, and no amount of reasoning will make her admit she has any connection to the kittens you insist on saying belong to her. Keeping the poor abandoned mites going with cow’s milk and eyedroppers was an iffy business. When they’re that young cow’s milk is too much for their digestion, and cats are so hard to milk.

Luckily my fears were laid to rest when Taffy and I crossed paths halfway between the coach and automobile, me with a kitten in each hand and her headed back to the Pierce-Arrow toting one of her relocated infants by the scruff of its tiny neck. It was a Sisyphean struggle, but she had the one mouth to my two hands so the numbers were on my side.

When I heard the ranch house station wagon's engine in the distance I'd just slipped the last furry little packet of protoplasm in and had propped the boot's lid open with another blanket, leaving a crack plenty big enough for Taffy to squeeze in and out of unless she tried to negotiate it with a mouthful of kitten. By the time I hotfooted it to the door of the shed, the station wagon was just a question mark of dust working its way up the ranch's long driveway. I didn't want to derail Nina and Emily's escape by getting myself tangled up with the other ladies, so I closed the shed door and applied an eye to a crack in it to see what would happen next.

I remembered then my mother taking me shopping in Memphis once when I was a kid, for what I have no idea anymore. Someplace in our travels we'd come upon a kinetoscope, even then an old-timey contraption that motion picture technology had rendered obsolete, but not so obsolete that a storekeeper who'd invested in one was ready to retire it. You put your money in a slot on the side of the machine, pressed your eyes to the view-finder, cranked, and, miracle of miracles, a little movie played, just for you. I've heard tell some kinetoscopes showed a lady peeling her clothes off, but I never saw one of those, particularly not while out shopping with my mother. The one I saw that day showed two cats in a miniature prizefighting ring wearing harnesses to lift their forequarters high enough to allow them to go at each other with tiny boxing gloves.

That day at the ranch the scene that unspooled for me when I pressed an eye to the crack in the shed door began with Nina at Coyote's window, gesturing vigorously. Emily joined her; they registered dismay at the fast-approaching automobile and ducked low behind the windowsill. As we watched from our separate vantage points, Max parked and hopped out to hold the passenger door open first on one side, then the other for the ladies fresh from Reno. Once all were under the overhang of the porch, Nina and Emily stood up again. Emily started to say something, but Nina held a finger to her lips and tilted her head, listening.

From my angle across the barnyard I could see what they couldn't, Max hurrying ahead to hold the front door for the ladies and closing it once the last had filtered through. A story above, Nina nodded when the door banged shut, then held up a hand—*wait.* I counted ten, same as she must have before raising the window sash and stepping through in her aviatrix ensemble of jodhpurs, white blouse, and high boots. Emily followed. She'd changed into more or less the same thing, aside from the equestrian boots. The first thing Emily put over the windowsill was her life insurance policy, the red varmints.

"I wish Portia were here to see," Emily said, looking petrified.

Nina had bounded off to find the keeper of the keys while we waited in the car. I'd parked alongside the hangar that housed her airplane to take advantage of a skimpy slice of shade. There hadn't had been time to clean up after the kittens before we left, so all three of us had piled into the sedan's front seat, Emily in the middle with her knees swept right so I could work the stick shift. Nina held her arms above the windshield like a kid on a roller coaster as we beat it out of there, hitting just the high parts of the bumpy gravel drive. "We're leaving this hot old world behind at last," she said, cupping her hands to catch the wind. "You'll love flying, Emily. Since it's your maiden voyage, we won't go high or stay up for long. The first time's free, chickadee, but every time after that I'm going to have to charge you the going rate, a dollar. And I won't charge you for the loan of the accessories this time, either."

"Oh? What accessories?" Emily asked.

"Goggles and a parachute."

"Why do I need a parachute?"

"In the unlikely event that you do not love flying, the quickest way down again is over the side."

Emily drew in a sharp breath. "I will not jump out of your airplane, I promise you."

"You say that now." Then Nina laughed and tickled Emily's knees. "I'm kidding, silly. You need a parachute in case we crash. Remind me to show you how it works before we take off."

After Nina got out, Emily didn't slide to the opposite end of the front seat like I'd expected. We were still close enough for me to feel her body trembling. "We got here so much faster this time," she said. "There was hardly any time to think."

"A stagecoach is picturesque, but it isn't speedy," I said. "You know, you don't have to go up in Nina's plane if you don't want to."

"I want to. I *asked* her to take me up. But now that we're here I can't stop thinking about Will Rogers."

Will Rogers, in case that name is unfamiliar to you, was a celebrity before the war. In vaudeville first, then the movies. Also he wrote newspaper columns everybody and their dog read during the early years of the Depression. One of his sayings that always stuck with me was, "Everything's funny as long as it's happening to somebody else." He'd died a few years earlier in a plane crash with the most famous pilot of the day aside from Charles Lindbergh.

"You know what's interesting about that Wiley Post," I said.

"Wiley Post? Who's he?"

If Emily wasn't thinking about the accident, the last thing I wanted to do was bring it up. "Wiley Post was Will Rogers's friend."

"Oh, wait. Yes, yes, yes. I'd forgotten his name for a minute there. He was the pilot who—" She looked relieved to have remembered that, then distressed when she remembered the connection. "Well? What's interesting about Wiley Post? Other than how he died and took Will Rogers down with him?"

"Oh," I said, "He was blind in one eye. But he could fly planes better with one eye than most people could with two."

"Until, *you know,*" Emily said.

"I don't think the plane crashed because he was one-eyed. I think it was equipment failure. That's the sort of thing that could happen to anybody, anytime."

Emily started trembling again. "Do you think the man with the keys to the hangar has gone home for lunch? If Nina can't find him, we might as well give up and go back."

"That's possible," I said. It was also possible that Nina, if she couldn't find the man she was looking for, would heave a rock through the airport office window and go through his desk to find the key. Or that she'd pick the hangar lock with a hairpin. If she'd had on her gun belt I wouldn't have put it past her to dig around in her pocket, find a bullet, and blow the hangar's lock off. Not being able to find the man who had the key to something didn't seem like enough reason for Nina to call it a day.

Emily took a firm two-handed grip on the stick-shift knob, as if she believed she'd slip to the floorboard and slide under the seat if she didn't hold on to something tight. "I'm afraid of heights," she said, squeezing her eyes shut. "Sometimes I get dizzy just looking down a flight of stairs."

"Then why on earth did you ask Nina to take you up in her airplane?" I asked.

"Because I'm every bit as dull as Portia says I am," she said, opening her eyes and giving me an earnest look. "I thought turning myself into the sort of person who flies around in airplanes would impress her. That's all I want in life."

"To impress a thirteen-year-old child?"

"Who is my daughter, yes. If I had that, I could die happy. Just talk to me until Nina's back, all right?"

"It messes with your depth perception when you're blind in one eye," I said. "Have you ever looked at photographs through a stereoscope?"

"A stereoscope?" she repeated faintly.

"Those wooden photo viewers with the long stick that has a rack at the end to hold two photographs of the same thing."

"Of course. My mother had one."

"Do you know how it works?"

She shook her head.

"It's based on human anatomy. The photos are taken from slightly different angles, the way each of our eyes sees everything we look at. When you just have the one eye, you don't get the other point of view, so it's harder to judge distances. Your perceptions flatten out."

Much later on, Emily had me recap that explanation for Nina's edification. Once I'd wrapped up my lecture, Nina said, "Given how far apart your eyes are, Em, you ought to be able to see clear through to the other side of things. Like those characters in comic books, the ones with X-ray vision. What color underwear do I have on today?"

Without missing a beat, Emily said, "You aren't wearing any underwear."

Nina applauded delightedly. "We should work up a vaudeville act," she said. "Take it on the road. Ward can drive our carnival wagon."

That day at the airport while Emily and I waited and wondered what had become of Nina, Emily closed both eyes, then cracked open the one closest to me. After studying me for a moment, she said, "This isn't making you look flat, but it is making my head hurt." She straightened up and closed one eye, then the other, staccato. "I see what you mean about the different angles, though. I'll have to find my mother's viewer. She had a box of photos of the San Francisco earthquake. You'd think she'd want to forget all about that, since we lived through it."

"You were alive then?"

"I was. Barely. I was three, so I don't really remember it. I looked at those photos so much growing up, though, that I've almost convinced myself I do. My mother always said the earthquake was really a blessing in disguise because it cleared out some awful slums."

"What happened to the people who had been living there?" I asked.

"They found someplace else to live, I suppose." Emily closed both eyes and collapsed against the seat. "Tell me another story, Ward. Quick."

It didn't seem like the time or my place to take on the right or wrong of her mother's assessment of those poor displaced unfortunates, particularly not when my own sainted mother might have said something pretty similar prior to becoming displaced herself. I was about to launch into the story about the kinetoscope and the two cats boxing when Nina rounded the corner of the hangar waving a ring of keys, the caretaker and the gangly kid trailing in her wake.

"But how can that thing fly?" Emily asked. "It doesn't have any wings."

The three of us stood in front of the hangar while the custodian and the gangly kid wheeled Nina's plane out by straps they'd threaded through its undercarriage. Where the wings should have been the plane was squared away into something resembling shoulders. Aside from that it looked a little like one of those plywood cars kids build to race in soapbox derbies.

"Watch," Nina said. "You'll love this." She climbed onto a wheel alongside the cockpit—the way I got to the driver's box of the stagecoach, I couldn't help thinking—and lifted an L-shaped metal pin on the fuselage's upper shoulder. Stepped off and stooped to free its twin down below. Trotted to the airplane's tail, grabbed what I realized was the tip of a folded-away wing, and swung it forward until its inner edge was flush with the cockpit. Then Nina slid the pins into fittings inside the wings, twisted the upright of the pins flat, and battened them down with little leather straps that snapped into place. Very small leather straps, narrower than my belt, joined with the sort of snaps you sometimes found on a pair of trousers. I glanced at Emily. She was very pale.

"Ta da!" Nina said. "Isn't it brilliant? When it isn't flying, its wings tuck against its body, the way a bird's do. For storage. One day everybody is going to have one of these babies in their garage. Now I'll just take care of the other wing and we'll get started."

"I am never setting foot in that death trap," Emily said.

On the way back to the ranch, nobody spoke for a long time. Finally Nina said, "My plane is not a death trap."

"I can't afford to risk my life, Nina. I have a child to think about."

"That's no excuse. Shackleton had children. Admiral Perry had ten."

"They're men."

"So? Why shouldn't *we* live lives just as full of risk and thrilling adventure, too? You're looking at this from the wrong end of the telescope, Emily. What we choose to do or not do should make our lives bigger, not smaller. Kids included."

Emily scowled. "That's easy for you to say. You don't have any children. You couldn't possibly understand what it's like."

"That's ridiculous. I know what having children is like. I am a child, after all. Was."

"And you'll stay one until you have a child of your own," Emily said.

"Look at me, Emily."

Emily looked. So did I. Nina was eyeing her roommate the way a cobra looks at a mouse that's about to become its lunch. I heard the scritch of gravel being kicked up from the highway shoulder, remembered I was driving, and looked back at the road again.

"Also, for the record, it's all right to be afraid for your own sake," Nina said. "You don't stop mattering once you give birth, you know. At least that's what my mother always tells me."

"There's no way to make you understand. We'll have to agree to disagree." Emily angled toward me, edging away from Nina and her messianic stare.

"Come on, Em," Nina said. She laid her left hand on Emily's right shoulder, grasped Emily's left hand in her right, and ratcheted her around to face her again.

"Don't be angry with me. I was scared when I first started flying, too."

In a small voice, Emily said, "I don't believe you were ever scared."

"I was! Half to death. I used to be such an unbelievable chicken, just like you."

"I'm not a chicken. I'm—"

"You are a chicken. Don't try to deny it. But you won't be once I'm done with you. *If* you come out the other side alive."

Emily said, "That's not funny, Nina. What is wrong with you?"

"So many things," Nina said. "Every now and then I decide to make a list, but inevitably I get bored and tear it up. Why bother, honestly, when there are so many more mistakes out there, just itching to be made? You don't learn as much from success as you do from failure, chickadee. That's why I'm wise beyond my years. In case you've been wondering what my secret is."

Chapter Five

We made it back to the ranch in time for dinner.

"What are we having tonight?" Emily asked brightly when Sam appeared at her left elbow with a platter of food. "It smells wonderful."

"Chicken," Sam said. "Ollie King."

"Chicken à la king," Margaret said, "is just a fancy way of saying chicken in gravy."

"Speaking of kings, I've met a prince. On my husband's yacht," said Mary Louise, a tall, well-put-together guest with the oversized blue eyes, corn-silk hair, and broad shoulders of a Viking daughter of the Midwest. She could have spawned a football team, that one, and for all I know she may have after she left the ranch. She was doing time with us after walking down the Ziegfeld Follies staircase into the heart of an industrialist who manufactured leather goods. She'd been married to him long enough to see some of the world, but not quite long enough to learn tactful ways of slipping what she'd seen into a conversation.

"Oh?" Margaret asked. "What was he prince of?"

"Some country. He was trying to do business with my husband and he wasn't interested in talking to me. He was older, frowned a lot, and wore this uniform to dinner that he'd stuck a lot of medals on because he would have looked look like a chauffeur otherwise. I guess he'd done something in the Great War."

Years later, when I was stationed in Europe during the next big one, I met a prince in an aid station. He was older, too, and frowning, though he was also bleeding like a stuck pig, so it hadn't seemed appropriate to ask if he'd ever been on an American industrialist's yacht.

Sam asked Emily, "Want some of this Ollie King chicken?"

"Yes, please."

I was coming along behind Sam with a basket of rolls, so I heard Nina lean close to Emily and whisper, "You're eating chicken? Cannibal." They exchanged a look, then stifled giggles. And just like that they were friends again.

The evening meal at the ranch was a ladies-only affair, the cowboys playing waiter, Max in the kitchen dishing out what Margaret cooked, and Margaret seated at the table to make sure the meal and conversation progressed smoothly. Back in those days people were wild for themed parties. Most nights we could have gotten away, easy, with calling our dinners "Cowgirls and Contessas." Guests who ambled around whistling "Home on the Range" with their thumbs hooked in their pockets showed up with their hands and faces clean but their boots and trousers militantly dusty, while the ones who could hardly wait to shed their dungarees at the end of the day dressed formally for dinner.

"I'd rather find my own, thank you." One of the contessa types, an effervescent older guest whose real name I can't recall now, took Sam's serving fork and started shuffling through the pieces of chicken on his platter. She was stoutish but still light on her feet, something I knew from dancing with her many, many times over the course of her stay. The sort of dowager Margaret Dumont would have played in a Marx Brothers movie, not always entirely on the ball but generally a good sport, pleasant enough to be around when she wasn't trying to convince herself and everybody else in Washoe County that she was a femme fatale.

"You must fall in love all the time here, Samson," she said, giving him the full Delilah while she had him at her elbow. "Hold on a minute, darling. Here's my breast. Do you see how perfect this one is?" She winked and moved her shoulders to give him a better angle on her cleavage while she transferred the piece of chicken she was after to her plate.

At the other end of the table, Emily shifted uncomfortably and Nina rolled her eyes. Nina had taken a dislike to that particular guest after she made the mistake of telling Nina she knew Nina's mother and then compounded it by going on at great length about a picnic they'd both attended in Newport before the war. "The War of 1812?" Nina had inquired sweetly. You had to give that lady credit. She'd laughed good-naturedly and said, "You'll be older someday, too, if you're lucky, miss. The hell of it is that you still feel young inside. Just you wait and see."

After that, Nina had called her the Zeppelin, Zep when she was feeling more charitable toward her. "Buoyant, but what a gasbag," she explained to Emily. "Watch yourself when you light a cigarette around her. She may explode if she gets too close to an open flame." That nickname stuck with me, alas, and the lady's real name didn't.

Sam, whose real name was not even Samuel, much less Samson, had grown up the eighth child on a dairy farm in Butterfield, Arkansas, where he'd learned early that the more you used your mouth for talking, the less of a crack you got at the vittles. Margaret remarked more than once that she felt Sam's being what you could call enigmatic made him seem even more like Gary Cooper than his looks did.

"Do I fall in love a lot? Well, yes, ma'am," Sam answered. "But I try not to dig up more snakes than I can kill."

"Our cowboys don't get involved with our ladies," Margaret added.

"Why not?" Zep asked.

Margaret always struggled with this explanation. The obvious one, "Because this isn't a whorehouse," seemed blunt. Sam asked the Zeppelin, "You ever caught a tadpole, ma'am?"

"Not lately," Zep said, handing the serving fork back to him. "No."

"Well, you catch a tadpole down at the pond, you take it home, run some water in the sink and slip it in. You mean to have it and hold it and so forth, but come morning when you visit it, like as not it's floating belly up." He carefully nestled the tines of the fork in among the pieces of chicken remaining on his serving platter. "That's why." He tipped the hat he wasn't wearing at her, then pushed through the swinging double doors into the kitchen, ones the set designer had modeled on the doors of a saloon.

Sam was devoted to Margaret. We all were. "That explanation you gave was very diplomatic, Sam," she said later, when the ladies were out of earshot. "Our guests will buy that one and feel good about it, even if it's not the absolute truth. It isn't a lie, either, though, which is what I like about it. We'll have to use it again, won't we?"

Sam nodded. "Always good to put the hay down where the goats can get at it," he said.

Since we men cycled in and out of the dining room with the plates of food, my experience of the ladies' chitchat came in snippets and what an affected kid from Shreveport, Louisiana, I went to college with in New Haven had called "aperçus." He wanted to be sure I, as a fellow southerner, understood there should be a little tail dangling under the "c" so that the stuck-up easterners who fancied themselves such aristocrats wouldn't catch me leaving it off and think the lot of us were hicks. He'd insisted on writing it out for me in the reporter's notebook I carried in my pocket back then for jotting down stuff people said that made me laugh, and to work out the random couplets I came up with when I made my feckless stabs at writing poetry. Let me tell you something: before I went to work at the ranch I had not realized how many words rhyme with "saddle." I toted around a boxful of those little spiral-bound reliquaries of my youth for many years. Gone the way of my copy of your photograph, I suppose. Lost, or torn out and twisted into wicks for lighting fires.

I still remember a few of my favorite exchanges, though. "You don't marry a man because he's perfect, you marry him because—" "—he's rich!" "He was taller when he was sitting on his wallet" came up a fair amount, as did some variation of "A fool and his money will soon be parted from his wife and shacked up with a chorus girl." I must have written down a fair share of the sorrowful aperçus as well, but only one stuck with me: "You know it's time to file for divorce when all your fantasies about your husband involve him being dead." Really, it's a wonder anybody who works in the divorce industry has the courage to marry, ever.

Where was I? Oh, yes. Dinner, after the airport. For the evening meal the table was set with a tablecloth, place cards, and a lovely set of china plates edged with gold. Max had wanted dishes with the Flying Leap logo wrapped around the rim, but the Hollywood set designer had advised against it, explaining that such plates would disappear into our clientele's luggage and that there were cheaper ways to advertise.

Sam got endless innocent pleasure out of setting the table with so many nice plates that matched, so that was always his job. Now and again, if dinner happened to be running late and the ladies were getting restless, to buy time Margaret sent Max into the dining room to say, "Sammy, don't you see this spot here on this cloth? We can't eat off this. Change it. *Now.*" Sam would nod, grab a double handful of tablecloth, and snatch. The tableware rattled but stayed more or less in place. The ladies cheered. There were no complaints about late service. I remember saying to Max once that there had to be a metaphor in that brilliant stall. Max pondered, then wagged a finger, chucked me on the shoulder, and said, "Keeping the magic of romance alive may require some sleight of hand."

Yes, yes, you're right. I did say place cards. They were exquisite, blank, and ordered in bulk from a Mrs. John L. Strong, Stationers, in New York City. Margaret had beautiful handwriting the nuns had taught her, and filled the place cards in at the same time she lettered a new guest's name on the wooden clothespins she used to keep laundry from getting jumbled on the clothesline. And yes. One reason Margaret used the place cards was to help the staff learn the names of the ladies we served, but the more important reason was to choreograph peace.

The upside of this particular seating arrangement was that it was easy to hear the questions Zep lobbed at Nina even when the kitchen's saloon door swung shut. Ditto Nina's answers. I was in the kitchen gnawing on a chicken thigh over the sink when I heard, "Your being from St. Louis, Nina, explains everything, doesn't it?"

"What does it explain?" Nina asked. I dropped the thigh bone in the sink, wiped my face and hands right quick, grabbed a water pitcher, and headed in.

"That's why you took up flying airplanes," the Zeppelin was saying as I swung through the door.

"I don't follow," Nina said.

"Charles Lindbergh," the Zeppelin said, "is also a native of your hometown. He named his airplane after it. *The Spirit of St. Louis.*"

"Is that so? Thanks for telling me. I hadn't heard that." Nina patted the knife and fork on either side of her plate as if she were thinking of using them to slice into the delectable breast on the other end of the table. "I'm not sure I've heard of this Lindbergh fellow, either."

"Really? That surprises me. I should think—"

"Yes, you should think. I'm kidding. Obviously I know who Charles Lindbergh is. I'm just sick to death of hearing about him. I'm sure Charles Lindbergh is sick of hearing about Charles Lindbergh, too, especially since being so famous made his child a target for—"

Emily looked stricken and grabbed Nina's forearm. "Stop," she said. "Can we please not talk about that? I can't imagine losing a child. I don't think I could survive that. I slept in Portia's room for ages after that kidnapping. Archer says that's when—well, it doesn't matter what Archer says. Not anymore." She looked at her lap and smoothed and resmoothed the napkin there.

Nina patted Emily's hand and said. "Shhh. All right. If you must know, Z—uh, ma'am, I took up flying airplanes because I enjoy looking down on people."

Margaret intervened with, "Who else here has been up in an airplane? Anybody?" Sounding so much like a schoolmarm that Mary Louise, in gold lamé, raised her hand to answer. "My husband and I traveled longer distances mostly by yacht, of course, or private rail car. But when I was growing up in Nebraska, I almost went up in an airplane once. With a barnstormer."

"I understand Charles Lindbergh began his career as a—" the Zeppelin began.

Margaret laid a hand on top of hers and shook her head almost imperceptibly. "Go on, Mary Louise."

"That barnstormer was so handsome," Mary Louise said, "and he'd been to France. That's where Paris is. He was a pilot in the war, like the men in that old silent movie that was playing at the cinema around then. *Wings.* Did you ever see that one, Nina?"

"Did I ever see that," Nina said. "The truth is, that movie is what got me interested in flying. I loved Gary Cooper in it. He stole the picture, if you ask me."

"That reminds me," Margaret said, looking around and spotting me. "Ward, will you ask Sam to serve the cobbler? I think we're all ready for something sweet."

"Yes, ma'am," I said. I dawdled a little more, though, refilling water tumblers. The cobbler would keep another minute and I wanted to see how the conversation played itself out.

"They say Gary Cooper stole Clara Bow's heart, too," the Zeppelin said. "I understand she was engaged to another man while she was making that movie, but those two had a fling. You must have wanted to be Clara Bow, Nina."

"Are you kidding? I wanted to be Gary Cooper. His character died doing something he loved. Right after eating half a chocolate bar. Never knew what hit him. Next stop, heaven."

"I remember putting on my nicest dress that day," Mary Louise continued, dreamily tracing a fingertip around the gold encircling her plate. "Parting my hair, and then redoing it, over and over, to make sure I got it perfectly straight. I imagined the pilot looking down on me, like you said, Nina, and noticing how careful I'd been with my part and thinking, 'That's the girl for me.' I know it sounds silly now, but I was young and I really didn't want to spend the rest of my life tasseling corn. Do you know, corn grows so fast that you can hear it? It moves and rustles when there isn't any wind at all. When I was a kid I was convinced a stalk of corn would come after me in my sleep, boil me, and eat me."

"Tell me, Mary Louise," Emily said, putting her napkin alongside her plate and leaning forward. "Were you at all nervous about going up in that airplane?"

"I imagine Mary Louise was, if the noise corn makes growing was enough to scare her silly," Nina said. "Although I suppose that's not as crazy as it sounds, come to think of it. It would explain why hunting is called 'stalking.'"

"Sure, I was nervous, Emily," Mary Louise said, studiously ignoring Nina. "But I had to do it anyway. The barnstormer was going to be my way out of Nebraska. A ride in his airplane cost a dollar, and a ticket on the Union Pacific to anywhere good cost thirty. A dollar I could afford."

"Fifteen minutes wouldn't have gotten you far, not even in an airplane," Emily said.

"Yes, but fifteen minutes was plenty long enough to get someplace with the pilot."

Nina tapped her fingers on her lips and considered Mary Louise. "Fifteen seconds probably would have done the trick if you made sure he got a good look at you," she said.

"Thanks," Mary Louise said. "I thought so, too. You know who didn't think that? The girl in line in front of me. She was telling her friend she'd kissed the pilot when he'd handed her his advertising leaflet the day before, and that he was probably in love with her already. She meant to take him home for dinner that night, to meet her parents. They'd get married, he'd give up flying and take over her father's farm when the old man died. They were meant to spend the rest of their lives together, she just knew it. She was so full of herself. But she was the prettiest girl in town, so you know." Mary Louise shrugged. "She was right, as it turns out."

"He *gave up flying*?" Nina asked.

At the same time Emily asked, "They got *married*?"

"No. When they were coming in for a landing she was waving her arms around and acting a fool. He got distracted by her hoo-ha, I guess, because he snagged a wheel in this barbed wire fence and flipped the plane. Splat. Killed both of them dead."

While we were cleaning up afterward, when we were alone in the kitchen, Margaret said to me, "I saw Nina smiling at you during dinner."

"So?" I said.

"She calls you Cashmere. Why?"

"She thought it was funny that I knew what cashmere felt like."

Margaret raised an eyebrow.

"The upholstery on the back seat of Emily's car is cashmere," I added hastily.

"What do you know about the back seat of Emily's car?" she asked.

"One of the cats had kittens there. That's all I know."

"I hope that's all you know, Ward. If there's a woman on this earth who could make a boy like you forget yourself, it's Nina."

"I am not interested in Nina," I said. "I'm not going belly-up like some poor tadpole in that woman's sink, I promise you. As far as I can tell she doesn't even know my name."

Chapter Six

Reno was a skillet in the summertime, sure, but its saving grace was the Washoe zephyr, a frisky little breeze that could be counted on most days to tumble down the mountains into the basin, fanning faces and fluttering through the trees its settlers had the foresight to plant all over town.

I liked to sit on a particularly shady bench while I waited for our ladies who'd booked appointments with the lawyers in the building close to the courthouse. As I watched the leaves flip forward and back, forward and back, anonymous tidbits drifted to me on the breeze: *"—last Thanksgiving, with my own sister—"* *"—of course I think the child is my husband's, but it's possible—"* *"—not a dime left in our bank accounts—"* *"Well of course I knew he was lying—"*

"—he hit me, so I walked—" "—he says he loves me, but I hate him—""—I love him, but he hates me—" It was like listening to a celestial radio that only picked up the saddest soap operas, its dial twisted slowly by the universe across the whole unhappy bandwidth without settling anywhere for long. I might not have had a set opinion of the right or wrong of divorce when I got to Reno, but the things our ladies went through before they came to us won me over to the necessity of it. Better to risk frying in hell than to suffer through a living one.

After Sam and I had done our best to scrub the back seat of the Pierce-Arrow clean, a couple of days later I drove it into Reno so Nina could deliver Emily personally to the law firm she always patronized. The seat was still damp and, it seemed, indelibly stained, so the three of us rode strung across the front seat again, Emily next to me like before and trembling. "I don't think I can go through with this," she said.

"Sure you can," Nina said. "Here's the lowdown on this law firm. It's called Stacks & Stacks. So named because of all the money they've made on my divorces."

"What? Is that really why—your lawyer—huh?"

Nina laughed. "Oh, chickadee," she said. She tapped the space between Emily's eyes with her right knuckle.

"Hello? Hello? Anybody home? Hmm. Sounds hollow. I thought you had extra brains stored in there."

Emily knocked her hand away. "Stop that," she said. "You're being mean."

"I'll stop when you stop calling me Stilts."

"I've never called you Stilts."

"I wouldn't mind if you did," Nina said. "Stilts O'Malley sounds like a very dangerous customer. I like it. As for the Stacks brothers, they're very dangerous lawyers. The best in Reno. You're seeing Michael, the younger one. He's absolutely ruthless. Archer won't have a cent when Mike is done with him."

I pulled over in front of the law offices to drop them off, and came around to open the passenger-side door. "It's not about the money," Emily said as I handed Nina out of the automobile.

"Don't kid yourself," Nina said. "It's always about the money when one half of the couple is loaded and the other isn't."

"Plenty of people have more money than I do."

"Yes, but Archer isn't one of them."

Nina had on her dove-gray visiting-the-lawyer dress and Emily her black one, brushed free of cat hair. "How do I look?" Emily asked as I handed her out as well.

"Like a million bucks," I said, "except—" I noticed one of the white tomcat's hairs still clinging to the shoulder of her dress and tweezed it away with my thumb and forefinger. "From your boyfriend Wally," I said, and held it up for her to see.

"Oh, I'm going to need that," Emily said, taking it back and replacing it on her shoulder. "For luck."

I parked the Pierce-Arrow across the street and had just taken my preferred seat in the shade when a second-floor window nearby rattled up. I heard Nina's voice say, "How can you stand it in here, Mike, with the window closed? All that fan is doing is moving the hot air around. No, not *your* hot air, I didn't say that, *the* hot air. Come sit over here, Emily, where you can feel the breeze." An unseen chair scooted across wooden floorboards. "Now, don't worry, chickadee. Nothing fazes Mike. He's seen it all and heard the worst. I'll wait for you in the car."

I decided to get up and amble around the block. Otherwise Emily might glance out the window, peg me on my bench, suspect me of eavesdropping, and as a result become too self-conscious to share her worst. After one circuit I headed back, figuring she'd be so engrossed in her tale of woe by then that she wouldn't look outside. On my return I was annoyed to see somebody had stolen my seat. A claim-jumper in a dove-gray dress. Nina.

"What are you doing here?" I asked.

"Hiding from photographers," she said. "Go away."

"But I always sit here."

"Well, stop talking about it, then, and sit." She slid to one end of the bench. Nina was sporting the sort of inward expression people get sometimes when they have stomach troubles or they're trying to remember something they feel like they ought to know.

"Are you all right?" I asked.

She didn't respond, but her color was good and she wasn't sweating so I decided she wasn't sick. "For the record, I don't mind you calling me Cashmere," I said. "But you know my real name's Ward. Right? It's short for Howard. That was my father's name, too. Once I was born he started going by Big Howard, and—"

"Hush," Nina said. "I can't hear what Emily's saying."

I realized then that what I had mistaken for the look of a person searching her mental filing cabinet was in fact her listening-in face. "Are you eavesdropping?" I asked.

"Shhh. Don't pretend you weren't trying to do the same thing. I saw you from the window."

Nina had my number. "I was not eavesdropping," I said anyway.

"I'm not judging you, Cashmere. I'm saying you were an inspiration. I saw you and realized I ought to move Emily's chair over by the window so it would be easier to hear her. Then I angled it so that it would be harder for her to look out and see the bench. I wish Emily would just tell me why she's dragging her feet about filing her divorce papers. Then I wouldn't have to do all this."

"Isn't she meeting with the lawyer now to get that ball rolling?" I asked.

"I hope so. I assumed Emily was ready to leave her sorry excuse for a husband, since she drove herself all the way to Reno the day she found out what he was up to. But I almost had to drag that woman here by her hair. Now I wonder if she has the guts to follow through." Nina shrugged. "He's the hell she knows, I guess. I go for hell I don't know, myself. Why not take a chance at winning big next time? People do."

"You sound like my uncle," I said.

"Oh? What kind of guy is your uncle? A die-hard optimist? Unrepentant romantic?"

"He was more a 'what's-in-this-for-me' kind of a guy."

"Was? Is he dead now?"

"No," I said. "Just dead to me."

Nina tipped her head and stared at me for a minute. "You interest me, Ward," she said. She stretched her fingers out in front of herself. They were long and elegant, but her nails looked like she trimmed them with a chain saw. After careful consideration she zeroed in on a hangnail, nibbled it contemplatively, then shoved her hands in her pockets and murmured, "Stop that."

"You really should," I said. "Nail-biting spreads disease, particularly if you don't wash your hands several times a day. Which not that many people do."

Nina furrowed her brow at me and said, "Thanks for the hygiene tip, pal. Now, shush, or we'll miss something important. Which would be irritating after I invested so much thought and energy into arranging the chair by the window."

At first the zephyr mostly flipped the leaves away from us, which meant we were treated to tantalizing fragments of what Emily said, her voice sounding more scraped-up than ever: "—mother said all men cheat, but there are limits—" "—a long blond hair on my pillow, *in the house I grew up in*—" "—and he said, 'I'm not your *lapdog*. You don't *own* me.' As if I—" The wind shifted in our favor then and we were able to catch complete sentences: "Archer said, 'You think you're so wonderful, Emily. Such a lady.

Well, I could walk down the street right now and meet five women better than you are.' I said, 'Ah, so that's where you meet your lady friends. Walking the streets.' Then he said—" The wind shifted again and we lost the rest.

"Good," Nina said. "She's sticking up for herself. Atta girl."

The wind shifted our way again, though not in time for us to hear Archer's comeback. "So I packed both our suitcases and Portia and I were all set to leave together," Emily said. "Then Archer started shouting. 'You can't take my daughter with you. If both of you go, I will die. Or sue you. Or die. Or sue you.'" An errant breeze bucked the rest away.

"Bully," Nina breathed. "Imagine shouting at Emily. And in front of their child."

"That's what bullies do," I said. "If you pound the table when you know you're wrong, maybe people will be too distracted to notice."

The breeze kicked back, just in time for us to hear, "Portia said—Portia said—Portia—" Emily's voice broke down, then rallied. "Portia said, 'I can't leave. You heard what Papa said. He'll *die*.'"

"Or sue her," Nina said.

"'Oh, Portia, honey,'" Emily continued, "I said, 'I don't believe Papa will—I mean, I hope—'"

"Although it would certainly make things easier for her if he dropped in his tracks," Nina said.

I shushed her. Nina smiled and patted me on the back. We missed the rest of Emily's sentence, but caught, "Who will have me now? I'll never find another husband. I'm damaged goods. I'm *old*."

Nina shook her head. "Oh, Emily," she said. We heard the rumbling, interrogatory rise of the lawyer's voice, if not the words themselves. Nina made an impatient gesture. "He's too far from the window," she said. "I couldn't get him close enough without asking him if he'd mind sitting in Emily's lap."

Another gust delivered Emily's answer. "I told you, sir, I packed her bag. I didn't *desert* Portia. She refused to leave if Archer wasn't coming with us. She wanted to know what he'd done that was so terrible. How could I explain? She's too young. He's her father and she loves him."

"Rumble rumble?" the lawyer asked. We couldn't catch Emily's reply, but then we heard the lawyer clearly. "You're right, my dear. It usually *is* about the money."

"How about that? She listened." Nina pounded my knee with a victorious fist. "I've been to this rodeo before, you know. Mike Stack said that very thing to me when I divorced my second husband."

The lawyer asked something else inaudible, to which Emily replied, "All I said was, 'Papa cheated.' She said, 'But he's always cheated!' I almost died on the spot. The idea that she knew when I didn't? Then Portia said, 'We just won't play Monopoly any more, Mama, how about that? Then Papa won't be tempted to cheat.'"

"I have news for that child," Nina said. "A man who cheats his own daughter at Monopoly cheats at everything. Cheaters cheat. It's what they do." She shook her head and tsked. "I don't want to hear any more," she said. "Let's go wait in the car."

"You know, I've hardly ever been in the front seat of an automobile," Nina said once we settled into the Pierce-Arrow. "This dashboard doesn't really look all that different from the control panel in my airplane. I believe I could teach myself to drive this thing without too much trouble."

"Or I could teach you," I said.

"But why? Trial and error is always the best way to learn, wouldn't you agree?"

"Not when it comes to operating heavy machinery. That's a good way to get yourself killed, and to take a few people out with you while you're at it."

"You sound like my flight instructor. A sweet man with a surprisingly pedestrian turn of mind, alas. Didn't read much, and when he did his lips moved. No way we could stay married, obviously. Look. Here she comes. Poor kid."

If you ignored her red varmint boots, Emily could have passed for a woman who'd just left a funeral. Black dress. Drawn face. Hunched, my-life-is-over posture. She waited on the other side of the street, wringing her hands and watching for a break in the flow of traffic so she could cross to us. It was a Tuesday afternoon and Virginia Street was the busy main drag, the very avenue the Pony Express riders had thundered down back in gold rush days. After what must have seemed like an hour to Emily but was probably three minutes, Nina said, "She needs help," and scrambled out of the front seat.

"I'll go," I said.

"You stay put," she said, and slammed the door.

Sir Walter Raleigh wasn't a patch on Nina. She hesitated on the curb, inserted her index fingers in her mouth, and let rip a head-swiveling whistle. Then she plunged into the street, her hands palms out to bring the automobiles to a halt, took Emily by the elbow, and escorted her across.

"There you go, my chickadee," Nina said as she held the car door open and handed Emily inside.

"Thank you, Nina," Emily said. "But you could have gotten run over."

"But I didn't. And here we are."

"How did it go?" I asked.

"It went," Emily said. Her eyes and nostrils were rimmed with pink.

I turned the key in the ignition, but Emily put a hand on mine. "Not yet," she said. "Can we sit here for a few minutes while I collect myself?"

"Of course," I said.

"Could I have one of your bandanas, please?" she asked.

I dug one out, and she sat twisting it between her hands. "For the record, I haven't been crying," she said, giving up the twisting long enough to point to the single strand of Wally's fur still adhering to her shoulder. "I'm allergic to cat hair. I'm sure of it now."

From where we were parked we had a front-row seat on the cavalcade flowing across the Virginia Street Bridge. The Bridge of Sighs, some poetic journalist or the Reno Chamber of Commerce had dubbed that span across the Truckee River. An unassuming little waterway that flowed shallow, bright, and noisy most summers, just like the town it cut through. Rumor had it that newly minted divorcées stood at the bridge's half-way point to throw their wedding rings into the churn below after casting off their husbands at the courthouse half a block away. A rumor also made up by business-men involved in the tourist trade, if you ask me. Who would be fool enough to do that when you could unload anything remotely precious at a pawnshop? Maybe the minimal payoff just wasn't worth the effort to women who were as rich as Croesus.

For a minute or two the three of us sat there, taking in the parade. Cars and pickup trucks and delivery vans, plus herds of tourists—pretend cowboys in stiff new denim hoofing it home from lunch; women in dark glasses who looked like movie stars or wanted you to think they did; gamblers half-drunk at 2:00 P.M. stumbling from or to casinos; and men dressed like the gangsters they might actually have been. So much money flowed through Reno during the Depression that crooks and money launderers called that little town in the middle of nowhere The Big Store. You could get anything there, it seemed, licit or illicit. Like Nina said, a twentieth-century Sodom and Gomorrah, where folks parted with their cash and inhibitions as if there were no hell, heaven, or tomorrow.

"Emily. Do you want to hear something funny?" Nina asked.

Emily nodded, then said in a small, scratchy voice, "Yes, please."

"See that older man just sitting in the blue sedan parked over there?"

"Yes?"

"That's Poppy."

Emily sat up straighter and looked more closely. "Your father?" she asked.

"Good lord, no. He's a photographer. I call him Poppy because of the sound his flashbulbs make when they go off. He's trawling for a catch. See how he has binoculars around his neck, and a camera propped on his steering wheel? If he sees anybody interesting coming out of the courthouse or the Riverside Hotel next door there, he leans out the window and takes pictures to sell to the newspapers. If they're interesting enough, he'll even get out of the car and chase whoever he has his eye on down the street."

"What makes someone interesting?"

"How rich you are, how rich your husband is, who's famous or infamous. Movie stars, society girls, titled aristocrats. That sort of thing."

"How do you know all that?" Emily asked.

"Because I broke one of his cameras the last time I was in town, divorcing Lord Whattamoron."

"I don't think a photographer would be interested in me," Emily said.

"They go for the pretty ones, too. Bonus points if you're crying. It makes me want to serve those guys a knuckle sandwich. But they always run so fast."

Emily patted Nina's knee and gave her a tight little smile. "I'm glad you're on my side, Stilts."

Nina wrapped her arm around Emily's shoulder again and hugged her close. "Me, too, pal."

"I am trying to be brave, you know."

"And you're doing a great job," Nina said. "Sometimes."

Emily rested her hands palms-up in her lap and studied them as if she'd written the answers to an exam there. "You know what I don't get, Nina?" she asked.

"What?"

"Why you're so nice to me."

"Except for when I'm being mean to you? Well, I'll tell you why. You have vast untapped potential, Em. I believe we'll make a rabble-rouser of you yet. Uh-oh, look out! Poppy's swinging into action."

The three of us watched as the photographer sat up, held the binoculars to his eyes with one hand, and lifted his camera with the other when an attractive and well-dressed young couple emerged from the courthouse and bounded down the steps. Poppy leaned forward, peered intently, then lowered his spyglass and let his head drop back against the seat. You could almost hear him thinking, *Just a couple of nobodies. Damn.*

"Poor Poppy," Nina said.

At the bottom of the stairs, the young man swept his companion into his arms and spun her around before kissing her deeply.

"They seem awfully happy about getting divorced," Emily said.

"Probably just got married," I said. "People elope to Nevada because you can get married the same day you get your marriage license. Heck, you can marry the same *hour.* If you want, you can get divorced and walk across the hall and get married to somebody else fifteen minutes later."

"Ugh," Emily said. "That sounds like giving birth at a funeral."

"Yes," Nina said. "Although *that* sounds like the kind of thing that would really cheer people up. See, folks! Life goes on! Shakespeare would have loved something like that, I think. Weddings, death. He ate all that stuff up. His comedies always end with people getting married, have you noticed? And the tragedies with somebody kicking the bucket. Really, it should be the other way around."

"Yes," Emily said. I'd eased the Pierce-Arrow out into traffic by then and she brushed away the hair that blew across her face as we picked up speed. Then she added, "I used to love *A Midsummer Night's Dream*. I took Portia to see the movie—"

"The one with Mickey Rooney playing Puck?"

"Yes. I didn't find it the least bit funny."

"Well, that happens when you marry an ass," Nina said. "Joke's on you."

"I suppose," Emily said.

She looked so dejected that I tried to change the subject. "They put that play on up at the college last winter," I said. "I took some of our ladies to see it."

"Oh?" Nina asked. "How was it?"

"Not bad, considering most of the students are there to study mining," I said. "The costumes were the best part, I thought. Showed real imagination. Bottom's in particular."

Nina said, "Let's drive around some before we go back to the ranch. Show me where this college is, Ward. I never went to college. Maybe I should enroll there since I'm about to become a citizen of Nevada again. Maybe if I had a university degree people would treat me with the respect I probably don't deserve."

Chapter Seven

It must have been around midnight when I heard it. I was lying flat on my back on my bed in the bunkhouse with my window open, sweating. Between the zephyr, the dryness of the desert air, and the way the temperature plummeted once the sun went down, I'd found Nevada after dark more bearable than the humid summer nights back home in Tennessee. As happened sometimes, though, for the last few days the manager of the big thermometer in the sky had forgotten to turn the heat down come nightfall, so I'd stripped off every stitch of clothing and lay spread-eagled on top of my sheets. After an hour or two of tossing and turning, I rolled off my bunk, got my towel, and wet it at my sink to spread over my torso. Sometimes that helped cool me off enough to sleep.

Passing the window, I was stopped in my tracks by what sounded like the muffled purr of the Pierce-Arrow's engine. The ranch being outside the city limits made it relatively secure, but every now and then a poor desperate soul from the real world wandered up the long drive looking for things to steal. Someone had crept into the tack room and stolen a saddle one night but not a horse, though the heavy, fancy saddles we used were probably worth more than any of our horses were. Another time our guests' lingerie had been nicked from the clothesline in broad daylight. Nothing major, so far; but for anybody thinking of making off with an automobile, Emily's would make a particularly juicy target.

The waxing moon put out enough light for me to see the shed door swing open and the dark shape of the convertible roll out. Top still down, headlights off, nosing out and swinging toward the bunkhouse on its way to the gravel drive. I couldn't make out the driver, but a tall figure closed the shed door behind the automobile and jumped in over the passenger-side door instead of opening it. I went for my jeans hanging on a peg by the window since I couldn't very well take out after car thieves stark naked.

But before I could reach my pants, I heard Nina's voice. "So what's this knob for?"

Emily hissed back, "No, Nina, don't pull—"

Nina must have pulled. The car's headlights blinked on, long enough to illuminate me standing at my open window as bare as Michelangelo's *David,* towel dangling loose in my hand. I jumped to one side of the frame and pressed my back against the wall the way a movie cowboy takes cover in a gunfight. The headlights flicked off again, but I could hear the two of them stifling laughter. Like Will Rogers said, everything is funny as long as it's happening to somebody else.

Once I couldn't hear the car's wheels crunching gravel I peeked out the window, towel wrapped around my bits this time. When the Pierce-Arrow was almost all the way down the long drive to the main road the headlights flicked on again.

Although I was so mortified I was certain I'd never be able to face either one of them again in daylight, I decided to wait up until Emily and Nina were back, just to be sure they made it home in one piece. But once I had a reason to stay awake, I fell asleep almost immediately.

The worst of that particular heat wave broke by the following afternoon. For the next couple of days I chose tasks that would keep me out of sight of Nina and Emily. I mucked out stalls when it wasn't my turn to, wormed the kittens, and weaseled out of serving dinner by offering to dish up food and scrub pots for Max so he could get out of that hot kitchen for a change.

I'd gotten over the incident entirely, or so I told myself, by the time Sam and I were scheduled to shepherd a late Friday afternoon trail ride. Emily had been slated to ride, but Nina hadn't signed up. That morning she'd been seized with the urge to join in, so the two of them asked Sam if it would be all right for them to double up on Dumpling, bareback. Both were slim, and the gelding had carried his share of guests who weighed as much as those two ladies put together more than once, so Sam agreed.

Oh, you've never ridden bareback, much less double? Well, it's definitely the way to go if both riders are friends and know their way around a horse. It lightens the load, of course, skipping the saddle, and also keeps whoever's riding in back from getting pinched by the shifting of the tack with every step the horse takes. The camaraderie that comes of it, well, that's an added bonus. Think of it as the equestrian equivalent of sharing a sundae with a friend.

Seeing those two riding that way reminded me of a couple of pretty little girls back home in Whistler. Hannah and Judy. Lovely, scrappy, barefoot sisters who rode their pony bareback all over town and used a halter equipped with hay-string reins in place of a bridle. Their features were as delicate as the flowers on my grandmother's hand-painted china, but they dressed in their older brothers' hand-me-downs and, like their brothers, would light into anybody on the playground they felt had slighted them. My heart's desire had been to ride that pony sandwiched safely between those two little warriors. When I begged permission to invite the sisters over to play, my mother said not under any circumstances. That, moreover, I'd get a switching if I ever put a leg across their mount or set foot inside their house. When I asked why, she said, "Because their father's folks are not our kind of people." Why this was so my six-year-old self did not question. When Miss Pam laid down the law she did not brook dissent.

Late one afternoon my mother realized she'd misplaced me, went looking all over, and finally spotted my Buster Browns poking out the front door of a little tar paper bungalow over by the railroad tracks. I'd followed the girls home and had been delighted to discover their house was only a few blocks away from mine. Their mother had been gracious enough to invite me in to have an after-school cookie. I dared not disobey my mother, so when Miss Pam found me, I was lying on my stomach half in and half out of their house with crumbs all over my face. My mother was not impressed by my ingenuity. Every detail of that afternoon was etched sharply in my memory, as any flagrant act of disobedience rewarded with a switching so often was.

Little did my mother know how valuable that afternoon's experience would turn out to be. During my interview with Margaret it struck me that she wasn't looking to hire some snooty formerly rich boy for the job of fetching and carrying for her ladies. So when she asked me to tell her about where I'd grown up, the house I described wasn't the Bennett manse astride a yard the size of a city block. It was Hannah and Judy's little bungalow.

On the trail ride that day I'd volunteered to ride rear guard while up ahead Sam indicated points of interest: A cow's skeleton picked bare by buzzards that the Hollywood set designer had insisted we leave there for "authentic desert texture." The gated field out beyond our trickling thread of a creek, fenced off because it was riddled with gopher holes that could snap a horse's leg. The ranch had lost Katie's first and only calf that way after the two of them had been turned out for a final ramble together before the calf was sold off to be bottle-raised and Katie started her life as the resident milk cow.

When we reached the water's edge, Sam invited everyone to dismount so he could point out all the animal tracks: rabbit and bobcat and the little x-shapes stamped in the earth by roadrunners, so perfectly symmetrical back to front that it was impossible to tell which direction the birds had been running. I stayed in the saddle watching some of our ladies climb off their horses and squat alongside Sam, nodding and murmuring among themselves.

"Maybe I should go in costume as a roadrunner at the masquerade tomorrow night," I heard the Zeppelin say. "I never know whether I'm coming or going either!"

I'd heard Sam's spiel a million times before and had given it about as many times myself. Both Sam and I could deliver it in our sleep. While he recited the points of interest I was mentally rehashing and feeling shamefaced about that sorry childhood episode with Hannah and Judy. That's why I hadn't noticed Dumpling slowing and falling in step with my mount. "Ahoy, Cashmere," Nina said, and flashed a grin. "Too bad we haven't been seeing as much of you lately."

"Nina, please," Emily said. She squared her shoulders and arranged her features carefully into a semblance of calm, but nonetheless blushed red. "About the other night, Ward. We wanted to ask—"

"—if your spotlight dance—" Nina jumped in.

"Nina!" Emily said. "What we wanted to ask, Ward, is for your forgiveness for the inadvertent intrusion. I'm sorry it took so long, but we didn't want to bring it up in front of all the others."

"No need to apologize, ladies," I said.

"Tell me, Cashmere," Nina said, "why were you standing there in front of your window in your birthday suit?"

"Oh, I stand in front of my window naked every Tuesday at about that time," I said. "Some of our ladies enjoy a midnight show."

"Do they?" Emily asked. "Well, I hope you're paid extra for that."

Now I felt my own face get hot.

"Emily," Nina said, "he's joking."

"Oh," Emily said, then buried her face between Nina's shoulder blades. "I'm an idiot."

"Sometimes, yes," Nina said. "But most of the people who are interesting are idiots at least every now and then. Proves your willingness to take risks."

"Actually, ma'am, I was worried somebody was stealing your car. I heard the engine, so I got out of bed to check."

"I'm so sorry, Ward," Emily said. "I should have told you we were going out. It was a spur-of-the-moment sort of a thing."

"I thought you hated driving," I said.

"It's not the driving I hate so much as the oncoming traffic. Other drivers are so unpredictable."

I nodded. "True enough," I said.

"I owe you another apology, Cashmere," Nina said. "I'm sorry if your backwoods accent has made me misjudge you. My darling Sam's grammar can be a little wobbly, but yours is excellent. Not that Sam's butchering of syntax makes me love him any less."

"You know what Sam says about underestimating people," I said, trying not to sound like I was lecturing her for talking down to me. Which I was.

"What?"

"No way to tell if an egg has a double yolk until you crack it open."

"Sam's such a philosopher," Nina said. "Do you know what he said to me the last time I was here when I kept complaining about my roommate?"

"What was wrong with your roommate last time?" Emily asked.

"Nothing particularly memorable. Certainly not as memorable as the advice Sam gave me. He said, 'Pull the weeds in your own yard first.'"

We three were still bringing up the rear when the lot of us got back to the barn. Nina said she wanted to help Sam with the horses, which freed me up to go help Max set up for cocktails.

When we got to the house Emily ran up the porch steps in front of me, then hesitated long enough to say, "You know, Ward, Nina can be tactless and condescending, but she has a good heart. By the way, I like your accent. Just because you don't sound like us doesn't mean you're ignorant. You haven't had the same opportunities we had, growing up." She snapped a rose from the climber and tucked it behind my ear, then turned and rushed into the house.

I hung back for a little while, wondering if Hannah and Judy's mother still lived in the little tar paper house she'd raised her family in. If she did, she was one up on Miss Pam. My poor mother. The thought of her darling son, Howard Stovall Bennett III, as a common laborer building the Boulder Dam already like to have killed her. I tried to imagine Miss Pam's face when Nina complimented my grammar. My mother, sprung from a long line of overeducated, underfunded folk, was a proud graduate of the University of Tennessee at a time when not many women bothered with college. I doubt I could have convinced her that such condescension from someone with less formal schooling than she had was in the least bit funny.

I found Emily standing by the hall table where the daily mail was fanned out, holding an envelope in her hands and studying it. "Did Portia write you?" I asked. "That's good news."

"Don't I wish," Emily said. "No, this one's for you. It's postmarked Whistler, Tennessee. Is that where you're from?"

"Yes," I said. "It must be from my folks."

"The return address says 'Daniel Horn.' Although this handwriting has so many curlicues that first name also sort of looks like 'Daniela.'"

I took the envelope and tucked it in my pocket without looking at it.

"Who's Daniel? Or is it Daniela?" Emily asked.

"It's Daniel," I said. "He's nobody. Just a man my parents used to know when I was a kid." I took the rose from behind my ear and stuck it behind hers. "You should keep this. It'll just fall in the sink while I'm doing the dishes."

I went into the kitchen to wash my face and hands and cover my dusty clothes with a clean apron. As soon as I was alone I took my uncle's letter out of my pocket, tore it to shreds, and shoved it into the garbage.

Chapter Eight

"Just because she was a fortune-*teller* doesn't mean she was a fortune-*keeper*," Nina was saying as I circulated through the library soon thereafter carrying a tray of Max's champagne cocktails, each with a bright red maraschino cherry bobbing merrily inside. Much of our guests' talk that afternoon, even during the trail ride, had been about ginning up the costumes for tomorrow night's masquerade at Tony's Spanish Ballroom in Reno. Nina plucked a drink from my tray and winked at me. "Thanks, Cashmere," she said.

Margaret looked at her wristwatch. "Well, I can see into the future," she said, "and I predict a photographer will be here in about half an hour to take our group picture. I asked him if we should set up sooner but he said no, the angle of late-afternoon sunlight is particularly flattering. He guarantees we'll all look gorgeous in his photo, and I said, 'Of course we will, because we are.' And not to worry, ladies, our man behind the camera teaches over at the university and develops his film in his own darkroom. None of his photographs have ever leaked to the press."

Margaret, bless her heart, ran through more or less the same speech every time the photographer came, and was always convinced her clientele would cherish this photographic talisman of their stay with us. I was never so sure about that. Try as I might, I never could imagine anybody hauling out a scrapbook, tapping the group shot taken at the Flying Leap, and saying, "Ah, here I am in Reno, cooling my heels until my divorce went through." I always figured those photographs got tossed into a wastebasket or shoved into the back of a drawer and forgotten. But, look here, this one you found must have meant something once to somebody, because the given names are penciled on the back. Martha, Theresa, Liz, Anna, Renée, Nina, Emily, and Mary Louise; Sam, Ward, Max, and Margaret. I think Anna might have been the Zeppelin's real name. Or maybe Renée. Hmm. Zep could have been Theresa, too, come to think of it. Oh, well. She'll always be Zep to me.

Would you like some of this Jell-O? No? I don't blame you. They keep trying to pass this stuff off as dessert, but it just isn't. Jell-O always makes me think of death. Every time I attend a funeral for a patient, I look over at the widowed partner or bereft children and think, "Hoo boy, I hope you like a Jell-O salad, because several dozen will be wiggling your way in the next week or two." How congealed salads jazzed up with marshmallows and pineapple tidbits got to be the go-to dish for the bereaved I'll never know. Of course, it's not the gift that matters. What matters is the impulse to give.

Meanwhile, back at the ranch—I can't tell you how long I've waited to have the chance to say that, so thanks, too, for giving me the opportunity to get that off my chest.

Meanwhile, back at the ranch, I wasn't surprised to see that Emily had changed for the photograph into something fresh and pretty I'd seen flapping on the clothesline earlier that day, a floral outfit figured in red and pink that went well with her varmint boots and the rose she still had tucked in her curls. Nina had also freshened up: hair brushed, face washed, divested of her revolver but not of her pearls, wearing a filmy lavender dress that made her eyes look a little lavender, too. Seemed like her only act of rebellion that afternoon was draping herself sideways across a chintz armchair instead of sitting in it facing forward with her ankles crossed as Emily Post decreed a lady should.

"She can't have been much of a clairvoyant if she couldn't foretell her own future," the Zeppelin said. She had her hands on the back of that armchair, which also happened to be her favorite place to sit. Nina willfully ignored her.

"Maybe she had a blind spot when it came to herself," Emily said. "Lots of people are like that."

"A blind spot big enough to steer an ocean liner through, sounds like," Zep said. "The woman built herself the biggest library in the state even though she didn't know how to read. If buying books you'll never read isn't throwing away money, I don't know what is."

"Gambling is throwing money away," Emily said. "Spending hundreds of dollars on clothes you'll never wear is throwing money away. Buying books is an investment in the future."

"Emily's right," Nina said. "Where there are books, there's hope. I have stacks of novels I haven't gotten to yet. It's the best reason to go on living I can think of."

"Because *you* know how to read," Zep said.

"I used to read the funny papers for Portia before she learned how," Emily said. "Maybe that woman had somebody to do that for her, to read her all those books she bought herself. The way Milton's daughters read to him after he went blind."

"Milton? Milton who?" Mary Louise asked.

Emily and Nina exchanged looks. "Milton Bradley," Nina said. "The board game guy."

"I didn't realize he was blind," Mary Louise said. "Gosh, I loved that Game of Life when I was growing up. I always beat my sisters, so they stopped playing with me. I had to play against myself."

"Did you win?" Nina asked.

"I don't see how I could lose if I was the only one in the game."

"People find a way to do that more often than you'd think," Nina said.

"What happened to her in the end, Margaret?" Emily asked.

"What happened to who?"

"That mining millionairess."

"Eilly Bowers?" Margaret said. "Oh. Her three children died while they were little and she outlived all her husbands. Also her money. Died broke, old, and alone in a poorhouse in San Francisco something like thirty years ago."

"I was a child then," Emily mused. "I might have passed her on the street. Imagine that. She could have warned my mother not to let me marry Archer. Although I doubt I would have listened to my mother or anybody if they'd tried to stop me. He was so handsome before all his hair fell out. Not that I minded that. Not like he did."

"All I'm saying," the Zeppelin said, "is that if the Bowers woman really had the gift of prophesy she should have been able to see what was coming. All clairvoyants are charlatans and liars."

"How do you know?" Nina asked. "She might have seen her future back when she was working her fingers to the bone over her washtub, scrubbing all those miners' dirty laundry. Couldn't believe anything she'd pictured would actually happen, that she'd be the richest woman in the United States one day, then dirt-poor all over again. Then it *did,* just the way she'd seen it. So she decided she had a gift for prophesy."

"Some gift," Emily said. "I can't think of anything worse than being able to see into the future. If I knew what would happen to me most days, I'd never get out of bed."

"I can think of something worse," Nina said. "Getting something you've wanted all your life, then realizing it wasn't what you thought."

The Zeppelin, God love her, was one of those chipper old broads who believed the secret to eternal youth lay in steering her ocean liner in the opposite direction of a conversation listing toward sadness. "Ladies, please.

We are straying from the question of the hour. What should I wear to the costume party? The easiest thing would be to go as a cowpoke, but so many other people will be doing that, and I do hate the way my dungarees squeeze all the blood out of my lower half every time I sit down."

Nina tipped her head back and groaned. "So don't sit down," she said. "Dance on tabletops. Start a riot!" She leaned forward and clinked her glass to Emily's. "To rabble-rousers, rousing rabble!"

"When I was your age, dear heart, I danced on my share of tabletops. But these days an ensemble that doesn't bind is the ideal." The Zeppelin clapped her hands together. "Everyone! I have decided. 'Clairvoyant' it is. As a matter of fact"—she gathered up a double handful of the fringed paisley cloth covering the library table—"I think this would be the sort of thing a fortune-teller would wear as a shawl." Looking terrifically pleased with herself, Zep snatched the tablecloth the way she'd seen Sam do it.

My tray of cocktails took a direct hit from a crystal snow globe that turned cannonball when the table flipped and everything on it went flying.

The Zeppelin clutched the cloth to her chest. "But Sam made it look so easy! I was so sure I—he made it look so easy!"

Nina jumped from the chair, her diaphanous dress splattered with champagne. "Who saw that coming?" she exclaimed, then ran to the window where the light was better and dabbed at the fabric with a napkin. The next time I looked at her she had buried her face in the drapes, her shoulders shaking with what I had to think was laughter.

Margaret pried the cloth from the Zeppelin's hands and said, "It's all right, shh, now, don't worry. Ward will have this cleaned up in no time and look, you're absolutely right, it does make the perfect shawl." She wrapped the fringed spread around Zep's shoulders and steered her to the favored armchair. The Zeppelin slumped in it, utterly deflated. For the first time ever I thought she looked as ancient as Nina pretended she was. What's funny to think about is that Zep was probably a good twenty years younger than I am now.

I set the table to rights and swept up all the broken glass, retrieved the books that had been on top of it, wiped down and replaced them, and returned the still-intact reading lamp to its place alongside the stack. Finally I spotted the snow globe over by the window, close to Nina's feet. When I went to scoop it up, she let go of the drapes, cast one forlorn look in my direction, and fled into the hall. I realized then that the table wasn't the only thing the Zeppelin had upended. Nina's face was streaked with tears.

I didn't think anybody else had noticed until I saw Emily staring after Nina, her lips parted in surprise. I caught her eye, touched a finger to my cheek, and trailed it halfway down. Emily nodded, got up, and followed Nina into the hall.

I picked up the snow globe, shook it, and watched the snow inside settle on the Eiffel Tower. Then I handed it to Zep. "This can be your crystal ball," I said. "When you tell people you're seeing Paris in it, you won't be lying."

"I've been to Paris several times," Mary Louise said. "It's in France."

Max smoothed his vest and shot his cuffs. "Well," he said. "Let's start this party over, shall we? Ward, can you fetch us another bottle of bubbly?"

I was grateful for an excuse to go find out what had become of Nina and Emily. I stopped by the kitchen first for the champagne. Sam was getting out dishes for the dinner service. As I put on a clean apron I outlined the ruckus in the library.

"She ought to of asked me how first," he said. "It don't work on a cloth with a fancy edge. The embellishment is what done her in."

"Bring this to Max, then tell her that," I said, taking

a bottle from the refrigerator and shoving it into his hands. "I'm sure she'll be glad to hear it."

I filled a tumbler with water and went looking for Nina and Emily. I found them sitting on the floor of the coat closet under the stairs, their knees drawn up to their chins and the hems of their dresses tucked demurely around their ankles. Nina had her hands over her face and her head half-buried in the lower reaches of somebody's lovely black winter coat, one that had been abandoned there a while ago.

I'd fingered that coat's fabric from time to time—*cashmere*—and checked its tag for some clue of who it once belonged to. *House of Worth,* the label sewn on its neck said, a French couturier I remember one of our clients gassing on about the winter before, so that coat had probably been hers. But if that designer-name-dropping matron couldn't be bothered to get in touch with us to ask after her missing coat, I couldn't be bothered to send it to her. I had about decided that, if a year passed and it was still unclaimed, I'd send it to my mother. Miss Pam hated wearing hand-me-downs when she was a girl, but now that she was poor all over again she might feel differently. I imagined she'd be pleased to have a decent overcoat again, whether she'd heard of the House of Worth or not. As for the woman who'd left that elegant wrap behind, I'd almost convinced myself she'd abandoned it on purpose. I pegged her as the type who'd rather die than be caught wearing last year's couture.

I handed Emily the glass of water I'd brought for Nina and asked, "Is Stilts all right?"

Nina took her hands away from her face long enough to say, "Stilts is fine. Stilts also speaks English, as well as French and a little Italian. Which she learned from a little Italian." She used the tail of the coat to wipe her face, leaving behind slug trails of mucus. Then she took the tumbler from Emily and raised it to me. "Unhappy 1938!" she said.

I raised my eyebrows and looked at Emily.

"Why don't you step inside and close the door," Emily said.

"It'll get pretty dark in there with the door closed," I said.

"It's pretty dark in here already," Nina said. "Come on in."

It was a big closet, I'll grant you, big enough that the previous owners of the house had hung hams in it to cure. But still, it was no Hall of Mirrors at Versailles. I wedged my toes in between their feet and pulled the closet door almost to behind myself. I left it cracked because I wasn't sure the door could be opened from the inside and I didn't like the idea of trying to explain myself to Margaret if the three of us got trapped inside.

"What's going on?" I asked.

"Tonight's the night," Nina said.

I started sweating. Whether it was from the lack of air circulation in the closet or the enigmatic nature of her statement or the whiff of the mortality of long-dead porkers, I wasn't entirely sure. "The night for what?"

"We weep. Or I do, anyway. Don't feel like you have to join in, if you aren't in the mood."

Emily's voice floated up from the darkness. "Nina lets herself cry once a year. Once and only once."

"The truth is I want to cry all day long, most days," Nina said. "But I fight it. Usually I do a pretty good job of beating back despair, but hearing Zep say her dancing-on-tables days are over set me off. The hell of it is that we'll be too old for it, too, someday, just like she said. We'll all wind up as tottery as she is."

"Zep isn't what I'd call tottery," I said. "Or particularly old. Even so, my understanding of that situation is that it doesn't happen all at once. You get to ease into it over the course of many years."

"I know, I know," Nina said. "But the tablecloth business! That's the stuff that really breaks my heart. Being so sure you can do anything you put your mind to, then one day realizing you can't anymore."

"If it's any comfort to you," I said, "the tablecloth business didn't go south on Zep because she's old. Sam said the fringe is what done her in. Did her in. The trick doesn't work if the tablecloth has an edge."

"Maybe that's what's wrong with me," Nina said. "I have an edge."

"There's nothing wrong with you," Emily said. "Aside from being tallish for a woman. It's getting stuffy in here," she added, and kicked the door open.

The Zeppelin's voice, as buoyant as ever, drifted in from the library. "I keep getting older," she said, "but my husbands don't!"

Emily took Nina's hands from her face and wiped her cheeks with the tail of the black cashmere coat. "Get up, Stilts. The photographer will be here any minute, and Margaret will come looking for us."

The two of them scrambled to their feet, brushed off their seats, and straightened their dresses. "How do I look?" Nina asked.

Emily plucked an errant maraschino cherry from Nina's hair and held it out to her by its stem. "Like a million bucks," she said. "With a cherry on top."

"A million? Is that all? Try five. Although every time I marry I end up with a little less." She took the cherry from Emily, pulled the fruit from the stem, chewed and swallowed it, and handed the stem back to Emily. "Don't say I never gave you anything."

"Happy birthday to me," Emily said, and dropped the stem down the front of Nina's dress.

Nina squealed and jumped. "Emily! How old are you?"

"Not as old as I'm going to be."

The three of us strolled back to the library after that, Nina leading the way. Emily grabbed my hand and held me back a little. "Let her go first, then me," she whispered, "so they won't think we've all been up to something." She gave my hand a little squeeze before she let it go.

"There you are!" we heard Mary Louise exclaim when Nina sailed into the room. "So what are you going to wear to the masquerade ball, Nina?"

"I'd rather be shot than dress up in a costume and go to that," Nina said.

That night I dreamed someone was trapped inside the hall closet, knocking, hoping a passerby would come along and free her. I opened the door, and there was Emily, nestled among the coats, as naked as a jaybird. She reached out, grabbed my hand, and gave it a little squeeze.

Even though I did my best to stay asleep, the knocking continued until finally I rolled out of my bunk and stumbled over to open the door. Nobody there, though the rapping grew more insistent. I realized it was coming from behind me, and when I turned I saw Emily's face at my window. She gestured urgently. *Sleeves,* I noted. Guess I wasn't still dreaming.

When I opened the window and leaned out, Emily was dressed in pajamas much like the ones I slept in. Although hers were probably boys' instead of men's, since she was small and they fit her pretty well. She was holding something lumpy bagged inside a pillowcase.

"What's up?" I asked.

"So you do sleep in pajamas," she said.

"So do you."

"Yes. I prefer men's pjs. I feel ridiculous sleeping in negligees."

"So do I," I said.

"Ha ha," she said, mirthlessly, and shoved the pillowcase into my hands.

"What's this?" I asked, and peeked inside. It didn't take a whole lot of moonlight to realize I was looking at Nina's gun. "Are you kidding? She'll skin you for taking this."

"She asked me to take it. Don't worry, it's unloaded. Hide it, will you?"

"I don't understand."

"You don't have to understand. You just have to hide it."

"Shouldn't Margaret be the one to—"

Emily made an impatient gesture. "No, Nina doesn't want to worry her. Nina told me to give it to you. 'Cashmere isn't a snitch,' she said. 'We can count on him.'"

"I don't know—" I said.

"I *do* know," Emily said. "Listen, Archer's father shot himself when Archer was a kid. He'd been a friend of my father's since college. Archer's dad had been struggling for years and my father felt like he should have seen that coming. Papa didn't think another man's troubles were any of his business, though, and then it was too late. I'm not making the same mistake. Take this. Hide it." She squeezed my hand again, said, "Thanks," and beat it back across the barnyard to the house.

After she was gone I turned on my reading light and checked the revolver's chambers to make sure they were empty. Then I stuffed the pillowcase under my bed. Tomorrow I could figure out a better place to hide it.

I was just drifting off to sleep again when I heard the engine of the Pierce-Arrow. I got out of bed, went to my window, and watched it creep down the driveway. Once it was too far from the house to wake anybody up, the limousine's headlights flickered on.

Chapter Nine

Emily and Nina didn't turn up at breakfast the next morning, so I assumed they were sleeping in. I knew they'd made it back from another of their late-night jaunts because on my way to the barn that morning I'd checked the shed to be sure the Pierce-Arrow was inside. I couldn't help wondering where that pair had gone every night for two weeks when they crept away from the ranch. None of our other night owls ever mentioned bumping into them in Reno in the usual hot spots.

If nothing else, ranch work taught me about the gap between who a person pretended to be and who she really was. I'd gotten a lesson in that early on from an older guest who proclaimed herself a teetotaler and carried around a glass of tap water to sip on throughout the day because, she explained, the desert air made her feel exceedingly dry. The first time I gathered her into my arms to dance, however, she'd reeked so of gin that it made my eyes water. When I mentioned as much to Sam, he'd said, "That old girl ain't been dry since Jesus turned water into wine. Reckon He turns her tap water into gin as a special favor because of they been friends since grade school."

When Emily and Nina didn't show for lunch, I asked Margaret if somebody ought to knock on Coyote's door to make sure they were all right.

"All right?" Margaret asked. "Why wouldn't they be?"

I thought about the gun in the pillowcase still under my bed. "No reason," I said. "It's just that Nina isn't one for missing meals. And they've got to be around here someplace. Emily's automobile is in the shed by the stagecoach, all the horses are in their stalls, and the ranch station wagon is parked out back."

Margaret eyed me. "Come 1940, Ward, you could probably get a job working for the census bureau," she said. "I saw you out there this morning, by the way, looking at Emily's car. I've noticed you go out and look at it most mornings."

"Just making sure Taffy and her kittens haven't moved back in," I said. "It's such a beautiful car. I wouldn't have minded being born in that back seat myself."

Margaret patted me on the shoulder. "I know," she said. "Don't let it eat you up inside, sweetheart, people having but not caring much about something you want but can't afford. It's the hardest part about coming to grips with working here, being around folks who have more than they need and still aren't happy. Give it enough time and you'll appreciate having what you need and knowing it's plenty. I don't envy our guests anymore. I have what most of them want but haven't found yet, and may not ever."

"What's that?" I asked.

"My Max. There aren't enough men like him to go around," Margaret said. My favorite thing about Margaret and Max was that they still seemed so deeply in love after so many years together. It gave a person hope.

As it turned out, Emily and Nina had left the ranch before breakfast that morning. "Emily asked if you could drive them," Margaret said, "because Nina has her thinking all Reno cabdrivers are gossip-column snitches. A few are, I guess." She shrugged. "Any other day I might have let her take you, knowing how you feel about that car. But I couldn't see having you gone all day and maybe half the night. I called a taxi for them."

"All day and half the night? Where were they going?"

"Who knows? As long as they don't leave the state, where they go and what they do is none of my business. But listen, the good news is you get to drive Emily's car after all. I asked her if we could borrow it to ferry some of the ladies into Reno tonight so we wouldn't all have to squeeze into the station wagon. She said that was fine by her, if we could find the keys. They aren't hanging on the key rack in the kitchen where she thought she'd left them. Nina says you must have them."

"Me? Why would I have Emily's keys?"

"Because you were the last one who drove her car, when you and Nina took Emily to see her lawyer."

"I don't have her keys," I said. I was about to add that Nina and Emily took that automobile out more nights than they didn't, but if Margaret had slept through all their nocturnal expeditions it wasn't my place to tell her what she'd been missing. Like Nina said, I wasn't a snitch. "I gave them to Emily as soon as we got back," I said.

Margaret looked annoyed. "Then they're probably swimming around in the bottom of her handbag, or forgotten in one of her pockets," she said. "That's the trouble with always having a staff do for you. You forget how to keep track of things for yourself."

As it turned out, Nina knew where the keys were, and lied to Margaret. She knew where they were all along.

My mother always assumed I wrangled cattle on the ranch, not ladies, so when I wrote home about going to my first masquerade dance in Reno I said I'd gone with a buddy I worked with, Sam, and that we'd dressed as cowboys because we had the clothes already and that was what we were. Soon after that a parcel from home arrived at the Flying Leap for me. I was touched to get it, figuring it might be a lemon pound cake, since my birthday was coming up and my mother had mailed me one of those during my year away at college. All the time I'd worked at the Boulder Dam I hadn't gotten a package with a cake inside, not once, so I took receiving her box that day as a sign that my mother's spirits were improving.

I carried it back to the bunkhouse to open, not because I didn't want to share but because I was worried seeing the lemon pound cake nestled in the box might choke me up. As it turns out, what was inside made me even sadder: a pair of saddle shoes and a crewneck sweater with a large *Y* emblazoned on its chest. A note in my mother's handwriting was pinned to the sweater. It said, *This is what you are.*

The saddle shoes were mine, bought with my mother in Memphis before I got on the train to New Haven. The sweater wasn't, though Miss Pam didn't know that. It had come from the lost-and-found drawer in the then-new, faux–Oxford University Sterling Library at Yale, where I'd shelved books for pocket money. I'd taken that job not because I needed cash then, but because I was fantastically lonely. You know, some medical professionals dismiss as hypochondriacs physically healthy patients who come into their offices and list ad nauseam every runny nose and hangnail. Not me. I have been there. Loneliness is a sickness, too, same as any other.

Like the cashmere coat at the Flying Leap, that Yale sweater had gone unclaimed for months, so before I left for home that summer I adopted it. I thought my parents would enjoy the joke of their brainy little Dumpling swaddled in an article of clothing my father, a Yale man himself, should have known went to star athletes, not the tubby likes of me. What I hadn't expected was the way my mother's eyes welled up when I stepped off the train wearing that sweater, or how she hugged me to her and choked out, "Oh, my angel, look at you! You earned a letter sweater!"

I hadn't had the heart to tell Miss Pam that I hadn't come by that sweater honestly. I wondered what sport she thought I'd taken up. Bowling? Darts? The Chemistry Decathlon? She never asked. I assumed Big Howard had some idea of the truth and kept it to himself. In retrospect, I wonder now if the real reason he didn't speak up was that he was easily duped, as my uncle had discovered and as we were all about to learn. The pilfered piece of clothing didn't return to Yale in the fall because I didn't either, not after the bottom fell out of our lives in Tennessee. I'd forgotten all about it.

The shoes still fit, though they were a little tight. The funny thing about the sweater was that my pick-and-shovel work at my previous job had given me the proportions of whatever careless athletic titan it originally belonged to. I wore it whenever I needed to play dress-up. Sort of an inside joke, worn on the outside.

So that Saturday night I squired our ladies into Tony's Spanish Ballroom in my Joe College mufti. Sam had on a loose-fitting cotton tunic and pants with the crotch down around his knees that our maharaja had sent him all the way from India after getting a load of how Sam danced. My cowboy colleague may not have talked much, but that boy could cut a rug. He specialized in a wild, unfettered Lindy hop, turning backflips when there was room, tossing exhilarated and slightly terrified women between his legs and over his shoulders, dropping to a split and pulling himself upright again using just the strength of his thighs. I think the day that package arrived from the maharaja may have been one of the happiest of Sam's life. No more dancing at a masquerade ball in unforgiving dungarees for him.

"Dance, ma'am?" Sam asked Mary Louise as soon as we arrived. He didn't have any special affinity for her—Sam was never much of one for playing favorites—but he knew she'd been a showgirl once and also she happened to be wearing trousers. Overalls, specifically—or, as Sam always called them, "overhauls." When I suggested once that they were actually called "overalls," Sam looked at me narrowly and said, "Don't you think I know that, son? My folks called them overhauls. That's how come I do."

I'll say this for Mary Louise—she may not have been the sharpest blade in the drawer, but she was a brilliant dancer. "Mercy," Zep said as we foxtrotted past that pair. "I never would have imagined Sam would be such a live wire on the dance floor." The Zeppelin was dressed like a soothsayer in layers of ruffles and swirling skirts and extravagant costume jewelry that actually might have been the real thing. I had the paisley library tablecloth draped over one shoulder because she'd found it too hot to dance in along with all the other folderol she had on.

"His sisters taught him," I explained. "They figured if they worked up a family act, it might get them off the farm. Into the movies, you know, the way dancing did that for Ginger Rogers and Jimmy Cagney."

"I guess it didn't work out."

"Oh, they made it to Hollywood, but they like to have starved while they were waiting to get discovered. So the girls went back to Arkansas. Sam said he'd rather die of hunger than go back there. Lucky for him, he knew a guy in Hollywood who knew Max. Sam's worked at the Flying Leap since day one."

"I wonder why Sam didn't want to go back to Arkansas? It's nice," the Zeppelin said. "I got divorced there once, in Hot Springs. Everyone was so friendly, and I saw Al Capone and Lucky Luciano eating pimento-cheese sandwiches on the porch of my hotel. Or two men who looked like them, anyway. I don't really like pimento cheese. Do you?"

"Pimento cheese is not for everybody," I said. "As for why Sam didn't want to go back to Arkansas, I guess that's his secret. Most everybody has one, at least."

Zep arched an eyebrow and dug the fingers of her right hand into my shoulder to pull me a little closer. "What's yours?" she asked.

I used to be a merchant prince, I thought but did not say. "If I told you it wouldn't be a secret anymore, would it?" I said, and winked.

Margaret had said during my interview that she liked hiring southern boys because even poor ones like me had nice manners and flirted with everybody they came across without setting any store by it. I was fine with the flirting but I confess it made me uncomfortable when somebody who was the contemporary of my dead grandmother tweaked me while we were dancing. Years later, during the war, if I found myself on leave and in a dance hall in Europe, I always tipped taxi dancers extravagantly.

"I think I know what your secret is," Zep said.

"Oh, do you," I said.

"Your mother taught you how to dance."

I hoped I didn't look as relieved as I felt. "Guilty as charged," I said. "How can you tell?"

"Because you dance like people my age do, instead of like a maniac the way Sam does."

"You're too kind," I said.

"Too old is more like it. Your mother must be almost as old as I am."

Give or take fifteen years. "She is," I said.

"Is she still with us?"

"Yes."

"And your father?"

"Him, too."

"Are they still married to each other?"

"Last I heard," I said. "Why do you ask?"

"Because as much as it hurts, I have to admit you're too young for me. So I was thinking maybe your apple didn't fall far from your father's tree."

"Aren't you sweet," I said. "But Miss Pam and Big Howard are still in love and living back home in Whistler."

"They're lucky," Zep said. "Are they still in the house you grew up in? On a farm, I'm guessing?"

"No, ma'am. I was a city boy. More a town than a city, really. My parents let the old house go a few years back and moved into a little place that was easier to take care of." I could still see my mother standing in the kitchen, sobbing into a tea towel after Big Howard told her we'd lost the house as well as the business. *But I've lived here half my life,* Miss Pam had wailed. *I thought I'd live here until I died.* There was nothing like the Depression for taking things away from people who thought it couldn't happen to them.

The Zeppelin laid her head against my chest and I closed my eyes and pretended I was dancing with my dead grandmother, also an armful, in our parlor back in Whistler.

I surprised myself then by saying, "If it's the last thing I ever do, I'm getting that house back. My children and my children's children will grow up there, trip over all the things I cherished, and say, 'What are we going to do with all this junk when Big Daddy dies?' "

Zep picked her head up, considered me, and nodded. "My parents gave our house to my oldest brother. Nobody asked for my opinion because I was a girl. I've never forgiven them, even though they've been dead for thirty years. You'll get that house back someday if you really want it."

"You think?" I asked.

"Of course you will. You're smart and you're male. The cards are stacked in your favor."

Before I could respond, Sam tapped on my shoulder to cut in. "Give me the keys to the Chevrolet," he murmured in my ear as I handed over Zep. "Your turn with cleanup." He tilted his head to indicate something going on behind her back.

I slipped him the keys. Sam and I traded off who got stuck taking care of the women who were about to get their business in a bad fix. As a rule our ladies weren't used to how heartbreak and high altitude affected their ability to hold their liquor, so sometimes things got messy.

As Sam artfully rumbaed the Zeppelin away I looked in the direction he'd indicated and saw a pair of women weaving unsteadily in my direction. The shorter one was dressed as a fairy, in a gossamer costume that looked familiar for some reason. Glittery wings and a disconcertingly expressionless full-face mask that I recognized once I got a load of the papier-mâché donkey's head the taller woman was wearing. They were costumes from the college's production of *A Midsummer Night's Dream.* The woman in Bottom's head also wore a string of pearls, and nothing else. Though I couldn't see her face, I recognized those pearls. Also, from the evidence on display, I gathered Nina was a natural blonde.

Chapter Ten

"But she had clothes on when we got outta the car," Emily said. "What happened to the rest of your donkey costume, N—?"

"Shhh," I said. "No names." Emily and Nina weren't titled aristocrats or Vanderbilts, but showing up at a costume party naked from the neck down might be enough to land a plain vanilla rich girl in the gossip rags on a slow night.

Nina's muffled voice fell from the lips of Bottom's papier-mâché head. "Too hot," she said.

The donkey's glass marble eyes rolled toward the ceiling, but its mouth was open wide enough for the person inside to see out. When I peeked in I saw the faint glimmer of Nina's eyes, the way you'll see light reflected in a possum's retinas if you surprise one rooting through the garbage.

"Hi, Cash," Nina said. "You see me naked?"

"Not anymore." I was swaddling Nina in the tablecloth I was now grateful to have draped across me. Once I had her wrapped up tight I tucked its fringed edge under one of her armpits as if it were a sarong.

"So now we even," she said. "I saw alla you, you saw alla me."

"That's right," I said. I scanned the crowd to see if anybody else had seen alla Nina. It really said something for what a hopping spot Tony's was that night that nobody seemed to have noticed the entrance of a six-foot-tall woman wearing nothing but a donkey's head and pearls.

"I tol' her, take off Bottom if it makes ya sweat," Emily said. "Meant tha head, not tha drawers. Why masks so hot? Ima take mine off."

"Nobody takes off anything else until I say so," I said. "Outside. Follow me."

Nina started shaking her head from side to side like a toddler with a dried crowder pea lodged in her ear canal. "Nuh-uh," she said. She stamped her foot and almost toppled over.

"Stilts," I said, "you're a mess."

"Whass new," she said.

"What's new is that it's time to go. Half past let's get out of here." I swept her into my arms and carried her to the exit, the way a mother forcibly evacuates a child from a birthday party when the kid's having a tantrum over leaving before the cake is served. "Chickadee, grab the back of my sweater and hold on tight."

Outside, I nipped into the mouth of the closest alley and propped Nina against the wall. Then I noticed something on the sidewalk that looked like roadkill coyote. "Is that what I think it is?" I asked, and pointed.

I'd hoped the fresh air would help the pair of them sober up, but both seemed even more intoxicated. Nina didn't respond at all. Emily at least turned her blank ivory mask in the direction I'd just pointed. Finally she covered one of her eyeholes, considered the thing for a year or two, and finally said, "Thass Bottom's bottom."

When I looked back at Nina she was sliding down the wall. I caught her before she hit the dirt and gathered her up in my arms again. She was so light that I wondered if her bones were hollow, like a bird's. Once I got the length of her arranged against me, I looked around to see Emily bent double, heaving. There are probably worse places to be sick than inside a full-face mask, but I can't think of one.

"Emily," I said. "Take off the mask."

Emily straightened, pushed the mask up onto her hair, and wiped her eyes. I realized that she'd been laughing. "Sa funny!" she said. "Bottom's bottom. Bot-tom's bot-tom."

I sighed. "What got into you two?"

"Shots," Emily said.

"I figured it was something along those lines." Nina seemed much worse for the wear than Emily did, which surprised me. "How many shots did Stilts have?"

"Too many," Emily said. She made a stab at calculating on her fingers, but was having a hard time finding one hand with the other. "Three. Or four. Five? Shickadee starta feeling sick, so starta tossin hers ina back seat. Always thinkin." Emily tried to tap her forehead but then gave up on locating that as well.

A horrible thought occurred to me. "The back seat? You were sitting up front with the cabdriver, doing shots?"

"No cab," Emily said. She shook her head, then put a hand against the alley wall to steady herself. "Ma car."

"Don't tell me you drove here like this," I said. "Please."

"I did not," Emily said, straightening up and enunciating carefully. "Nina did."

We followed the bread crumbs of Nina's costume around the corner of the building and toward the river, Emily picking up every piece we came across. She only fell down once. I couldn't help her to her feet, either, since I was carrying an armload of ass-headed millionairess. That evening I think I must have started codifying the advice I would someday pass along to parents of idiot children whose foolish hijinks landed them in the emergency room. Better here than in the morgue, I'd say. Now is not the time to lecture. Save it for tomorrow, when your little knuckleheads will have a better appreciation of how lucky they are to be alive.

The Pierce-Arrow, when we found it, was over by the river, top down, front doors open, keys still in the ignition. It was a wonder somebody hadn't stolen it. After a few tries Emily managed to open the back door for me. What looked like one of the bedsheets from the ranch house had been spread across the back seat, something I was glad of but Margaret probably wouldn't be. I eased Nina down onto it, holding her upright with one hand while I pulled the donkey's head off with the other.

Nina's hair was plastered to her head with sweat. She blinked a few times and squinted at me. "Cash!" she said. "Izz you!"

"Who did you think was carrying you?" I asked. "Emily?"

"Nope," Nina said, and kissed me full on the mouth. She smelled like peppermint gone sour, and tasted like it, too. "You so pretty, Cash," she said when I pulled away. "Why?"

"People say I look like my father," I said, "who looked like his father. The Bennett genes are strong."

"No," Nina said. She shook her head vehemently, almost tumbling from the seat to the floor. When I righted her she put a lot of thought and effort into making a fist and thumped the middle of my chest. "Y," she repeated. "Shouldna Y be a scarla A? Ors scarla A jus for girls?" Then she flopped back across the seat and closed her eyes.

I circled the Pierce-Arrow once to check for damage. Miraculously, there was not a scratch on it. I picked up the donkey's head and put it in the trunk, then looked around for Emily so I could take Bottom's bottom off her hands. The gray terry cloth pieces lay abandoned in a pile. Alarmingly, there was no sign of Emily anyplace.

She hadn't wandered far, though. I found her kneeling by a storm drain, the tips of her wings tucked neatly under her ankles and her empty-eyed mask flipped to the back of her head. I knelt alongside her, eased the mask off, and held her hair while she retched. After she finished, I scrambled down the riverbank and dipped a bandana into the cold, fresh river water. Emily wiped her face with it and sat back on her heels. After a few deep, shaky breaths she said, "Drinking too much is less fun than Nina made it out to be."

"Yes," I said.

"When I was pregnant with Portia I threw up all day long, for months," she said. Her purge seemed to have sobered her up considerably. "My doctor worried I'd starve to death. Only thing I could hold down, and only sometimes, were saltine crackers."

If I had been to medical school already by then I could have explained that her problem might have been hyperemesis gravidarum, a somewhat rare condition experienced mostly during first pregnancies. The other thing we doctors used to call that was "nature's birth control." It took a brave woman to step up for another at-bat after suffering through it once.

I hadn't been to medical school yet, however, so I said, "That couldn't have been much fun."

"It wasn't," she said. "Do you know, my husband never held my hair for me when I was sick? Not once."

I helped Emily out of her wings and put them in the trunk while she crept into the front seat for the drive back to the ranch. When I fired up the ignition I could see in the light from the dashboard that her face was sweaty and a few shades paler than her mask had been.

"Not yet," she said. "Let's wait until my stomach settles?"

"Fine by me," I said.

She took a deep breath and exhaled it. "I don't think I'm cut out for Nina's thrilling adventures." Her voice sounded even croakier than usual.

"I thought she said she'd rather be shot than come to a masquerade."

"Maybe that's why she asked me to have you hide her gun," Emily replied. "To avoid the temptation."

"Where were your car keys?" I asked.

"Nina found them in one of my boots."

"After she hid them there."

"Probably so."

"So she planned on the two of you going to the party all along?"

"It was going to be a surprise."

"And Nina drove all the way to Reno with Bottom's head on?"

"Of course not," Emily said. "Nina isn't crazy. She couldn't see well enough to drive with it on. She realized that after we turned onto the main road and ended up in a ditch. Lucky for us, the ditch was shallow so we were able to drive out of it. I pushed."

"Lucky, yes," I said. "Go on."

They'd stopped first by a liquor store, then parked the Pierce-Arrow by the river and started drinking. I was relieved to hear they hadn't been quite as irresponsible as I'd thought. More like a couple of giggly, boneheaded teenagers who'd taken in a lot of alcohol, too fast, without eating dinner first. Rookie mistake, like the kids say now. Still, I assumed Nina had done enough dissipating to know how to go about it better. I guess I had misjudged her.

Emily wrapped up her account with, "I left the top down so the schnapps in the upholstery would have time to dry out before we drove home."

"Schnapps!" I said. They really were like teenagers.

"It tasted like mouthwash," she said. "Peppermint flavored."

That explained the flavor of Nina's kiss. "And who, exactly, was going to drive home, since neither of you was in any shape to?" I asked.

"You were," Emily said. "We meant to steal you away. Well, not steal, not exactly. Nina says we have dibs on you for as long as we're on the ranch."

"Is that so?"

"She said Margaret told her we could take you whenever we wanted."

"I see," I said. "I guess I should be flattered that you two think I'm worth taking. Speaking of things worth taking, did it occur to you that leaving the keys in the ignition was an open invitation for somebody to steal the car?"

"Nina left them there because she was afraid she'd lose them."

"I can understand that, since birthday suits don't come with pockets," I said. "I thought she didn't know how to drive."

"I taught her," Emily said. "We had lessons almost every night."

"Because everybody knows the best time to learn how to drive is between midnight and two A.M."

"The car has headlights," Emily said.

"Yes. I remember."

She laughed, then covered her mouth with her hand.

"Go ahead. Laugh," I said. "I'm glad you thought that was funny."

"I think I may be sick again," Emily said.

"Oh," I said. "In that case, close your eyes and put your head between your knees until it passes."

The two of us sat there, listening to the music the Washoe zephyr delivered to us from the dance hall while Nina sawed logs in the back seat. You wouldn't have thought it, but her percussive snoring made a nice duet with the Johnny Mercer ditty they started playing, "You Must Have Been a Beautiful Baby." Emily picked her head up when she heard that one and started humming along. Then she groaned and collapsed back against the seat. "Take me home, Ward. If we wait until I feel better, we might be here all night."

"You're the boss," I said. I put the car in gear and pulled away from the river. In the back seat, Nina shifted and stopped snoring. Emily tipped the mirror down to see if she was still asleep. When she tipped it up again, she said, "That's part of Nina's charm, you know."

"Her snoring?" I asked.

"How she believes that anything worth doing is worth overdoing. She says that's what she wants engraved on her tombstone. Do you know what she thinks will be carved on mine?"

"What?"

"'I told you that was dangerous!'" She laughed. It was oddly silvery, given how gruff her speaking voice was. Then she groaned and put her head between her knees again.

Chapter Eleven

Nina slept splayed across the back seat all the way back to the ranch. Once I got the Pierce-Arrow backed inside the shed, I roused her, pulled her upright, and asked, “Stilts, do you think you can walk into the house under your own steam?”

“Nope.” She raised her arms like a small child and commanded, “Up.” I slid my arms under her knees and carried her into the ranch house. Without the donkey head she was a lot easier to manage.

I toted my tablecloth-wrapped bundle into the library and settled Nina on the couch while Emily scrounged a couple of paisley pillows from the arm-chair by the library table. When I peeled Nina’s arm free of my neck her eyes fluttered open, she whis-pered “Cash,” touched the cleft in my chin, said,

"Looks like a baby's rump," and kissed me on the lips again. When Emily tucked pillows under her head, Nina kissed her on the lips as well, then said, "Nighty-night," and promptly started snoring again. Emily covered her feet with a throw and draped another over her bare shoulders. We watched her for a minute to be sure she was settled in.

"Is it all right to leave her here?" Emily whispered.

"I wouldn't be surprised if she had to sleep down here before," I said. "No menfolk are allowed upstairs after dinner, so if she got this pickled when she stayed with us before she probably ended up here. It happens. If you want to carry her upstairs yourself, be my guest."

"Oh. Never mind."

I switched off the lamp on the library table.

"I can't remember the last time Portia kissed me good night," Emily said. "Not even on the cheek."

"Come on," I said, and touched her hand. "We'd better clear out before the others get back and start asking questions you're too tired to answer."

Emily twined her fingers with mine and let me lead her out into the hall. "I am tired," she said. "I'm too old for this."

"You aren't old," I said.

"Easy for you to say. All this overdoing is exhausting." She looked at the stairs as if they were Mount

Everest. "Where are my fairy wings when I really need them? I wish you could carry me up to bed and tuck me in."

I was reminded of that conversation many decades later, when I stood at the bottom of the stairs in the house my father had built for my mother when they married. I realized that night that, much as I loved the place, the steps had become an almost insurmountable obstacle. I felt like I was spending half my days descending them, clinging for dear life to the railing, and the other half hauling myself upstairs again to go to bed. Where were my fairy wings when I really needed them? I should have considered sleeping in the guest room on the first floor, I know, but that would have meant admitting I'd been bested by old age. So I hung on, making my painful way up and down that cursed flight until I had a fall. It's a wonder it didn't kill me. Sometimes I wish it had.

Oh, you're kind to say that. Yes, I bought the old homestead back as soon as I was able, and still own it. I can give you the address if you want to drive by. It's locked up, all the furniture under sheets. I just can't bear to let it go. I understand now how my mother felt when she was crying into that tea towel when my parents lost the place. The current undertaker in Whistler has been after me to sell it to him. Fellow's name is

Barrymore, can you believe it? As if he were a character out of Dickens. You ever noticed how the loveliest old houses in small towns end up as funeral homes? I suppose that's who's willing to buy smack in the middle of town now. Proximity to local business is not the boon it used to be in the days before the automobile, when people walked to stores and carried their purchases. Like as not the beautiful homes of yesteryear that haven't been pulled down for "progress" are now sandwiched between a Kentucky Fried Chicken and the parking lot for Kroger.

That night at the bottom of the ranch house stairs Emily said, "I remember the last time I carried Portia up to bed. She'd fallen asleep in my lap in front of the fire. She was five or six, and had gotten so big. I struggled all the way to the top with her and when I got there I knew I'd never be able to carry her upstairs again. I thought my heart would break. I had no idea when she was little how much heartbreak having children lets you in for. How much joy."

"Get some sleep," I said. "Take some aspirin and drink a lot of water. You'll feel better in the morning."

About the time she disappeared upstairs I heard the sound of tires crunching in the drive and decided to disappear myself. I slipped out through the kitchen and kept to the shadows of trees and outbuildings on my way to the bunkhouse. As I passed the barn, what looked like a white rag blew across my path. Caterwaul, I realized, on the prowl.

The next morning, Sam and I shuttled back and forth between the kitchen and the dining room, laying out the morning buffet. Zep, an early riser, had planted herself squarely in our path, chattering about the night before, until Margaret shooed her off. I was about to ask Sam if any of the ladies had noticed I'd gone missing from the masquerade when Zep's voice drifted in from the library. "Oh, look, Sam," she called out. "Here's the tablecloth! Hallelujah! I thought I'd lost it."

"Uh-oh," I said, and put down the platter of bacon I was carrying.

Before I could intervene I heard a thump and a yelp. When Sam and I got to the library door, Nina was stretched out naked and blinking at the Zeppelin's feet. "I'm so sorry, Nina," Zep said, looking aghast and clutching the tablecloth to her bosom. "That pillow over your head and the throws! I didn't see—Nina, why, I never meant to—"

Nina hauled herself upright with admirable dignity, brushed herself off, patted Zep on the shoulder, and said, "It's the edge that did you in again. You really have to get Sam to teach you how to do that trick right."

Then she fingered her pearls, selected a book from the stack on the library table, opened it, and ambled our way. "Gentlemen," she said, and winked at us as she shouldered past and headed for the stairs.

Zep, still dithering apologies, stood with Sam and me as we watched Nina's ascent. She took her sweet time about it.

"I used to be just that slim when I was young," the Zeppelin said once Nina disappeared into the upstairs hall. "I really should have walked around naked more."

While Sam and I were gathering up the dirty plates after breakfast, he shook his head and started chuckling. As funny as Sam was, it was almost impossible to make that man laugh. If I managed once a year, I felt like I'd accomplished something.

"What?" I asked.

"Old Zep," he said. "She's a sly one."

"How do you mean?"

He pitched his voice an octave higher. "'Nina! Why, I never!'" He hooted, then dropped back into his usual range. "Zep's been on the prowl for ways to take Nina down a peg ever since she got here."

I had no idea what he was talking about at first. Then it hit me. "You mean that business in the library? You think the Zeppelin did that on purpose?"

"Think about it, son," Sam said. "Zep had to put her back into it to dump Nina off that couch. When she found her rolled up in that tablecloth, out cold, she must of thought, 'Hot dog! Here's my chance.' Nina being buck naked inside it, well, that was the icing on the cake." Sam shook his head and grinned. "Then dang if Nina didn't see her bid and raise her one."

It occurred to me then that maybe Sam was a little bit in love with Nina, too.

As was often the case after a big blowout of an evening, things were quiet at the Flying Leap the following afternoon. Most of our ladies who had made it down for breakfast or lunch had retreated to their bedrooms to sleep through the hot part of the day.

I'd taken advantage of the quiet to help Margaret by hanging the laundry on the line. On days when the sun was fierce and the wind stiff, the first sheets I hung were about ready to be taken down by the time I pinned up the last. I'd just clipped the second corner of the final one in place and was walking down the aisle between the bedclothes to make sure everything was securely attached when a gust snapped a sheet horizontal and revealed Emily, looking square at me. When the wind dropped it again I raised the sheet and asked, "Were you looking for something?"

"Yes," she said. "You. Margaret said I'd find you here hanging out laundry and I wanted to see it for myself. You certainly do know your way around a clothespin." She ducked under the clothesline to join me on my side.

"I'd tell you to pull up a chair, except the show's over now," I said, dropping the sheet behind her.

Emily was wearing a loose, white, ankle-length shift that looked sort of like a nightgown but might not have been. She was barefoot, though, and her hair was mashed flat on one side. "I could use a chair, after last night," she said. "I'm still a bit shaky." Her eyes were squinty and a little bloodshot.

"You aren't feeling well?" I asked. "Did you remember to take aspirin?"

"I'm not sure," she said. "I thought I did, but—" She put two fingertips to each temple and grimaced. "I feel about as rotten as I must look right now."

"You look all right," I said. "But if you don't feel good why don't you go back to bed? That's where everybody else is."

"Nina says the best cure for a hangover is floating in your back on a lake. Apparently there's one nearby that's known for its curative waters."

"Pyramid Lake," I said. "People do say that about it. So you're headed there? Sounds like as good an idea as any."

"Yes! Terrific! Nina said you'd be up for going. I wasn't sure you would be after what we put you through last night."

It took longer than it should have for the light to dawn. "Emily, I work for Max and Margaret, not you two hooligans. I can't just up and go wherever, whenever."

"Nina's asking now if they can spare you," Emily said. "Look! Here she comes."

Sure enough, Nina scrambled down the trellis and pelted across the barnyard, running straight for the mouth of our corridor of sheets. A large canvas bag swung behind her and she was wearing what looked like the fairy costume minus its wings and mask. "Is this the new clubhouse?" she asked breathlessly when she joined us among the flapping linens. "Club Three Sheets to the Wind?"

"Is that my fairy costume?" Emily asked.

"I found it wadded up on the bedroom floor. Finders keepers."

Emily tsked. "Look what you've done. You snagged the chiffon on the thorns and tore it. Here and here. Oh, Nina. How could you be so careless?"

"Just doing what comes naturally," she replied, plucking clothespins from the closest sheet, tossing the pins into her bag, then gathering the sheet up and stuffing it in after.

"I'll have to stitch it up later," Emily said. "I'm glad I brought along a sewing kit." This, from a woman who'd buy a new car rather than clean its kittened upholstery.

"Of course you did," Nina said. "Come on. Let's get out of here before the others realize we're going swimming and ask to tag along." She helped herself to two more sheets and a few towels after feeling several to see which were the closest to being dry.

"Hang on a minute," I said. "Margaret—"

"Margaret said to help ourselves to whatever we need."

"And she knows you're helping yourself to me?" I asked.

"Yes, yes," Nina said. "Now hurry up. The Zeppelin was just knocking on our door, asking how I was feeling. She thinks we should be friends now, just because she's seen me naked. As if that were such an exclusive club. Let's go!"

"What did you say when Zep knocked?" Emily asked.

"I didn't say anything. I stuffed a tissue in the keyhole and pretended I wasn't there." Nina tugged at the neck of the fairy costume. "This thing is choking me. I think I might have it on backward."

"You do," Emily said. "The 'V' goes in front. Pull your arms in and I'll turn it around for you." Nina dropped the canvas bag and did as she was told. Emily fingered the tattered spots in the fabric and shook her head before she spun the dress around. "At least the rips won't be as noticeable in the back," she said.

"Let me run this empty laundry basket back to Margaret and grab my swimsuit," I said. "If I can remember where I stowed it."

Nina reinserted her arms in the opposite armholes and shimmied until the costume fell into place around her. That outfit had raked the floor when Emily wore it, but on Nina it was more what you would call tea length. "Margaret said to leave the basket here so she can use it to bring in the sheets," she said. "As for swimsuits, I have everything we'll need right here." She picked up the canvas bag again and patted it.

"You have my bathing suit?" I asked. "Where was it?"

"Speaking of things that have been shredded by wild things, a coyote pulled your swimsuit off the clothesline and ripped it to pieces after you wore it the last time. Alas, it was beyond repair."

"What?"

"That's what Margaret said. She didn't have the heart to tell you when it happened. She feels awful about it, so she's loaning you Max's."

I'd never seen Max in a swimsuit. "Max's?" I asked. "What does it look like?"

"It has a tank top and pants that go below the knees. Margaret said Max was wearing it when they met on the beach in Atlantic City twenty years ago."

"Max and Margaret met in Atlantic City twenty years ago?" I was so taken by this tidbit of intimate history that I didn't ask all the questions I should have.

"Didn't I just say that? Come on. Let's get out of here."

Nina grabbed Emily's hand, raced to the car, and shoved her into the front seat before climbing in behind her. When the Pierce-Arrow was halfway down the driveway I looked in the rearview mirror and saw Margaret in the yard, semaphoring with a kitchen towel. "There's Margaret," I said. "I'd better go back and see what she wants."

Nina turned around and looked. "Keep going. She came out to see us off. That's all." Nina waved at

Margaret vigorously, blew a few kisses in her direction, and settled into the seat facing forward again.

"It won't take a minute to—" I tapped the brakes.

"Don't you trust me, Ward? Fine. Turn around. Ask Margaret if I'm lying. While you're working all that out, Zep will have plenty of time to round up all the others. Liz. Theresa. Martha. Dopey. Grumpy. Think of what fun our little party will turn into with the Seven Dwarfs along."

"You're terrible, Nina," Emily said. "You have no idea how aggravating it is, being short. Everything you need the most always seems to be just out of reach. Anyway, there are only six of them."

"Six? There are seven dwarfs. It's right there in the title. *Snow White and the Seven Dwarfs.*"

"Yes, but there are only six other guests. Six of them, plus the two of us."

Nina made an exasperated noise. "What difference does that make, Emily?" She leveled that cobra gaze of hers on me again. "The point is, Ward, you could go back, or you could keep driving. Your call."

I gave the car the gas again.

Chapter Twelve

It was late afternoon by the time the three of us piled out of the Pierce-Arrow at Pyramid Lake, a vast body of water an hour north of the Flying Leap. The lake was on a Paiute reservation—still is, as far as I know—and had been left pretty much untouched back then, aside from a road that connected Reno to the reservation and the old fishing camp on the lake edge that had once doubled as a stagecoach stop.

I parked on a pebbly beach, far enough back from the water's edge that the wheels wouldn't get mired in sand. The lake stretched immense and placid, a bathtub for the gods, its azure surface stamped here and there with silvery scales where the wind and insects tipped it. The inland sea it once was had shrunk over the millennia, leaving behind sand dotted with fossil-covered rubble and a surround of terraced hillsides, the edge of each giant step down to the water's edge an abandoned shoreline.

"If you told me time began here, I'd believe you," Emily said.

"It did," Nina said. "Starting now." She took Emily's hand and the two of them raced barefoot across the scorching beach, hair and dresses flying, like children let loose on the first day of summer. They stood on the cool wet sand at the water's edge waiting for me, moseying along in my cowboy boots and carrying Nina's canvas bag.

"It's so lovely," Emily said to Nina as I caught up to them. "But where are the other people?"

"What other people?" Nina asked.

"The other people who are always all over every other lovely beach I've ever been to in the summertime."

"Not right here, right now," Nina said. "This lake is so remote that I've always had it pretty much to myself in the late afternoon. Except for the birds. They're what brought me here the first time. I was flying along, following the river, because that's the easiest way to navigate when you're just tooling around. Then I fell in with a flock of enormous pelicans, the white ones that have the black-tipped wings. I recognized them right away because they had them at the St. Louis Zoo. Turns out the pelicans were on their way to their nesting grounds on that flattish island over there. That one's named Anaho. The pointy one is called Pyramid. For obvious reasons."

While they were talking I lay a sheet on the sand and emptied the bag of everything else Nina had taken from the clothesline. "I don't see any bathing suits here," I said. I shook all the sheets and towels to make sure the suits hadn't got twisted up inside something larger, but no such luck.

Nina took the bag from me, turned it upside down, shook it, then peered inside again. "Oops," she said. "I must have left the swimsuits on the kitchen counter. Oh, well. We'll have to do without." She pulled the fairy costume over her head and handed it to me. "Hold this," she said. Based on the past two days, if I hadn't seen lingerie clamped to our clothesline by wooden pins marked "Nina," I wouldn't have believed she wore undergarments, ever.

Nina splashed out into the water, then dove under. Just as I was starting to wonder if we'd ever see her alive again she came up for air some distance out. "It gets deep fast, just so you know," she shouted, treading water. "Come on in. It isn't cold."

Emily cupped her hands around her mouth and shouted back, "I. Don't. Have. A. Swimsuit."

Nina shouted back, "You. Don't. Need. One."

Emily put her hands on her hips. "I'm not the kind of person who goes swimming without my clothes on."

"Oh," Nina called. "I thought you were tired of being that kind of person. Pardon me." She dove under again and didn't surface until she was a discreet distance from the shore. Then she flipped on her back and floated.

Emily stared after her for at least a minute. Then she looked up at me, her forehead wrinkled and her eyes suddenly full of tears. "Ward," she said. "Do you know the difference between an elephant and an aspirin?"

"No. What is it?"

"Then I'd better not send you to the car to see if there are any aspirin in the glove compartment. Ha ha." The "ha ha" was so very small and sad. "That used to be Portia's favorite joke. I do have such a headache, though. The trouble is, now I can't think about aspirin without thinking about an elephant. Those two things will be tied to each other in my brain for the rest of my life."

"No wonder you have a headache," I said. "It must be so crowded inside your skull."

She gave me a blank look. "What?"

"It's like that old gag," I said. "Would you care to join me in a cup of tea? Why, yes, but won't it be awfully crowded in there?"

Emily took hold of the dimple in my chin the way Margaret was fond of doing. "You're a boy after my own heart, Ward," she said. She let go and sighed. "My husband hasn't thought anything I said was funny since I don't know how long. Portia used to. She doesn't anymore."

"Tell you what, ma'am," I said. "I'm going to drive over to the fishing camp and fill up the car with gas. If you want to swim, go swim. No one will see that you aren't wearing a swimsuit aside from Nina and the pelicans."

"Will you do me a favor, Ward?" she asked. "Before you leave, will you see if there are any aspirin in the glove compartment? I seem to remember a bottle in there. If you find it, please bring me a couple. If there's an elephant inside, let the poor thing out."

"Sure thing, ma'am," I said, and tipped my hat. I located the bottle she remembered, shook out two, and brought them to her. "I found your aspirin, but I don't have any water for you to take them with," I said.

She held her hand out and I dropped the pills into her palm. "Down the hatch," she said, tossed them back and smiled at me. "Who needs water?" she said, then coughed. She swallowed again, and grabbed my hand with such urgency that I worried she was choking. But when she found her voice again she said, "Please, Ward, *please* don't call me ma'am. It makes me feel like I'm your grandmother."

She surprised me then by pulling her dress over her head, same as Nina had, and handing it to me. The difference was that Emily said, "Happy birthday," and she was wearing underclothes. Still was when she plunged into the water and swam out to where Nina floated.

To get a grip on myself as much as anything before I got behind the wheel, I built a beach cabana of sorts in case the ladies came out of the water before I got back from the fishing camp and wanted shelter. First I weighed down the spread-out sheet with rocks so it wouldn't blow away. I was careful to find pretty ones imprinted with the fossils of ancient bivalves, laughing a little at myself for making the effort since I doubted either of them would notice. After that I folded all the towels and their clothes and tucked the lot inside the canvas bag, then went back to the Pierce-Arrow, hoping to find something I could wedge upright in the sand. I opened the trunk and the papier-mâché donkey's head eyed me accusingly. I lay Bottom's deflated body across his face while I rooted around under the fairy's wings for something I could use to create some shade, but no dice.

I walked around the vehicle, scratching my head and thinking. Then I noticed a little door in the back, on the passenger side, like something Alice would have crawled through into Wonderland after drinking from the bottle of magical shrinking liquid. I opened it out of curiosity and found a set of golf clubs and an enormous golf umbrella that fit the space so perfectly, I figured it must have been a custom job. That was the way-too-wealthy for you. Always finding inventive new ways to spend more money.

As it turned out, the clothespins Nina had tossed into the canvas bag came in handy for constructing a nice little beach pagoda of sheets clipped to the foundation I built of that golf umbrella strapped with my belt to a tent pole made of golf clubs. I wished the Hollywood set designer had been there to see it. I think he would have applauded my ingenuity.

Since sunset in Reno during the high summer came so late, while I was at the fishing camp I bought a jug of water and sandwiches in case Emily and Nina wanted to stay out past dinnertime. I thought I might call Margaret from the store there to give her a heads up, but they didn't have a pay phone. I told myself she would put two and two together since Nina was helming our adventure. They would forgive us for missing dinner.

When I got back to the pebbly beach, Nina came out of my makeshift beach pavilion wrapped in a towel. She waved the fairy costume over her head. "Ahoy, Cash," she called. "I thought we'd been abandoned at sea, but Emily promised you were coming back. We're so thirsty, and Emily refused to let me drink lake water."

Emily joined her, also wrapped in a towel. "There were *fish* swimming in it," she said. "One swam past me that was as long as my arm."

The two of them turned and went inside the tent. I overheard Nina say, "You should have been more sympathetic to that poor fish. Couldn't you see that his heart was broken? This lake was just a puddle before he filled it with his tears. That's why the water's just the tiniest bit salty, you know."

"Oh?" Emily asked. "Why was the fish crying?"

"His soul mate left him. Big fish looking for a deeper pond. You know how it is. She ended up in Scotland."

"Are you talking about the Loch Ness Monster?" Emily asked.

"Please," Nina said. "Nessie is not a monster. She's just larger than the average girl, and very misunderstood."

From the way they were rustling around in there, it seemed they were getting dressed. In case my delicate edifice of sheets collapsed from all the action inside I headed back to the Pierce-Arrow for the sandwiches. When I opened the auto's trunk to retrieve our bag of refreshments my eyes fell on the fairy's wings again. I took them out and strapped them on. They fit all right once I adjusted the buckles some. I amused myself by thinking how the wings would help me mix with the other waterfowl around the lake. I pulled off my cowboy boots and socks, too, and rolled my dungarees up my calves. Might as well get a little wading in if I meant to mingle with those other birds.

As I started picking my way gingerly down to the beach I realized that I'd become the very definition of a tenderfoot. When I was a kid and the weather started getting warm, I couldn't wait until I achieved what we kids in those days called our "summer feet." How long had it taken for my soles to harden into hooves? I couldn't quite remember. My mother hated to see me skipping around without my shoes on. In the first place, Miss Pam couldn't understand how a child with such nice ones would ever want to go without them. In the second, she saw the world outside our house as one big rusty nail lying in wait to deliver a deadly dose of lockjaw. To be fair to Miss Pam, there was a real element of danger in going barefoot before the tetanus vaccine was invented. It was so much harder on a woman's soul to be a mother in the days when a kid could be snatched away by an infection or a disease in the blink of an eye.

But I digress.

The ladies were sitting on the sheet, still wrapped in towels, when I rejoined them. "One of the pair was gone from the exhibit so long that I got worried," Nina was telling Emily. "So I asked the zookeeper in charge of the Flight Cage what had become of it. He said it had a hurt wing."

"Was it broken?"

"Maybe. Probably. I don't remember exactly. I do remember that the zoo vet had the wing bound against the pelican's side to immobilize it until it healed. They let me visit it in the sick bay."

"They did? That was sweet."

"Not sweet so much as smart. They knew my grandfather was obscenely rich, even by St. Louis standards. Made his money manufacturing dog food, which the zookeepers could give to the jackals in a pinch when people didn't throw enough of their awful little children into the jackals' pen."

"Nina!" Emily said. "You're awful."

"I know," Nina said. "Such a shame I managed to climb out of the enclosure before the jackals got me, isn't it? So anyway, I told the zookeeper who my grandfather was, and the next thing you know I was visiting my injured friend. The zoo vet assured me that my pelican would recover. Not enough to live in the wild again, but he was never going to be set free anyway. Oh, look, here's Cash. Bearing gifts." Nina jumped to her feet and ran to me, took my paper bag, and peeked inside. "What are those bundles wrapped in waxed paper? Could they possibly be sandwiches?"

"They are," I said. "Swimming always made me ravenous when I was a kid."

Nina threw her arms around my neck and kissed me, on the cheek this time. "Decorative as well as useful. You're going to make some lucky girl very happy someday." She scampered back to Emily with the jug of water and the sandwiches. "Look what our boyfriend brought us."

By the time I reached the sheet, the two of them were kneeling on it, unwrapping the food I'd brought. Emily seemed as delighted to see me as Nina had been to see the sandwiches. "Oh!" she exclaimed, putting the salami and cheese I had sort of wanted for myself on the sheet beside herself to clasp one of my hands in hers. "Look how beautiful you are in my wings!"

Nina switched the salami and cheese sandwich for the egg salad sandwich she'd just made a face at.

"*Your* wings? You mean the wings you stole from the college?"

"I thought we might as well get a little more mileage out of them before you take them back," I said. I could feel my pants slipping down my haunches without my belt and hitched them up. "The pelicans invited me to a party. The invitation said, 'White tie or wings, please.' I didn't have white tie."

"You couldn't possibly look any better than you do right now, not even in white tie," Emily said.

"I don't know about that," Nina said. "You could put an orangutan in white tie and he'd look like the Prince of Wales. They did that at our zoo once, you know, when they threw a fancy dinner to celebrate the opening of the Ape House. They seated the Prince of Wales at the head table, by an orangutan in a tuxedo. We were at the next table so I saw it with my own eyes."

"They seated an orangutan in a tuxedo next to the Prince of Wales?" Emily asked. "Please tell me you're lying."

"It's not so much a lie as a plausible fiction," Nina said. "In fact, they seated the orangutan next to Mayor Kiel. The mayor wasn't the dandy the Prince of Wales is, of course. More magisterial. I prefer that, actually. Do you want this other sandwich, Emily?" She'd finished the salami and had moved on to the third wax paper bundle.

"What kind is it?"

Nina unwrapped it. "Egg salad."

"No, thanks," Emily said. "I don't like egg salad much."

"Neither do I," Nina said. "Oh, well." She proceeded to make short work of it anyway, watching a pair of pelicans wheel overhead while she ate. "Look how magisterial those pelicans are when they're flying. Once they're on the ground all dignity evaporates. They waddle around like old drunks."

"Well," Emily said. "Word is they drink like fish." She held up a finger. "No, wait, excuse me. I meant to say, they *drink* fish. I saw several do that just this afternoon." She tossed her head back to demonstrate, saying, "Glub, glub, glub," then loosed her tinkly laugh. Emily picked up the sandwich in front of her, took a bite, looked confused, and pulled back the bread on top. I was about to point out that one of the sandwiches was meant for me when she said, "Oh, well. I'm so hungry I could eat a horse. Please don't tell Dumpling that I said that."

"By the way, we aren't taking the wings back," Nina said. "The theater department at the college doesn't need those costumes anymore. They're going to buy themselves a lot of new ones."

"How do you know?" Emily asked. A seagull landed close to the edge of the sheet and eyed her sandwich.

"Because I mailed them a check and attached a note that said, 'If you've noticed a couple of your costumes missing, go buy yourselves a lot of new ones.' I signed the note 'A Friend.'"

Emily shooed the seagull away and nibbled on her sandwich. "Won't they figure out who their friend is when they see your name on the bottom of the check?"

"I wrote them such a large check, I expect they'll be willing to forgive and forget."

The seagull landed a little closer this time. Emily tossed it the rest of the sandwich. "Now go away," she said. "Nobody likes a beggar." The gull took off, the crust of egg salad sandwich clutched in its beak.

I got up then and wandered down to the water. I don't know how long I glared at the pyramid-shaped island, trying not to brood about Nina and Emily eating my dinner. Those two were like children, oblivious to other people's needs as long as theirs were being taken care of. But so many of our guests were like that, as I'd had ample time to witness. No point in working myself into a swivet about it. They'd be gone back where they came from soon enough. I'd learned early on that, for the sake of my sanity, it was best to hold my irritation in check until an irritating guest packed her bags and left.

I'd about talked myself out of my upset when the pair of them showed up at my elbow, their hair dry and wild and their bodies still wrapped in towels, holding three delicate-looking little paper dinghies pinched between their fingers. "Look what Nina made, Ward," Emily said. "Boats. She used the waxed paper the sandwiches you brought us came in."

The two of them knelt in the water at my feet and released the trio of launches onto the water. "The wax makes the paper waterproof," Nina said. "Or at least more waterproof. My mother taught me how to make them when we'd picnic on the beach at our summer place at Lake Leelanau. I always got the hiccups because I ate my sandwiches so fast. I didn't care about the sandwiches, but I couldn't wait to make the boats. Mumsie always insisted I finish eating before we made them."

"I thought you didn't get along with your mother," Emily said as the two of them stood up again and readjusted their towels.

Nina shrugged. "We were as thick as thieves when I was little."

"Portia and I used to be like that." Emily sighed. "I guess I should count myself lucky for having those years instead of wondering why they couldn't go on forever. Anyway, if by some miracle Portia starts speaking to me again, in ten years or so she'll marry and I'll lose her all over again."

"Ten years? Try four," Nina said. "I ran off with my flight instructor when I was seventeen."

Emily closed her eyes and pressed a hand to her heart. "Please," she said. "I can't stand the thought of losing my baby. Let's talk about something else."

"All right," Nina said. "Look how beautiful our little boats are."

Emily opened her eyes. "They are, aren't they? They remind me of that poem. The one about the owl and the pussy-cat, pushing out to sea in a beautiful pea-green boat. I used to read it to Portia at bedtime, over and over, until she fell asleep."

I was about to pipe up with the fact that Miss Pam had read "The Owl and the Pussy-Cat" to lull me to sleep, as well, when my stomach growled noisily.

"Is that your stomach, Emily?" Nina asked. "You should have finished your sandwich, chickadee. Think of the starving Armenians. Cash, we'd better—"

"Don't call me Cash," I snapped, so suddenly that all three of us were a little taken aback. In my defense,

I was hungry. Of course, a reasonable person, Sam for example, might have said, "That was my stomach, ma'am. I'm a mite peckish."

Nina tipped her head to one side and studied me. "But you said you didn't mind me calling you that," she said.

"I said I didn't mind you calling me *Cashmere,*" I said, which only made me feel more foolish. I stumbled out of the water and back to the sheet, and sat heavily, not even exactly sure right then why I was so upset.

The ladies knelt on either side of me, still wrapped up in their towels. "I'm so sorry, Ca—Ward," Nina said. She reached for what I thought would be my shoulder, but her hand touched the tip of one of my wings instead. "I won't call you that ever again. I promise. No more nicknames for any of us, fair enough? We'll just be our own true selves from here on out."

I think all three of us were as startled by the sincerity of her apology as we had been by my outburst. "Fair enough," I said.

"You've taken such good care of us, Ward, and we're so grateful," Emily added. "Just look at the bower you've made for us. Exquisite." She picked up one of the rocks I'd used to weigh the sheet down. "Every one of these rocks is embedded with a lovely fossil, isn't it? Don't think I didn't notice."

"It's true! When Emily started talking about fossils I thought she was trying to tell me that Zep had tracked us down," Nina said. "Watch me make this old fossil skip." She picked up a stone and winged it into the lake, torpedoing one of the little boats and swamping the other two. "Oh, well. We'd better go, hadn't we? Margaret will be wondering what's become of us."

She retreated into the pagoda, but Emily just stood there looking at me. "Can I help you with something?" I asked at last.

"With so many things," she said. "But what I need most of all right now is dry underwear."

In the end, Emily put her dress on with nothing on beneath it, à la Nina. I used the clothespins to clip her wet underthings to the archer crouched on the Pierce-Arrow's hood so the breeze would dry her lingerie before we got back to the ranch. The plan was, we'd stop before we swung into the driveway and Emily would put it on again. It wasn't seven o'clock yet, so we were sure to be home before dark.

Unfortunately, all three of us forgot the plan by the time we got back to the ranch.

Chapter Thirteen

When we got back to the car I held the back door open for the ladies, the way a proper chauffeur would. Nina looked at me like I was crazy. "Are you kidding?" she asked. "Backseat driving is so much easier when you're sitting in the front." She opened the front door on the passenger side for Emily, and gestured for her to climb aboard.

On the way back to the ranch Emily put her head on Nina's shoulder and Nina wrapped an arm around her. They fell asleep that way, Emily tucked under Nina's wing and Nina's face mashed against the half-open passenger-side window. Every time I hit a pothole I stole a glance at them to see if the bump had waked them. They slumbered on.

As we approached the ranch my stomach started growling even louder than before, and I felt annoyed all over about Emily eating half my sandwich and throwing the other half away. But I promise you that's not why I forgot about Emily's underthings clipped to the hood ornament. I just forgot.

I pulled up to the stagecoach shed and put the car in park. Emily and Nina slept on even as I hopped out to open the shed's double doors, climbed in again, and backed the Pierce-Arrow into its spot alongside the coach. I hated to wake them, but I had to figure they wouldn't be happy if I left them in the car overnight. "Emily," I murmured. "Nina. Wake up."

Nothing. I put a hand on Emily's shoulder and was fixing to give it a little shake when I looked up and saw a girl framed in the open shed door, staring at me like a murderess fingering the blade of a newly sharpened knife. Right away I realized who she was. For one thing, she looked just like Emily. For another, I heard Margaret calling, "Portia! Where are you? I think your mother's back!"

Emily jerked awake, disoriented, and gasped, "What?"

Nina bolted upright, equally out of it, put a hand to her hip, and said, "What is it? What's going on? Where's my gun?"

The girl said, "Blindfolding the archer with your panties, Mother? Is this another of your stupid jokes?" She snatched Emily's underthings from the hood ornament and flung them at the windshield.

Are you familiar with the concept of the Hail Mary pass? It comes from football, a sport I'm not particularly fond of given all the broken bones and concussions I've been called to the emergency room to take care of over the years. However. In the 1930s there was a big game between a Catholic university and some state school, I forget which. A halfback on the Catholic side by the name of, get this, *Bill Shakespeare* threw a desperate, last-ditch pass in the final seconds of the game, a play that didn't seem to have a prayer of succeeding yet resulted in a game-winning touchdown. One of the headlines trumpeting the game's results summed it up like this: *Church Beats State with Hail Mary Pass.*

This was in the middle of the Depression, when uplifting stories were few and far between, so some version of that event ran in all the papers. I was at Boulder Dam then and read every newspaper I could get my hands on from cover to cover, even articles I wasn't much interested in. The papers were my only companions, see, as I wasn't any better at befriending my fellow man there than I'd been at Yale. I'd learned the hard way not to mention my Ivy League past when I was working at the dam after someone who hadn't had the opportunities I once had punched me in the face when I brought it up in conversation.

The doctor who pushed my broken nose back into alignment prescribed aspirin, sleeping sitting up until the swelling went down, and keeping my year of fancy college education to myself going forward. "If anybody asks how this happened, tell them you were fighting over a woman," he advised. I didn't know near as much about women then as I was about to learn at the Flying Leap, so I decided I was better off not say anything. I really knew precious little about women until I got myself mixed up with Doorknockers. After that I guess you could say that Emily and Nina saw to it that I left the ranch with a graduate degree.

Where was I? Oh, yes. I was telling you how Portia ended up at the ranch. Dropping her off to spend what should have been her mother's last couple of weeks at the Flying Leap was Archer's Hail Mary pass. If he couldn't talk Emily out of divorcing him, he figured Portia might be able to.

Emily climbed over Nina in her eagerness to get to her daughter. Nina pulled herself together and got out of the car in time to waylay Max, who was bearing down on me with the determination of a man ready to administer a tracheotomy with his thumbs.

Don't get the wrong idea about Max. He was one of the most genial men I have ever known, at least until you crossed him. I only saw him angry twice: once when a liquor supplier tried to cheat him, and the second time when a cast-off husband showed up at the ranch and made a show of bullying one of our ladies into going back to him. When Max was angry he didn't turn red in the face or yell. He went icy, like one of the cold-blooded killers from a gangster movie he styled himself after sartorially. He refused to keep firearms at the ranch, however, not even a rifle for shooting coyotes, as he felt gunplay was not only hell on tailoring but also always made bad situations worse. When a crisis cropped up, he strolled into the thick of it with a keen spade propped on his shoulder like a baseball bat, looking you over as if he were trying to decide the best way to cut you up so that your parts would fit into a compact hole. Let me tell you, neither of those men stuck around long enough to find out if Max actually intended to dismantle them.

Max hadn't picked up the spade yet when Nina intervened, but it was clear he wasn't happy. Of course, it was all Nina's fault that I was in trouble in the first place.

"Max, Max, Max," she said, grabbing his wrist and intertwining her fingers with his. "Don't be mad at Ward. I told him I'd ask Margaret if he could escort us to the lake this afternoon but I got distracted and then I forgot. I am so very sorry. I hope we didn't inconvenience anybody."

Max glanced from her face to mine. I'm sure I looked as startled as I felt, although I shouldn't have been surprised to hear this. His expression softened and he wagged a finger at her. "I should have known you had something to do with this," he said. "Well, you'd better run tell Margaret. She's at her desk right now, writing out a listing to send to every paper in Nevada to advertise for Ward's replacement."

Nina threw her arms around Max's neck and kissed his cheek. "Of course, you darling," she said, and trotted off across the barnyard. She was still wearing that ridiculous fairy costume. Or maybe it wasn't so much ridiculous as custom-made for her, given the power Nina wielded over people thanks to a magic combination of good looks and great personal charm, backed up by lots of money. As for me, a humbled-by-circumstance working stiff, I was shaken to the core by my close call with unemployment. I had been both idiotic and too trusting. I swore nothing like that would happen to me again.

"He was smote," Mary Louise said to me when I hustled into the house to find out what was going on with Emily and Portia. She was in the front hall at the phone table by the stairs, her fingertips resting on the receiver she'd just returned to its cradle and a single tear trailing cinematically across her lovely cheek.

"Who was smote?" I asked.

"My husband. He had a heart attack while he was breaking one of God's commandments."

"Which commandment?" I asked.

"'Thou shalt not cover thy neighbor's wife.'"

The urge to laugh bubbled up inside me while I fought to maintain my poker face. "Cover" was just a consonant away from "covet," after all. Instead of laughing I managed, "Your husband—is he all right?"

"If by all right you mean dead as a doornail, yes, he's fine. I've been wishing that old fool would die ever since he threw me away so he could marry that harpy he's been covering once our divorce goes through. A *schoolteacher.* In her *forties.* Now that he's dead I don't know how guilty I'm supposed to feel about it. Him up and dying is my fault, after all."

"Whoa there, ma'am," I said. "It is *not* your fault. Hearts give out. Particularly older ones."

"It *is* my fault," she insisted. "Remember the barnstormer? And the girl in line who was so sure she was going to marry him? I wished them both dead, and look what happened. All I have to do is pray on it and the Almighty takes over for me. Dammit." Then she let loose a flood of tears that the Boulder Dam itself would have been challenged to contain. "I'm going to miss that old fool," she wailed.

"Now, now," I said, and patted her shoulder. "The Almighty has his hands too full with war and pestilence to drop everything to smite one fornicating old man for you."

You're right. I didn't say that last bit. Only thought it.

Mary Louise wiped her face with her palms. "At least now I get all his money, instead of just some lousy settlement. He was too busy slipping it to the neighbor to change his will and I wasn't about to remind him. I can afford to marry anybody I want to next time. Heck, I could marry you."

Portia tore past us then and pounded up the stairs. She must have been sprung from Margaret's office, because Emily and Nina came out the office door soon after. "Which way did she go?" Emily asked.

I pointed upstairs just as clothing started raining down the stairwell like manna from Saks Fifth Avenue. I recognized some of Emily's dresses and blouses as they fluttered into the stairwell. A pair of peach silk panties settled themselves onto the newel post and tilted jauntily to one side, a lingerie beret.

"Portia isn't wasting any time helping you move out of Coyote," Nina said.

"I guess I should go talk to her," Emily said.

Nina laid a hand on her arm, shook her head, and went upstairs instead.

Mary Louise, meanwhile, plucked Emily's drawers from the newel post and peered at them. "Hmm. Store-bought," she mused. "I have all my underclothes handmade by Spanish nuns. Also my husband just dropped dead."

I think Nina was as grateful to have an excuse to go after Portia as Emily was to stay behind to gather up her store-bought unmentionables and offer condolences to the freshly widowed Mary Louise.

"Thank you," Mary Louise responded after Emily had administered the usual platitudes. "But the old boy had it coming. I loved him, but he was an infidel. That's why I had to file for a divorce, you know."

After some rapid-fire blinking, Emily asked, "Because of his infidelity?"

"That's right," Mary Louise said. "He was a cheater. Like all men are."

Reflexively, the two of them turned their eyes on me. "I'm sorry," I said.

"Oh, you don't count, Ward," Mary Louise said. "I meant real men, like Emily's husband."

"Yes," Emily said, "I suppose he is an infidel."

"Cheaters cheat," I said. "It's what they do."

I wasn't in on the negotiations with Margaret over the new sleeping arrangements at the Flying Leap. All I know is that Emily moved into Scorpion and Portia took over her mother's berth in Coyote. "We'll let Nina work her magic on her," Margaret explained to me later. "She'll have that girl eating out of her mother's hand in no time."

I thought of Nina charming Emily into scrambling down the trellis and skinny-dipping and stealing costumes and drinking schnapps to excess. Of Nina's revolver tucked under my bed.

"And Emily was all right with this?" I asked.

"Not just all right. Relieved," Margaret said. "She's at her wit's end with that child. Emily's in a delicate situation, you understand. Portia is Archer's daughter, too, so it would be wrong to bad-mouth him to her, no matter how much he may deserve it. Nina's confident she can talk some sense into the kid. Rebellious daughter to rebellious daughter."

"I guess that could work," I said. Who was I to judge? I had no children of my own. Never did, alas. Not that I know of, anyway, ha ha.

In retrospect, Portia's arrival at the ranch was like somebody tossing a lit match on a stack of dry kindling. I've always wondered if what happened between Emily and me would have come about if Portia hadn't shown up to stir the pot. Because before Portia had been at the Flying Leap a week, Emily and I were covering the bejesus out of each other.

Chapter Fourteen

"Can I tell you a secret?"

It was an unfamiliar female voice, and just past sunup. I was on my back on the floor of the empty stall next to Dumpling when I heard two sets of footsteps coming along the breezeway that ran down the middle of the barn.

Well, give me a minute and I'll tell you why I was lying on the floor there. We had more stalls than we had horses, so I'd swept the pounded-dirt floor clean in the unused enclosure next to Dumpling and converted it into a kindergarten for Taffy's kittens. The shoulder-height walls kept them from straying into danger while their mother was out hunting, and the slats that ran the rest of the distance to the ceiling were widely spaced enough to let Taffy slip through when she came home to give them breakfast. Before my day got started, I'd been coming to spend a few minutes with the kittens so they wouldn't grow up feral.

"A secret? Sure. Who doesn't love a secret?" I heard Nina say, then realized the other voice must belong to Portia. The pair of them had stopped in front of Dumpling's stall, just a couple of feet away from my head. From where I lay I saw Dumpling's ears pass the slatted part of the wall between us like the periscope of a submarine as he shuffled to the front of his stall and poked his head out to greet his visitors. I couldn't see Nina and Portia, so I was fairly confident they couldn't see me. I started picking kittens off my shirtfront so that I could stand up and announce myself.

That's when the kid said, "It's about that cowboy. The handsome one."

I froze, holding a freshly disentangled orange kitten clutched to my chest. The kitten's teeth were just coming in, so he started gnawing on my thumb. I let him have at it, the way a mother plugs her infant's mouth with a pacifier while she catches up on a favorite soap opera.

"If you ask me, both our cowboys are beautiful," Nina said. "Excuse me, sir. Take your lips off my face now, please."

I heard some snuffling noises, and Portia giggling. "He's kissing you," she said.

"Yes, well, Dumpling has always been a sucker for a good-looking dame with a sad story or two tucked in her pocket and also maybe a sugar cube. So. Tell me which one of our boys you think is 'the handsome one.'"

"The one with the dark hair and the cleft chin. I keep wondering what it would be like to kiss him."

After that there was no way I could stand up to announce myself. The kid would die of embarrassment. I might, too.

"Aren't you a little young to be thinking about things like that?" Nina asked.

"No," Portia said. "How old were you when you kissed a boy for the first time?"

"Twelve."

"I'm almost fourteen."

"My situation was different."

"Different how?"

"I was desperately in love. I figured we'd better get the kissing part behind us before we got engaged."

"People don't get engaged when they're twelve."

"Tell that to the royal families of Europe," Nina said.

"Was he a *prince*?"

"I thought he was. But no. He was my next-door neighbor. We were friends from the cradle onward. Don't make the same mistakes I have, Portia. Listen to your mother, and remember that beauty isn't everything."

"My parents have been friends ever since they were born, too," Portia said. "My mother likes to tell people that she and my papa took their first bath in a grown-up bathtub together. When they were babies." After a beat she added, "At least she used to like to tell people that. I guess she doesn't tell that story anymore."

Nina said, "Hey. Hey. Oh, geez. Come here."

"No. I'm all right," the girl said, though she didn't sound it. "I always hated that story anyway." I heard more snuffling noises, and then Portia was giggling again.

Nina said, "Dumpling, you old tart. Kissing another woman right in front of me." I heard the stall door click open, and Dumpling's ears floated out into the breezeway. "We're going to try something new today, Portia. No saddle, no bridle. You'll lean the way you want to go, you touch his neck, you use your knees. It's a test."

"A test?" Portia asked. "For what?"

"My flight instructor at Lambert Field rode in every day on a horse he called Proctor. Anybody who came for lessons he asked to ride Proctor around the hangar three times without a saddle or a bridle. That was his entrance exam. He swore the people who could guide a horse without a set of reins to saw on were born aviators."

"Are you going to teach me how to fly your airplane?" Portia gasped.

"I'm going to show you my airplane, and explain all the controls to you," Nina said in a solemn tone of voice I'd never heard her use before. "If you strike me as someone who might have a knack for flying *and* all involved parties are in agreement, then we'll see."

Portia was silent for a moment. Then she asked, "Is that true? About equestrians and aviators?"

"It sounds true, and that's what matters, isn't it? Look. You fly an airplane with your whole body, the way you ride a horse. Both feet working pedals that control the rudder, hands on the joystick that lifts and lowers the ailerons and elevators. It can be a lot at first unless you're already good at something else that calls for the same sort of skills."

"So if you failed the entrance exam, your flight instructor wouldn't give you lessons?"

"If you failed he charged you three times what he charged the other pupils," Nina said. "Now, put your foot in my hands and I'll give you a boost up. One, two, three, hoop-la."

I heard Dumpling grunt a little when the kid landed on his back.

"How's the air up there, Ace?" Nina asked.

"Excellent," Portia said. "I have a question."

"Yes?"

"How did you talk my mother into this?"

"Into what?"

"You teaching me how to fly your airplane."

"Don't go counting your chickens just yet, miss. Nobody's agreed to teach anybody anything. First we test for aptitude. If all goes well, then we petition the authorities for clearance. Now, grip tight with your knees and grab a fistful of Dumpling's mane. If you fall off and break a leg, you fail the entrance exam."

Portia clucked to Dumpling and the old gelding began plodding down the breezeway.

"Hey, wait a minute," Nina said. "Aren't you forgetting something? What's Ward's secret?"

"Who's Ward?"

"The dark-haired cowboy."

"Oh, that," Portia said. "I almost forgot. He's—" Her voice sank to a confidential murmur, frustratingly harder to hear as Dumpling ambled away. Whatever the kid thought my secret was, I wanted to be in on it. I plunked the orange kitten unceremoniously on the floor beside me and sat up right quick. He mounted a mewling protest.

"Whoa, Dumpling," Portia commanded. The hoofbeats stopped. "Did you hear that, Nina?"

"Hear what?"

"It sounded like a kitten."

"It probably was a kitten," Nina said. "One of the barn cats had a litter right after your mother got here. In the back seat of her car, in fact."

"That's my father's car. My mother bought it for his birthday last year."

"Fine. Your father's car. I think Ward said the kittens are living in the stall next to Dumpling."

"Oh!" Portia said. "I love kittens. I want to see them!"

I held my breath.

"When we get back," Nina said. "Those kittens aren't going anywhere. So what's the secret? Don't make me beg."

"Well," Portia said. Dumpling stepped out of the breezeway into the wider world then, so I couldn't hear the rest.

Just before dinner I was walking a bucket of Katie's milk up to Margaret when I noticed Nina and Portia on the porch roof outside Coyote's window. The two of them were poring over an oversized tome that was either Leo Tolstoy's *War and Peace,* a textbook on basic aeronautical principles, or a titanic potboiler called *The Many Secrets of Howard Stovall Bennett III.* That last one, I should note, was still a work in progress.

I was so lost in wondering which title the two of them had chosen from Nina's collection of canned remains that I came very close to bumping into Emily. When I finally saw her in my path I slammed on the brakes, spilling a little milk when I did so. The cats that had been tailing me from barn to house set upon it eagerly before it soaked into the earth.

"I'm so sorry, Ward," Emily said. "I assumed you saw me coming. What were you thinking about? You looked like you were a million miles away."

"I was calculating the chances that I'd get to the house without spilling any of this milk," I said. "The cats would like to thank you for keeping that from happening."

"Where have you been all day?" Emily asked.

"Here and there," I said.

"Well, you must have been here when I was there. Every time I thought I'd run you to earth, you evaporated. It was almost like you were avoiding me."

"Why would I want to do something like that?" I asked. My eyes wandered guiltily to Nina and Portia huddled on the roof, maybe or maybe not plotting a thrilling aeronautical adventure. Emily's eyes followed mine.

"Look at those two, would you?" she asked. "Aren't they dear together? Margaret was so right about Nina. She is a miracle worker. Portia has been almost civil to me all day long."

I put my burden down at my feet, flexed my right hand, and massaged my palm where the bucket's wire handle had cut into it. "Good," I said. "Well. I'd better get going with this milk. Margaret's waiting for it."

"You are such an enigma sometimes, Ward," Emily said.

"An enigma?"

"I'm surprised you don't know that word. You've always struck me as someone who's surprisingly articulate, given your background. An 'enigma' is a mystery."

"Thank you for explaining that," I said.

"You're probably wondering why I'm calling you a mystery."

"I guess you have your reasons."

"I do. Here's one of them." Emily took a piece of paper from her pocket and handed it to me. "I took a telephone message for you this morning."

I looked down. *Daniel Horn* was written on the paper in her girlish script, followed by a number I didn't recognize. It couldn't be my parents' number, because they didn't have a telephone anymore. Thanks to Daniel Horn.

"He says he really needs to talk to you," Emily said. "He also says that he's your uncle."

"Thanks," I said, and put the piece of paper in my pocket.

A scrum of cats, God bless them, chose that moment to take advantage of my distraction to mount an attack on the bucket of milk. They tipped the whole thing over, drenching my boots and the two ringleaders, Cataclysm and Catapult. The cats washed themselves off, but an unpleasant whiff of curdled milk never came out of my boots. Not in the next couple of weeks, anyway, before I threw them and all my other cowboy gear away.

"Margaret will be waiting for that milk for a long time now, won't she?" Emily asked.

"Yes," I said, and picked up the empty bucket.

"Are you going to call your uncle? I said you would."

"Sure," I said.

"Is everything all right at home?" Emily asked. "Is there anything you want to talk about?"

"Everything is fine," I said, even though I had an uneasy feeling that everything was not.

Chapter Fifteen

The first time Emily kissed me, it was Nina's idea.

The next day the lot of our guests were going into Reno for a morning of shopping and what have you, the sort of adventure Emily and Nina usually opted out of. But Portia wanted a cowboy hat, and moreover she wanted Emily to come into town to help her choose it, an invitation that had Emily all but swooning with joy. So in we went, in caravan with the rest of the gang in the ranch's Chevrolet. Nina had asked Margaret if she and Max could spare me to chauffeur the three of them into town in Emily's automobile, as Nina had plans to meet a friend once their shopping was taken care of. You'd better believe me, I stood right at Nina's elbow when she requested my services to be sure she actually got around to asking. I couldn't be too careful.

When Nina mentioned that business about meeting up with a friend, I figured her "friend" was just a fabrication, invented so she wouldn't have to ride into town jostled between Zep and Mary Louise. I believe she almost regretted her decision not to ride with the others when, as they waited on the porch for Sam to pull the wagon around, the Zeppelin said, "Kudos, Mary Louise, for outliving an awful husband. How I've wished some of mine would be polite enough to drop in their tracks. Or on their cheap floozies, as the case may be."

"Oh, you can go to hell for wishing somebody dead," Mary Louise said. "That's what my pastor kept telling me. So I prayed for it instead."

"I'd like to be a fly on the wall for the rest of that conversation," Nina said as she climbed in the back seat of the Pierce-Arrow between Emily and Portia.

"Shouldn't Mary Louise be leaving soon for her husband's funeral?" Emily asked.

"What? And spoil the rest of her vacation? Shouldn't her husband have kept his pants on until after their divorce went through?" Nina asked.

"Nina!" Emily said. "There are children present."

"Oh. Sorry, Ward," Nina said.

Portia giggled. I looked in the rearview mirror and saw Emily smile and reach across Nina to pat Portia's knee. "It's nice to hear your laugh, buttercup," she said.

I also saw Portia pull her knee away.

Sam cooled his heels in the station wagon while the Zeppelin, arm in arm with Mary Louise, shepherded the rest of her entourage, the various guests in your photograph, Liz, Theresa, Martha, and so forth, to a storied Reno lingerie emporium much beloved by dowagers and showgirls alike. "To negligees and new beginnings, ladies!" Zep called as she opened the door and waved the others inside.

"I suppose this also means that Mary Louise will be cheating on the Spanish nuns with some cheap store-bought panties," Emily said.

"They won't be cheap," I said. "Even if they're store-bought. Not in that place."

"Why are you so interested in Mary Louise's panties?" Portia asked me. "Is it because you're—*oof*—"

I looked into the rearview mirror in time to see Nina removing her elbow from Portia's ribs and holding a finger to her lips. I looked to see Emily's reaction to that mysterious exchange, but she seemed oblivious. "I hope the nuns weren't depending on Mary Louise's business," she said.

"The Spanish nuns have more important things to worry about," Nina said. "Don't you read the papers, Emily? The Falangists and the Communists are fighting to the death in Spain. Blood is running in the streets. Come on. Let's go find Portia's hat. You, too, Ward. We need your professional opinion."

The four of us ambled into Parker's Western Wear together and wandered its aisles with cowboys both real and of the drugstore variety. You've never heard of a drugstore cowboy? Oh. Well, in the early days of Hollywood that's what they called men, some in fact real cowboys, who turned up at studio gates looking for work as extras in movie westerns. Since there were no chuck wagons handy, those cowpokes ate at drugstore lunch counters nearby where food was cheap and the coffee tasted as if it had been stewing in a tin pot since Prometheus brought mankind the gift of fire. Once other actors realized *acting* like real cowboys might land them work, they adopted the wardrobe, squint, frontier accents, and colorful sayings. People started calling the lot of them "drugstore cowboys." Sam had done time as one before he gave up and headed for Nevada. His doppelgänger Gary Cooper, too.

I hung back a bit while the women examined the hat display. Nina plucked a towering ten-gallon from its peg and asked, "What kind of cowboy would choose a hat like this?"

"The kind Sam calls 'Big hat, no cattle,'" I said.

"You could give a baby a bath in that hat," Portia said.

"Have I ever told you the story about the first bath I had in a grown-up bathtub?" Emily asked Portia. The kid started to roll her eyes, rethought, then threw her arms around her mother's waist. "Only about a million times," she said. "So you do miss Papa, don't you?"

Emily looked like she might crumble to dust and blow away. She stroked her daughter's head hesitantly and said, "Maybe just a little."

I noticed a pair of drugstore cowboys, his and hers editions, trying on ten-gallon hats together in front of a three-way mirror. "If you want to know what kind goes for a hat like that," I murmured, and inclined my head in their direction.

The ten-gallon cowboy slipped his hand into his ten-gallon cowgal's back pocket and pulled her flush against himself. They kissed, and their brims collided. The man's hat bucked off and landed upside down on the floor behind him. Underneath the hat his head was as smooth as an egg.

Nina snickered, but honestly, I felt a little cheap for making a joke at the lovebirds' expense. If I learned anything in my time at the Flying Leap it was that passion in any relationship could be so fleeting that any evidence of it should be celebrated, not laughed at. When Emily looked up to see what was so danged funny, she stiffened. Portia followed her mother's gaze to the couple, mirrored in triplicate. Portia gasped, let go of her mother, and fled.

"What just happened?" Nina asked. "Hasn't Portia ever seen a bald man kiss a woman before?"

"Yes," Emily said. "Not that woman, though."

She spoke hardly above a whisper, but even from half a showroom away, there was no mistaking that voice. The bald man unlocked his lips, looked up, and exclaimed, "Emily!"

"That's her?" the woman asked. "The wife you came here to unload?"

Nina hissed, "I'll go after Portia." She gave me a discreet shove in Emily's direction. "Emily," she said. "Kiss Ward."

"What?" I whispered.

"No," Emily gasped. "Why?"

"Archer's going to try to talk to you otherwise. Can't you see that?"

Emily looked at Nina, then at me. I gave a little shrug of assent.

When I was a kid an older boy had described his first osculatory experience to me, saying: "When she kissed my lips, it was like she'd unbuckled my belt with her tongue." At the time I didn't see how such a thing could be anatomically possible, but that afternoon in Parker's Western Wear, I understood what a poet that young man was. Doorknockers had actually taught me very little, I realized. By the time Emily had finished ascertaining that my tonsils were in the places indicated by the illustrations in *Gray's Anatomy,* Archer and his lady friend had vanished. The sad, empty giant of a hat that lay upended on the floor was the only evidence that ten-gallon infidel had ever been there.

When she pulled away from me, Emily croaked, "Sorry."

"No harm done," I said. "Happy to help out in any way I can."

We finally found Portia crumpled between Nina and Sam on the shady bench I liked to sit on. Nina had her arm around the kid.

"Here's your mama, miss," Sam said when he saw us coming. He hopped up, took off his hat, and swept the bench with it, then directed Emily to sit. "I'll be going now."

"Don't go, Sam!" Portia wailed.

Sam looked a little startled, but said, "All right, miss," and stood there turning his hat around and around in his hands as he stared off into the middle distance to give the ladies the semblance of privacy.

Emily sat beside Portia and put her arm around her. "It's all right, sweetheart. I'm here," she said.

Portia burrowed into her mother. "I thought that if we came into Reno every day, Mama—" She gulped and started over. "It occurred to me we might just happen to—and then you'd see him and—oh! But not like that!"

"Shhh, sweetheart, it's all right."

"I didn't know—that—that—Mama, who *is* she?"

"I don't know, honey," Emily said. "I've never seen that one before."

"That one? Are there others?"

Emily didn't answer.

Nina said, "Take them home, Ward."

"No!" Portia howled, shrugging off her mother's arm and pushing her away. "Not without my h-h-hat."

Emily took a deep breath. "We'll buy you a hat another time."

"I need a hat," Portia said angrily. "You don't care if the sun makes me go *blind*. You don't care if I *die*. No wonder Papa hates you. You know what? I hate you, too." Raising children is not for the faint of heart, you know. In my years of practicing family medicine, many mothers asked me how infants they'd carried inside them, who grew into toddlers who clutched their legs and yelled "my mommy" whenever other children approached, could turn into teenagers capable of saying such hurtful things. Well, I'd said, who better to test their fangs on than someone who'd love them no matter what? They will outgrow it, I said. And if they don't, disown them. Then the mothers and I laughed, but only on the outside.

I must have shaken my head at Portia's outburst because the kid all but spat at me, "Why are you here? What business is this of yours?"

She made a valid point. "I'll go wait in the car," I said.

"No. Stay," Emily said.

"Can't you ever be on my side, Mama?" Portia snapped.

Emily pressed her lips together to keep from saying anything she'd live to regret while I eased back a step or two and did what I could to blend into the scenery. Nina, I noticed, was about to chew off her thumb. She looked sadder than I'd ever seen her look.

The cavalry, in the person of Sam Vittori, rode to the rescue. "Miss?" he said, holding his hat out to Portia. "Why don't you have mine?"

Sam had always been so good with kids. Comes of having so many brothers and sisters, I suppose. He always knew just what to say.

Portia stopped crying abruptly, the way very little children and people at their wits' end do. She looked from Sam to the hat to Sam again. "It's a nice hat," she said.

"Thank you, miss. Every night I go over it with a hat brush and then I leave it sit on a post down at the corral to air out till morning. You take care of your hat, and your hat will take care of you."

"I can have it? Really?"

Sam smiled at her. "I got another," he said. I knew he didn't. "If it suits you, you're welcome to it."

Portia ground the heels of her hands into her eye sockets, then took the hat and mashed it on her head. It fit her as neatly as Cinderella's slipper. "Thanks," she said, then got up and headed for the Pierce-Arrow without uttering another word. Emily watched her go.

Nina watched Emily watch Portia, then touched Emily's cheek. "She isn't mad at you, you know," she said.

"I know," Emily said.

"Go on, Ward," Nina reiterated. "Take these ladies home. I'll see you back there."

"Aren't you coming with us?" I asked.

"I'm meeting my friend," Nina said. "Remember?"

"I forgot," I said, not wanting to admit I thought Nina's "friend" had been another of her plausible fictions. "I can drop them off and come back for you," I offered.

"That's all right," Nina said. "Sam will make sure I get home in one piece. Won't you, Sam?"

"Yes, ma'am."

Nina hooked her arm through Sam's and said, "Let's buy you another hat. Then I'll introduce you to my friend."

"Oh, now, you don't need to be doing that," he said as Nina dragged him away.

When I saw Sam the next day in a new version of his same old hat, I asked, "Did Nina buy you that?"

"I tried to stop her," Sam said, "but she like to of broke my arm."

"Did you meet her friend?"

"Yep."

"What was her name?"

"Hugh. She was a he. He was her husband. Is."

"The one she's about to divorce, you mean? Holy Joe. What was he like?"

"Well, let's see. Good-looking fella. Tall and blond, like Nina. Was waiting for her on the sidewalk, with his bicycle. Brought that bicycle on the train, he said. Bought a ticket for it and everything so he could keep it right next to hisself the whole trip. Says he takes that bike everywhere, then rides the thing around ever new place he visits. Thinking a opening a bicycle store someday if he finds a place he'd like to settle."

I loved Sam like a brother, but sometimes getting the right details out of him was like pulling teeth. "Sam," I said. "I don't care about the bicycle. I want you to tell me about Hugh."

"Right. Sorry. I got sidetracked. It was a nice bike. I always wanted a bicycle growing up, but my folks never had the money for it. I never even rode me somebody else's. City kids had bikes. Not the likes of us." He scratched his head and lapsed into silence.

"Sam. Let's talk about the bike later. Right now I'm interested in hearing about Nina's Hugh."

"Yep. Yep. Sorry. Don't know where my head is at today. So this Hugh was real polite. Shook my hand, introduced hisself, looked me in the eye when he done it. He and Nina seemed awful glad to see each other. Hugged for a good long time. Said they loved each other when they said goodbye. Like to of broke down when they said it. You know how it is."

I did not know how it was. None of what Sam had just said made a lick of sense to me. "They love each other? Still?" I asked. "Then why are they getting a divorce?"

Sam took his hat off, turned it around in his hands a few times, and stared off into the middle distance again. Finally he shrugged. "Didn't ask. Wasn't none of my business."

Chapter Sixteen

But I'm getting ahead of myself again. Let's circle back to the day before. The trip home to the Flying Leap that day was painful. We'd hardly gotten underway when I heard Portia say to her mother, "Don't touch me."

I glanced into the rearview long enough to see Emily's hand hover above Portia's shoulder. Then I turned my eyes back to the road.

"Listen, baby—" Emily said.

"I'm not a baby," Portia said.

"Sweetheart, I'm sorry about what happened back there. I tried to keep you from knowing what—"

"Stop talking," Portia said. "Whatever you're about to tell me, I don't want to hear it. This is all your fault."

After a pause, Emily asked, "And how is it my fault?"

"If it isn't your fault, whose fault is it?" Portia asked. "Mine?"

"Oh, Portia," Emily said. I saw a flicker of movement in the rearview that was Emily scooting across the seat, arms extended to gather her daughter into a hug.

"I said *don't touch me,*" Portia said. "If you need something to pet to make yourself feel better, ask the cowboy to fix you up with one of those kittens."

Emily sighed and retreated to the opposite end of the seat. I reached up and adjusted the mirror a little to check on her. Watched her press her cheek against the cool glass of the window and close her eyes. Neither Emily nor Portia said another word for the rest of the trip.

Back at the ranch, I hopped out and opened the car door for Emily. Portia wanted no help from anybody. She threw her door wide and flung herself out so violently that she landed on her knees. Emily winced but didn't say anything as the kid scrambled to her feet and slammed into the house.

When I handed Emily out of the automobile she tried to smile, but it was more of a grimace. "I'm sorry you had to hear that," she said.

"I've heard worse."

"It's kind of you to say that, even if it isn't so."

After I backed the car into the shed I saw Emily on the porch, gripping the railing and looking down. For a brief, crazy moment I wondered if she might be thinking about jumping. That porch wouldn't have made much of a launching pad from this life into the next. At most, she'd sprain an ankle. Then Emily stepped away from the railing and I saw she was in her socks. She'd been using the cast-iron jack Margaret had installed there to pry the varmint boots from her feet.

I closed the shed door and headed into the house to see if I could find some lunch. Emily had left her boots on the porch and the front door standing open. I gathered up the varmints to carry inside, took off my hat with my free hand, and hesitated in the doorway, blinking, while my eyes adjusted to the dimness of the hall beyond. Portia was nowhere to be seen, but Emily was at the mail table, holding something in both hands. An envelope. "Ward!" she exclaimed, when she saw me. "You startled me. I didn't hear you coming." She dropped the envelope on the table.

"Cowboy boots," I said as I hung my hat on the rack by the door. "The cat burglar's shoe of choice." I walked over and twisted my neck around to look at the envelope she'd dropped on the table. It was addressed to me. I got the sense she'd been about to hold it up to the bright rectangle of doorway before I'd eclipsed it, in order to make out what might be inside it. "I brought in your boots," I said.

"Oh, thanks," she said, and picked up the envelope again. "There's a letter here for you. From your uncle. There's something inside it. Two somethings. Round."

"Trade you," I said, and handed her the boots.

She handed me the letter. "You should probably read that," she said. "He sounded upset when I talked to him the other day."

"I will later," I said. I worried the letter with my thumbs and located the two circlets inside. Suddenly I was as hot to find out what they were as Emily seemed to be. I slipped a thumb under the envelope's flap and tore it open.

Two gold rings sprang out, dinged onto the floor, and rolled in her direction. She stooped and captured both, stuck the larger of the two on her thumb, and held the smaller one up to examine it. "There's an inscription inside," Emily said. "HSB to PKH, 3/12/12," she read, slowly. "I'd be lost without you."

I already knew what the inscription said. What I couldn't figure out was what the rings were doing in that envelope. I scanned the first line on the page folded up inside. *Ward,* it read, *both your parents are deceased.*

I didn't read any further then, as I was having trouble breathing.

Emily looked up at me. "Is everything all right?" she asked.

"No," I said, my voice cracking. I let go of the letter about the same time Emily dropped my mother's wedding ring. A puff of wind blew through the open door and picked up the pieces of paper that had fallen from my hands. Next thing I knew the two of us were on our knees, trying to gather up the shattered pieces of my heart.

The ring had rolled under the table. I crawled after it as the letter's pages drifted past behind me. Emily caught both and looked at the one on top just long enough to get the gist. I located Miss Pam's ring and stuck it on my pinkie while I struggled to my feet again. I misjudged the distance between Emily and me as we both made to stand and we cracked foreheads on the way up. In any other situation this would have struck me as funny, but it wasn't something we'd ever laugh about. Not then. Probably not ever.

"Oh, Ward," she said. "I'm so sorry."

"That didn't hurt half as bad as it sounded like it should have," I said, rubbing my forehead. "Are you all right?"

"You know that's not what I'm talking about," she said. "Come here. It's about time you got to use one of your own bandanas for a change." I stood there while she rooted one out of my pocket and started wiping my face. She put a hand behind my neck to crank me down to where she could get at me better. Then somehow she was using her lips to dry my face. Then her lips were on mine.

The sound of approaching footsteps tore us apart. Emily gave me a wild-eyed look, grabbed her varmint boots, and ricocheted up the stairs, bounding from one side of the staircase to another, skipping some steps entirely. I remember noticing she didn't make any noise at all racing up in her sock feet.

I turned away and was sorting the mail as if the future of the human race depended on it when Margaret's hand fell on my shoulder. "I thought I heard somebody out here," she said. "Where's your fan club?"

"My fan club?" I asked. My voice sounded odd and tinny to me, but Margaret didn't seem to notice.

"Nina and Emily and Portia," she said.

"Oh, them," I said. "Nina's still in town and Emily and Portia are upstairs, I believe."

"Hmm," Margaret said. "I didn't think any of you would be back for hours. Are you hungry?"

"We got something to eat in town," I said, then panicked. Where had we gone for this fictional lunch? I needed to have an answer ready in case Margaret asked. I appreciated for the first time then how nimble Nina's brain must be, given her constant rejiggering of facts.

Emily's voice floated down from the second floor. "Margaret," she called. "Is that you down there? Do you know where Ward is?"

Margaret stepped away to look up the stairwell. "Emily," she said. "Stop leaning over the railing. You're going to fall head over heels and break your neck if you aren't careful."

I looked up, too, and saw Emily hanging almost upside down over the banister, her hair dangling across her cheeks like curtains and her face a little red from the angle, or else what we'd just been doing. "I'm always careful, Margaret," she said. "Have you seen Ward anywhere?"

"I'm here," I said. My voice still sounded foreign to me.

"Oh, good. Margaret, can I borrow Ward for a minute? He said he'd help me carry something in from the car."

"Have him for as long as you want," Margaret said. "I didn't expect anybody to be back for hours. I'd planned to use this afternoon to catch up on bills and update my ledger." She patted me on the shoulder and disappeared down the hall.

Occasionally when I can't sleep I think about Margaret's ledger. An earthly version of the book Saint Peter is said to refer to at the Pearly Gates, a record of who's deserving and undeserving of being welcomed into paradise. Sometimes I wonder if Margaret noted down my name there, and what aperçu she wrote alongside it if she did. I imagine something along the lines of *Howard Stovall Bennett III: Seemed trustworthy. Wasn't.* Although of course that's just my guilty imagination working overtime. For all I know Margaret never found out what I got up to there at the end.

Despite my overactive conscience I am not a Catholic, so I've never been inside a confessional booth. There was something about sitting next to Emily in the semidarkness of the parked stagecoach, though, staring at the tufted leather seat opposite us instead of at each other, that made me think of that. "You don't have many private places to talk around here," she said as she opened the door painted with the Pegasus insignia of the Flying Leap.

"I'm not sure this is a good idea," I said. "I'm not ready to talk about my parents."

"Oh," she said, looking honestly surprised, "I wanted to talk about us." The things folks choose to focus on when they hear tell of a crushing loss never cease to amaze me. I remember telling the wife of a patient once that her husband had been killed on his way home from work when some old man who had no business driving anymore ran a red light. The first thing the wife said was, "I wonder if he picked up the dry cleaning." She was in shock, of course. Though that was hardly Emily's excuse. Her parents weren't the ones who'd died.

"Us? What about us?" I asked as I climbed into the stagecoach and settled in beside her.

"I think the last time I was in here, I was with that tomcat, Wally. I may start sneezing at any minute," she said. I handed her a bandana, which she proceeded to crumple and uncrumple as we talked. "I want you to know that I'm ashamed of myself. I don't know what got into me. It just that you're so young and good-looking, Ward. I hated seeing you so upset, and I let myself get carried away. Now I feel like one of those old men who pinch cigarette girls in nightclubs."

"You aren't like them. Those old men are not ashamed, for one thing."

"Let me finish. I'm also sorry I kissed you because if there's one thing I despise, it's a cheater."

"I don't think it qualifies as cheating once you've filed for divorce," I said.

"I'm not talking about me cheating. I'm talking about you cheating. On Mary Louise."

I didn't have the least idea of what she meant by that. "Me, cheating on Mary Louise? I don't follow."

"You don't have to pretend, Ward. Portia told Nina your little secret, and Nina told me."

I twisted around to face her. "What's my little secret?"

"That you and Mary Louise are engaged."

"What makes Portia think I'd want to hitch myself to Mary Louise?" I asked. "I can find Paris on a map without someone always reminding me where to look."

"Nina said Portia told her she overheard Mary Louise ask you to marry her."

"Oh? When?"

"Right after she found out her husband was dead. I gather Portia ran past you in the hall just as Mary Louise proposed."

Then I remembered the kid whisking past us. Given how today had unfolded so far I had to laugh to keep from crying.

"Portia misunderstood," I said once I regained my composure. "Mary Louise wasn't asking me to marry her. She was telling me she was free to marry anybody she wanted to now that she was rich. Even the likes of me, a man Sam would call about as broke as the Ten Commandments."

"Oh!" Emily said, and then was overtaken with a fit of sneezing. "I'm glad to hear that. Mary Louise is closer to your age and very pretty, but she's really nothing special." She sneezed again.

I was both appalled and relieved that our misbegotten kisses were what Emily had wanted to discuss. Sure, if Margaret had caught us necking like a pair of teenagers on prom night I would have been let go, but with my parents dead, getting fired was the least of my worries. "Let's get you out of here," I said. "Your boyfriend Wally's hair is all over everything."

"I almost forgot," Emily said when I handed her down from the coach. She went around to open the Pierce-Arrow's trunk and reappeared with the papier-mâché donkey's head. "I feel ridiculous asking you to carry this in. It isn't heavy."

"Why are you taking this inside? Are you that lonesome up in Scorpion?"

"I told Margaret I needed you to carry something in from the car for me. It was this or the fairy wings."

I noticed then that she still had Big Howard's wedding band on her thumb. "While you're handing things over I should probably take that ring," I said.

"Oh. Of course," she said. She pulled it off and put it in my free hand. Both of us looked at it lying in my palm until she closed my fingers around it. "That was your father's," she said, and touched the one lodged on my pinkie. "And this was your mother's."

I nodded. As long as I didn't acknowledge their passing out loud it was like they weren't dead. "Please don't tell anybody," I said.

"I'm so sorry, Ward. Do you have brothers? Sisters?"

I shook my head. "I have nobody. Not a soul."

"What about your uncle?" she asked.

What about my uncle, indeed. Daniel Horn, my mother's brother. He'd always been so quick to clap me on the back and go on and on about how alike he and I were. Cut from the same cloth. Two peas in a pod. Like twins. Always to my horror.

My father, you see, had made the mistake of allowing his brother-in-law, a recent graduate of a business college over in Nashville, to take over the books Miss Pam once kept at Big Howard's cotton brokerage. My mother had been the best bookkeeper he'd ever had—it's how they'd met—and he'd assumed, naïvely, that Daniel would be just as good. My no-count uncle then proceeded to skim proceeds and cook the books to cover his malfeasance. In the best of times it might not have been enough to run the business into the ground, but the Crash came along and finished off the job. By rights my uncle should have gone to prison for embezzlement, but Miss Pam and my father refused to press charges. Big Howard said it was his own damned fault for not exercising more fiscal vigilance, and my mother about ate herself up over the whole squalid affair. I've always believed the pain of Daniel's betrayal is what did her in before her time.

If my mother were still alive, she'd be approaching a hundred years old now. Miss Pam was under half that when she died. Lay down for a nap, never got up. Forty-six years old. A stroke? A heart attack? I wasn't there when it happened, so I'll never know for sure. What I do know is that losing my mother was one loss too many for my old man. First his business, then the house he'd built for Miss Pam, then Miss Pam. He was so deranged by the pile-on of grief that he decided it would be best for everybody if he went with her. It doesn't matter how he did it. What matters is that it happened. Maybe it wouldn't have, if I'd been there. We'll never know.

By the time I found out they were gone they'd both been in the ground two weeks.

I will say this for Daniel. He wrote me regularly, both at the dam and at the ranch. I have no idea what his letters said as I always tore them up, except for that one.

After that grabby opening sentence, *Ward, both your parents are deceased,* followed by the bald facts of their demise, my uncle's letter continued, *When I didn't hear back after repeated attempts to reach you, I was forced to liquidate your parents' remaining worldly goods to pay their funeral expenses and cover my travel costs. Alas, this sad enterprise did not yield near enough. I was reduced to negotiating with the funeral director, old Mr. Schaefer, who eventually agreed to front a portion of the remaining amount. I convinced him you'd be good for it. Took some doing!*

Your parents' rings wouldn't have brought enough $$ to cover lunch at the train depot in Memphis when I took a last few bits and bobs into the city to pawn. Diamonds have some worth as they can be reset, the gentleman behind the counter told me, but wedding bands are a hard sell as the typical pawnshop customer is superstitious and doesn't want to invite a curse on a new union. So I enclose them here for you.

I'm headed now to New Orleans to look for employment in the cotton industry. Wish me luck! I hope once I am settled you will come visit. You are the closest kin I have left in this world now. Your devoted uncle, Daniel Horn.

I have wondered more than once whatever became of Miss Pam's engagement ring. For many years I searched the window of every pawnshop in Memphis and, later, New Orleans for it. I don't suppose I would have recognized her diamond even if I'd seen it. More than likely the stone had been reset, as Daniel mentioned. Still, I looked.

Chapter Seventeen

It surprises me how entirely forgotten the phenomenon of the Reno divorce seems to be. Heck, it was on the cover of *Life* magazine just the summer before the one I've been telling you about. Just goes to show that divorce isn't such a big deal anymore. And honestly, who even remembers *Life* magazine?

It's nice to see you again. I was worried I'd run you off with my endless gabbing. It's a real pleasure for me to have the opportunity to talk about all this stuff, you know. When you get to be my age, things that happened fifty years ago start seeming more real to you than what happened yesterday. And yes, I've had all this tucked away for a good long while. Well, now that the dam's busted, watch out. Raise your hand when you need to come up for air.

Give me a minute, will you, and let me turn this television set off. I'll just do it the old-fashioned way, with the knob here. I can never find that danged remote, so what's the point of having it in the first place? That's correct, that was *The Thin Man.* Yes, it is a good one. You know, when the 1960s rolled around, I was thunderstruck by how much Jack Kennedy's wife, Jackie, favored Emily. But to be honest, Myrna Loy reminds me of her even more. Jackie always seemed so serious, and when she talked, that whispery voice of hers wrecked the illusion. Myrna didn't sound like Emily, either, but she had her sense of fun. Her lightness.

I met her once. How about that? Myrna Loy, I mean. At one of those Hollywood canteens the USO set up during the war. Cinema stars would volunteer at these doughboy social clubs, I guess you could call them, to give a thrill to all us men in uniform. They'd dance with us, serve us food, chat us up, and so forth. Yes, good point. Very much the way we pretend cowboys were called on to entertain the troops of divorcées who marched through Reno. Anyway, there I was, hanging out with my buddies from Fort Ord at the edge of the dance floor, and I felt this tap on my shoulder. I turned around and said, "Oh. You're Myrna Loy." Myrna Loy, asking *me* to dance.

"I am," she said. "Want to dance, soldier?"

"Yes, ma'am," I said.

"Please don't call me ma'am," she said. "It makes me feel like I'm your grandma."

That turn of phrase, so like Emily's, made me trip over her feet as well as mine. I'm sure I wasn't the first soldier dumbstruck at having the flesh-and-blood Myrna Loy in his arms after so many years of seeing her likeness projected onto a screen. She was kind enough to ignore my clumsiness and did her best to draw me out. "So where are you from?" she asked.

For some reason, I said, "Reno."

"Oh, I know Reno," she said.

"Why's that?" I asked. "Did you get divorced there?"

"Just did, as a matter of fact," she said. "Doesn't everybody?"

"Not everybody," I said.

The night after I found out my parents were dead and buried was another scorcher. I lay on top of my sheets again, naked as the day I was born, twisting Miss Pam's ring on my pinkie finger and Big Howard's on the one next to it. When I'd said goodbye to them years earlier on the platform at the Memphis depot, I never imagined that would be the last time I'd lay eyes on them.

I was finally, *finally* pushing off to sea in that beautiful pea-green boat when I heard a quiet little tap on my window frame. I sat up, and there was Emily. "May I come in?" she whispered.

This time I wrapped the sheet tight around myself before I went to the window. "Sure," I said.

Emily looked up at me, in her boy pajamas and a pair of moccasins she must have bought when she got the varmint boots. "If I'm going to come in, you're going to have to give me a hand."

"Oh, you mean *come in* come in."

"Yes."

I had nothing to lose anymore, so when she put a moccasined foot on the wall I grabbed her wrists and pulled. Over the course of the last few weeks Nina had turned Emily into a good little climber. Once she was inside, she said, "I hoped you'd still be up. Were your ears burning? Nina and I were just talking about you."

"Oh? What were you talking about?" I asked, tightening my sheet around my waist.

"Nina's revolver. Where did you hide it?"

"Why?"

"Nina asked me, and I said I didn't know. Which was true. But after she went to bed, I started wondering where it was. Then I couldn't stop wondering. Maybe if you tell me where it is my brain will stop chasing its tail and let me fall asleep."

"It's under my bed," I said.

"Under your bed?" she asked. "Is that safe?"

"It's still in the pillowcase."

"Shouldn't it be under lock and key?"

"I don't have anything that locks with a key. I think it's safe enough under my bed. It's unloaded."

"Yes," she said. "I remember."

The two of us stood there in the moonlight, looking at each other. Finally I asked, "Is that all you wanted?" Somehow I managed to stop short of saying, "ma'am."

"I have one more question you might be able to answer," she said.

"I'll do my best," I said.

She cleared her throat. "Nina told me I shouldn't base my opinion of all men on Archer. That I'm selling half of humanity short by assuming all of men are bad bets in one way or another. She says I deserve better than him, but I said I couldn't imagine who that better man would be, or whether he'd want me now, if in fact he existed."

I figured she was fishing for an answer, but what answer I didn't know. Eventually I volunteered, "I don't think you're damaged goods, if that's what you mean. I think any man on earth would be lucky to be with somebody like you."

"Someone *like* me?" she asked. "Or me in particular?"

"You in particular. Of course you. All sorts of men are going to fall in love with you. You'll see."

"How about you?" she asked. "Could you imagine falling in love with me?" She stared at me pointedly, then started fumbling with the buttons on her pajama top.

I realized then that hadn't been so much a question as an invitation. Once I got over my surprise, I said, "Where are my manners? Let me help you with those buttons."

Of course it was a bad idea. But I was heartbroken and lonely and a woman who was also hurting, whose company I enjoyed, was taking her shirt off, right in front of me, with intent. We might not have been in love, but it seemed like as good a way as any for us to cheer each other up.

From that night forward Emily and I got together every chance we got. Day or night, indoors and out. It didn't matter. Whenever we saw an opportunity we jumped right on it and each other. You may wonder how we managed not getting caught with our pants down, but as the weather grew very hot our guests tended to lose interest in excursions. Everyone who could spent the afternoon hunkered down under a fan, napping.

I will admit that the danger of what we were up to was a welcome distraction, too. The illicit delight of a quick and dirty coupling in the kittens' stall, for example, after Emily asked at lunch if I'd be willing to take her to visit the furry little varmints. Or a session in the stagecoach, which squeaked and rocked so alarmingly that I transferred us midway to the back seat of the Pierce-Arrow. Also on a saddle blanket I spread out of sight of the house in the no-man's-land of the gopher field, below the rim of a dry wash that turned into a raging creek during the rainy season.

Somehow in the midst of all that fornication I fell in love with Emily. Fell hard. That's the danger but also the wonder of that sort of thing, isn't it? First bodies entwine, then hearts. Does it ever really happen any other way? I'm not so sure.

You can't exactly blame me for believing she'd fallen for me, too. Not after the morning I woke her up to send her back to Scorpion before the sun came up. Emily opened her eyes, smiled sleepily, and said, "Oh, Ward. I'd be lost without you."

One night as Emily climbed back into her pajamas in the bunkhouse before lighting out, she heard the sound of a toilet flushing on the other side of a wall and froze. "What's that?" she whispered.

I held up a finger until we heard a door click shut. "Sam," I whispered back. "We have sinks in our rooms but we share the rest of the facilities. The bathroom is between my room and his."

"Oh. Do you think Sam can hear us?"

I said, "When he's in his bedroom? I don't think so. Which reminds me. How in the heck are you getting in and out of the house without anybody hearing you? That staircase creaks and grumbles like Zep's stomach once she gets a whiff of lunch. It's not like you can climb down the trellis in and out of Coyote anymore."

"Oh, you have our friend Nina to thank for that," Emily explained. "When she was here for her first divorce, years ago, she figured out how to sneak down to the kitchen for food after everyone was supposed to be in bed. When we were first roommates and I was too upset to fall asleep, Nina taught me how to navigate the stairs. Memorizing all those moves was sort of like learning to play chess."

That explained the way Emily had ricocheted silently up the stairs the first time we kissed. "Those chess lessons have certainly come in handy," I said. "Good thing you asked Margaret to let Nina be your roommate."

"I asked Margaret to let Nina be my roommate? What do you mean?"

"I overheard Nina tell Margaret that it was your idea to share Coyote."

Emily shook her head. "You must have misunderstood. It wasn't my idea. However it happened, though, I'm glad it did. Nina's the best friend I've ever had. I love her. So does Portia. So does everybody. She's sort of irresistible, don't you think?"

"Not as irresistible as you are," I said.

"That's the right answer," she said.

I wonder if Emily would have loved Nina quite as much if she'd realized what Nina and Portia were up to while the two of us were busy with other things. On the other hand, I don't think Emily and I could have gotten away with as much as we did if those two hadn't been involved in forbidden business of their own.

I can't remember exactly how long Emily and I had been going at it when I came down to help Sam saddle up for the late-afternoon trail ride and found him in the breezeway of the barn, holding Dumpling's tack and looking flummoxed.

"What's wrong, Sam?" I asked.

"I got Dumpling's gear here, but no Dumpling."

"What do you mean, 'no Dumpling'?"

"Have a look," Sam said. "His stall is as empty as Jesus's tomb the day after Easter. I wonder if the coyotes got at him somehow."

As it turned out, the coyotes had. The capital "C" Coyotes, Nina and her new roommate, Portia.

Since we were a horse short and our ladies were confident in Sam's ability to keep them safe, I stayed behind while they rode. Emily was upstairs, asleep in her little bed in Scorpion, I supposed. I hoped so, since she wasn't getting a lot of sleep when she was in my little bed. As for me, there was no rest for the weary. It would hardly do for me to disappear to sleep the afternoon away. So I kept myself awake and visible practicing rope tricks Sam had been trying to teach me. The guests ate that kind of drugstore cowboy hotdoggery right up, but I was never any good at it.

I was out in the barnyard, giving it my inept all, when the Coyotes guilty of making off with Dumpling trotted up the ranch drive, riding bareback and without a bridle, in the company of a handsome and willowy young gentleman in a light cotton suit, a bow tie, spectacles, and a straw boater. On a bicycle. Hugh.

I gathered up the rope in coiled loops and hung it from the post I'd been casting at.

"Before you start scolding, Ward," Nina said, "there was an emergency. The three of us had to be somewhere, and we couldn't all fit on Hugh's bicycle."

Hugh propped his bike against the corral fence, tipped his boater, and shook my hand. "I'm Hugh," he said.

"I guessed," I said. "I'm Ward."

"Ward! I've heard a lot about you. A pleasure."

"I've heard a lot about you, too," I said.

"You have?" Hugh asked.

"About your bicycle, anyway," I said. "Sam told me all about it. He always wanted to ride one when he was a kid. Never got the chance."

"Ah. Well, we can't have that, can we? I'll have to show our friend Sam the ins and outs of mine when next we meet."

"Where's my mother, Ward?" Portia asked.

"Why are you asking me?"

Portia gave me such a sour look that I worried she might be on to us. "I don't see anybody else to ask. You win by default."

"Still a win," I said. "I'll take it. But I don't know where your mother is."

"She's probably having a nap in her room," Nina said.

"She's always asleep lately," Portia said. "I wonder if she's coming down with something."

"Oh, it's pretty normal for our guests around about this time," I said. "Their hearts need rest to mend, the way a sick person's body does."

Nina swept a leg over Dumpling's rump and slid to the ground. Portia followed her example.

"Where have you three been?" I asked.

"Nowhere in particular," Nina said.

"At the airport," Hugh said.

"None of your business," Portia said. She gave Hugh the evil eye first, then me, then stomped off to the house, slamming the front door behind herself hard enough to make the windows rattle.

"What did I say?" Hugh said. "Don't they call that scrubby path by all the sheds and airplanes an airport? It's hardly Lambert Field back home, but one must make do with what's on hand."

"The truth is, Ward," Nina said, "we did go to the airport. It hardly bears mentioning to anybody, but Portia wanted to see my airplane. I let her sit in the cockpit while it was parked in the hangar. Wings still tucked away. In case anybody should ask."

"Nina has been trying to get me to go up in that unwieldy beast of hers for years," Hugh said. "No, thank you. Whereas Portia—"

"My plane is not unwieldy, Hugh," Nina snapped. "I've never crashed. Never even came close. How many times have you wrecked your bicycle? I can think of three grisly incidents, off the top of my head."

"Not as far to fall, my love. You don't see me wearing a parachute, do you?"

"More people are killed riding bicycles than—"

"Look," I said. "I was just making conversation. Portia's right. Where you've been is none of my business. It is my business, though, if you run off with one of the horses without telling us. It throws everybody else's schedule off. You ought to know better, Nina. You need to go fess up to Margaret."

Nina groaned. "How would she find out? You wouldn't tell on me, would you?"

"You know I'm not a snitch. But what do you think the chances are that where you got off to this afternoon won't come up at dinner?"

Hugh intervened with, "This whole kerfuffle was my fault, I'm afraid. There was a miscommunication. I meant to carry Nina to the airport on my handlebars. I didn't realize there would be three of us going. The trouble is, I don't drive automobiles."

"Doesn't anybody in St. Louis know how to drive a car?" I asked.

"Between the streetcars and the chauffeurs, there's

really no call for it," Hugh said breezily. "Well, I'd better be getting back to town. Don't want to get mowed down by a motorcar, riding my bicycle on a country road after dark. I love you, my darling Nina." He kissed both her cheeks. When they pulled apart he smiled and touched the strand of pearls around her neck. "I see you're still wearing the pearls I gave you," he said.

"Always," she said.

"I knew they'd suit you."

"Of course you did."

Hugh hopped on his bike. "Toodles," he said, and cycled off.

"Thanks, Hugh!" Nina called after him. He waved without looking back at her. Probably a good thing, because Nina was fingering those pearls and giving his retreating back a look of such naked longing that it was almost painful to see.

Once Hugh was out of earshot, I couldn't resist asking, "Why are you divorcing this one?"

"None of your business," Nina said. She hunched her shoulders and headed for the ranch house.

When Sam got back from the trail ride that afternoon I explained who'd been behind Dumpling's disappearance.

"Figures," Sam said. He kept nodding for a good long time after he said that. Once we had all the horses and the saddles squared away, he said, "I can't help but notice that you're looking rode hard and put up wet these days, Howard. What ails you, friend?"

I hadn't told anybody about my parents, but the sympathetic look Sam gave me, combined with the fact that he was calling me Howard, convinced me that he must have found out about their deaths somehow. "How did you know?" I asked.

"It sounds like you've been killing hogs over there in your room every night. It's too hot out to be killing hogs. Plus we got no hogs here to kill."

"Oh," I said.

"I'm worried about you, son," he said. "Be careful. Like as not these rich ladies will toss you out like a used tissue when they're done with you."

I should have listened to Sam's advice. That's the thing about advice, though, isn't it? You only listen to what people tell you when they say the things you want to hear.

Chapter Eighteen

Surprisingly, Emily seemed more rattled by the idea of getting caught than I was. Or maybe she just reveled in the drama of our forbidden connection. Who can say? All I know is that it didn't take much to spook her.

"I crept into my room this morning, turned on the light, and almost fainted," she told me one night in the bunkhouse as she lay across my naked chest. "There it was on my bedroom chair, just looking at me with its beady little eyes. You should have heard me shriek. It's a wonder I didn't wake the whole house."

"Good thing you didn't," I said. I wasn't ready to lose my job before I'd given some thought to where I might go next. "What was it? A scorpion?"

She sat up abruptly, pulling my sheet to her chest. "A scorpion? Is that why my bedroom is named Scorpion? Because scorpions live there?"

"Yes," I said. "How did you get along with all the coyotes living in your room back when you were sleeping in Coyote? Of course that's not why your bedroom is named Scorpion. A scorpion is one of those things people think about when they think about the desert. Finish your story, please. What was looking at you?"

"Bottom. His top, anyway. His head. I'd forgotten all about him. The way his glass eyes catch the light is terrifying. You would have screamed, too, I bet."

"I'm sure I would have," I said, grinning.

"Just you wait. I'll show you, and when you least expect it. See if it doesn't wipe that cocky smile right off your face."

So I shouldn't have been surprised a few days later when I opened the stall door neighboring Dumpling's and found Emily on the other side wearing boys' pajamas, red varmint boots, and that donkey's head. She was kneeling in the midst of a scrum of kittens frolicking around her with joyful abandon.

I let out a yelp, then slumped against the stable door and started laughing. "Fine. Good. You got me. Congratulations."

Emily stood, holding a tortoiseshell kitten, and turned the donkey's glinting marble-eyed regard on me. I remember noticing she wasn't sneezing. That's how it can go with your milder cat allergies—one cat will make you sneeze while another cat will not.

"Nice touch, by the way, telling me you were going back to the house to take a shower and try to get some sleep," I said.

I started to feel uneasy when she didn't answer. With good cause, as it turned out, since it wasn't Emily inside Bottom's head.

"Portia," I said after the kid dragged the thing off and glared at me. "I thought you were your mother."

"Oh yeah? Why's that?" she asked.

"You're wearing her boots and her pajamas," I said.

"These are my boots now. My mother said I could have them. And what do you know about her pajamas?"

"I help Margaret with the laundry," I answered with a coolness I did not feel. "We pin everybody's wash up with clothespins marked with their names so things don't get mixed up."

"So I hear," Portia said. "Tell me where I should I leave my boots so you can polish them." She shouldered past, clutching Bottom's head in one hand and the kitten in the other.

I followed her out into the breezeway. "Wait a minute there, miss," I said. "Where are you going with that kitten? She's too young to take away from her mother for very long. Best to leave her here."

Dumpling poked his head out over his half door and watched us with his ears pricked forward. The old boy was on my side, if you ask me, based on our long-standing relationship. Also Portia was holding the head of a decapitated equine.

The kid focused on my boots for a good minute or two, considering.

"Sorry about my boots," I said. "You can smell them, can't you? They got soaked with milk, and it went rancid. They stink the worst first thing in the morning. Margaret keeps telling me to go into town and buy another pair, but I haven't been able to find the time to do it."

"Your boots aren't all that stinks around here," Portia said. She handed me the kitten, smirked, and said, "Have fun rounding up the others."

I realized she hadn't been looking at my boots. She'd been watching the tortoiseshell kitten's half dozen siblings make a break for it through the stall door I'd left ajar. She'd waited until the last one was on the lam before she handed over her hostage.

By the time I made it into the house after chasing down all the kittens, some of the ladies were enjoying their second or fourth cup of coffee and a few had moved out to the porch for cigarettes. "It's about time you showed up, son," Sam said as he handed me the coffeepot. "I been busier than a three-legged dog locked in a smokehouse this whole entire morning."

Portia came down for breakfast directly. Emily was a no-show, so I pulled out a chair next to Nina for Portia. Instead of thanking me, the kid said, "Look what the cat dragged in," and took her plate out to the porch.

Nina looked up at me. "What's eating her?" she asked.

I shrugged. I could see Portia through the open window, sitting on the porch stairs and shoveling her breakfast in with one hand while waving cigarette smoke away with the other.

"Where is that child's mother?" Zep asked nobody in particular.

"I think she's sleeping in, ma'am," I said. It might have been my imagination, but I felt like Portia's fork paused midair when I said it.

"Emily has been sleeping a lot lately," Mary Louise said. "I wonder if she's sick."

"Morning sick, if you ask me," the Zeppelin said. "Smart play on her husband's part if he means to hang on to her, which I gather he's eager to do." She rubbed a forefinger and thumb together, making the universal sign for money. "No woman wants to be on her own when there's a baby on the way."

Nina looked up from her plate. "If he's eager to hang on to her, maybe he ought to stop hanging on to other women." She snapped a piece of bacon in two. "Emily isn't pregnant. She's having trouble sleeping in the heat. That's all."

The Zeppelin made an exasperated sound and wiped her mouth with her napkin. Nina came close to aspirating her coffee when Zep said, "I know you think I'm full of hot air, missy, but not everything I say is wrong just because I'm old. I have a feel for these things, you know. I could list a dozen pregnancies I've diagnosed before anyone else was the wiser. Let's see, there was my good friend Betsy Collins, and—"

"Please don't list them for me," Nina said, as she plucked the last two biscuits from the platter I was on my way to the kitchen to refill. "I wouldn't know any of them, and even if I did I wouldn't care. Emily was my roommate until just lately. She had her monthly. End of story."

"Say what you will," Zep said. "I'm usually right about these things."

"A stopped clock is right at least twice a day," Nina said.

The Zeppelin banged her palm on the table with such force that all the place settings danced. Mary Louise was so startled she spilled milky coffee down her front.

"Would it kill you, Nina, to go a day without correcting me?" the Zeppelin asked.

Nina looked at the ceiling as if she were giving the question serious consideration. "I'm afraid it might," she said. Then she pushed away from the table, took her plate, and headed for the porch as well.

The Zeppelin called after Nina's retreating back, "Have some respect for your elders, you impudent hussy!"

Nina tossed back, "Impudent hussy, huh? Who taught you that zinger? Marie Antoinette?"

Mary Louise, who was dabbing at her blouse with her napkin, paused mid-dab. "Marie Antoinette?" she said. "I have a set of porcelain that serves fifty that used to belong to Marie Antoinette. The antique dealer who sold it to me said she was queen of France before the Great War. Do you know her?"

"I'm not quite that old, dear. Here, let me help you with that." Zep plunged her own napkin in her glass of water and started in on Mary Louise's blouse.

"Thank you," Mary Louise said. "Why doesn't Nina like you? You're so nice to everybody."

"I think Nina doesn't like me because she can see how alike we are." The Zeppelin leaned back to examine her handiwork.

Mary Louise tucked her chin to look down her shirtfront. "Did we get it all?" she asked.

"Almost," Zep said. "It's more than that, of course. Nina's so hurt and unhappy and mad at life. And young. I have been there. I would not be her age again, or yours. No, thank you." She sighed. "I shouldn't have let myself lose my temper. That wasn't nice. What I was really doing"—she paused to dunk her napkin again—"was shaking my fist at my younger self for wasting so many years worrying about things over which I have no control."

Good old Zep. I ducked into the kitchen and came out with more biscuits, said, "Straight from the oven, ma'am," when I offered her the platter, and asked if she'd like me to refresh her coffee while I refilled Mary

Louise's cup. The Zeppelin nodded as she blew on her fingers after dropping a hot biscuit on her plate.

"I'm going to change my shirt," Mary Louise said, picking up her coffee and hesitating long enough to kiss Zep on top of her head as she passed by. We only had a dozen or so people at the ranch at one time, guests and staff included, but we had enough cups to serve fifty, à la Marie Antoinette, as our ladies left them everywhere. Margaret claimed not to mind their carelessness. It transformed a humdrum day of housekeeping into an Easter egg hunt, she always said.

It was just the two of us in the dining room after that, Zep and me. I moved around the table, gathering up abandoned plates, while she buttered her biscuit lavishly. Then she erupted with, "Zeppelin! Ha!"

For a horrible moment I wondered if I'd called her by her nickname without realizing I had done it.

"That's what she calls me, you know," she continued.

"Who does?" I asked, feigning innocence.

"Nina. Who else? Let me tell you something, Ward." Zep wiped her face with her napkin. "I'd rather be a dirigible than a bag of bones. Slender women shrivel up like raisins as they age. I don't find that withered look attractive. Do you?"

"No, ma'am," I said, and pushed through the swinging doors with my armload of empty plates. In the safety of the kitchen, I wiped my brow with one of the used napkins I'd harvested from the table. It wasn't the last time I would regret my immature unkindness, always mentally referring to that pneumatic, good-natured woman as "the Zeppelin." A score of years later, when I was finally able to buy my parents' house back for the future generations of Bennetts I never ended up having, Zep was one of the people I most wished I could tell. Take that as a lesson, will you? In this life there will be those you may dismiss on first meeting who you'll grow very fond of eventually. Given that, it's wise and best to treat everyone you come across with equal measures of kindness.

Through the kitchen window that opened onto the porch that fateful morning, I could see Nina leaning against a column, holding her breakfast plate in one hand and wiping her cheeks with her napkin. Sweat? Tears? I didn't have the unwavering courage of my convictions that Zep had, so I couldn't have said for sure.

When I was back in the dining room gathering up the last of the plates, I heard the roar of an engine pulsing up the ranch house drive. I looked out the dining room window again in time to see Nina straighten up, smile, and wave. "Ahoy, Hugh!" she called out.

Her smile, I noted, didn't make it all the way to her eyes.

Somehow, somewhere, Hugh had acquired a motorcycle with a sidecar. Also a pair of goggles, and a gauzy scarf he'd tied over his boater to keep it from blowing off his head. "It is a noisy cuss, compared to my bicycle," he said to Sam and me when he was showing it off to us. "But I suppose that doesn't matter so long as I'm not trying to sneak up on anybody. It is somewhat wonderful, isn't it?"

"Somewhat," Sam said.

"Go on," Hugh said. "Give it a straddle."

"Oh, no," Sam said. "Not for me. Although I would like to try that bicycle of yours out sometime."

"We'll have to make that happen, won't we?"

Hugh was waiting for Nina and Portia while they gathered up their things for their day's adventure. Emily stumbled out onto the porch in her pajamas before they emerged, her curls in mad disarray and a sleep mask perched on top of the tangle like one of those ridiculous little pancake hats the British call a "fascinator." She looked like a woman out for blood.

"I had finally, *finally* fallen asleep," she said. She cast an indignant upraised palm at Hugh and the motorcycle. "Is this what was making that infernal racket?"

Hugh's face fell. "Oh, dear," he said. "So sorry. I hadn't thought it possible that anybody might still be sleeping at this late hour. I promised I'd take Nina and Portia out to the airport today, and alas, a bicycle built for three is not to be had in all of Reno."

"The airport?" Emily asked.

"Did I say 'airport'? Ah. My mistake. When I think 'Nina' the word I think of next is 'airport.' I meant 'desert.' We're off in search of the route of the Pony Express. Nina and I whiled away many an afternoon in my tree house when we were young'uns, reading aloud to each other from dime novels that described those brave and lightweight fellows' acts of derring-do. Both of us were desperate to ride for that service, but I believe at eleven we were both already too tall to qualify for the job. I was always one to remind Nina that they wouldn't have taken her anyway because she was a girl, until one day she shoved me out of the tree house. Nothing broken, luckily, though I did end up with some painful bruises. Ah. Here come my ladies now. Nina. Portia. Your chariot awaits."

Now, I am not a fan of motorcycles. "Murdercycles" would be a better name for them. Can I tell you, entre nous, what we in the emergency room used to call people who rode motorcycles? "Organ donors." I would no more let a child of mine ride one than I would a hoot owl. I guess it's just as well I never had any offspring of my own.

Oh, sure, there was a time when, like most young men, I found the idea of riding a motorcycle thrilling. You know what cured me of that? Being in a motorcycle crash. It happened during the war. Every moment of our lives seemed so dangerous then that things that should have scared us simply didn't. I got a concussion, dislocated a shoulder, hurt my back. I'm convinced that old wound is why I have to use this blasted walker to get around today. Arthritis, exacerbated by a history of injury. If I'd never straddled that cursed machine I might still be actively practicing medicine. Oh, well. Like they say, hindsight is twenty-twenty.

On the upside, the French nurse who took care of me was a darling, capable of joking around in both French and English, and absolutely unflappable. When bombs fell close enough to the hospital to make the bedpans rattle and orderlies dive under tables, she went about her business without breaking stride. I did my best to convince her to marry me and move to the States after the war. Every time I asked, she thanked me graciously and explained that, *hélas,* that would be impossible. She could not leave behind Mother France and her French mother, who wasn't going anywhere once she got her château back from the Nazis. Bad luck on my part, not being born in France myself. Then I might have stayed on there forever, too. That nurse struggled pronouncing "Howard," so you know what she used to called me? "Quartier," the French word for "Ward." I thought that was funny, because, well, I'll get to that. Her name, get this, was Emily. Which I was able to forgive her for since she spelled it the French way. E-m-i-l-i-e.

"Are you going to let your daughter ride in that thing?" Zep asked our American Emily as Portia climbed into the sidecar after breakfast that morning.

Emily looked thoughtful for a minute. "Yes," she said. "I'm going back to bed."

"Wait! I forgot my hat!" Portia said. She hopped out of the sidecar, dodged her mother, and pounded up the stairs.

"I brought along another scarf for you to tie your hat on with," Hugh called after her, waving it exuberantly overhead. Nina, doubled up on the motorcycle seat with Hugh, was already tying on the scarf he'd been thoughtful enough to bring along for her.

I headed inside to help Margaret with the dishes, and found Emily at the mail table, flipping through an issue of *Life* magazine that had just been delivered. "I know I said I was on my way to bed, but *Life* intervened," she said.

I looked around quickly to make sure that we were alone. Then I stepped close to her and said, "Emily, I have to tell you something."

She looked around, too, then murmured, "Is it that I look more beautiful than you imagined possible right now?"

"Yes, yes," I said. "But that's not what I need to tell you."

Her smile dribbled away. "Oh," she said. "Is something wrong?"

"I'm not sure," I said. I outlined what had happened in the kittens' stall and what I'd said to Portia before I realized she, not Emily, was inside Bottom's head. I finished with, "I'm not sure what to make of it. I'm not certain how much of what I said she understood."

"Do you think she heard any of it?" she asked. "With that thing on it's almost as hard to hear as it is to see."

"I'm not sure about that, either," I said.

Emily frowned. "Well, she hasn't said anything about it to me. Of course, she never says anything to me if she can help it. I wonder when she got her hands on that awful old thing. I swear I saw it in my room last night before I came to visit you. While I was changing my underwear I was trying to decide when I was going to have the chance to scare you with it."

"Do you think Portia came into your room in the night, looking for you, and took it?" I asked.

"While I wasn't there, you mean?" she asked. "Oh. Dear. I don't know." She paused, considering. "Let's not panic yet. I'm not sure the head was in my room last night. Maybe it was the day before that I'm remembering. I've lost all sense of time. I blame you for that." We looked at each other, and then I guess we must have gotten lost in each other's eyes. Emily grabbed my dimple and pulled my face down to hers and kissed me. "I doubt Portia made anything of anything she might have heard," she said. "She's just a kid."

If that had been true at the beginning of our conversation, it certainly wasn't true by the time Emily released my chin. When the two of us disengaged, Portia was standing at the bottom of the stairs with Sam's old hat in her hands. She hadn't made a sound coming down those steps. When Portia was feeling sad and couldn't sleep, Nina must have taught her to play the same game of squeaky-floorboard chess she'd taught Emily.

Chapter Nineteen

"I guess you and Papa are even now," Portia said. Her voice was calm and her facial expression inscrutable. Then she mashed Sam's hat onto her head and left us.

Emily followed Portia at a remove and stood on the porch watching as her daughter climbed into the motorcycle's sidecar. As the three of them roared down the driveway, Nina turned to wave to Emily; Portia did not.

When I joined her on the porch, Emily murmured, "That went about as well as could be expected, didn't it? Portia and I will talk about it as soon as she gets back."

I wasn't convinced that it had gone as well as all that, having seen Portia's face over Emily's shoulder. She'd given me the sort of calculating look Max gave when he hefted his shovel onto his shoulder. The look that Max himself might give me soon enough if Portia reported catching me with my hand in her mother's cookie jar. A wiser, more mature man than I was might have backed off then. But remember, I was lost in sorrow, and not quite twenty-five years old yet. I'm not a mind reader, so I couldn't have explained Emily's reasoning then to you.

That night, as we lay corkscrewed together on the slim ledge that was my bunk, Emily said, "You know, it's not like that with us."

"What's not like what?"

"I'm sorry. Of course you have no idea what I'm talking about. I've been thinking about what Portia said. With us, it's not the way it is with my husband and his—his—"

"—his cheap floozies?" I traced a finger up her sternum, spread my hand flat across her chest. I was able to span almost the entire distance between her shoulders with my fingers and my thumb. Emily really was a tiny thing. Lucky, that. If I'd hitched my wagon to Nina, we never would have been able to fold the both of us into my small bed.

Despite the heat, Emily shivered and closed her eyes. "This is different because I love you," she said.

"You what?" I asked. No woman I'd been entangled with had ever said as much to me.

Emily propped herself up on an elbow. "I know you're from a humble background, Ward, but I promise I'm not taking advantage of your ignorance. I'm not slumming with you, the way Archer does with his floozies. I *love* you."

I could see that she was serious, but I confess I was taken aback by what she said about slumming and my ignorance. I'd sort of assumed Emily recognized me as a princeling in disguise, not some semiliterate cowboy. The very stuff of fairy tales and Shakespeare's lighthearted romances and all the best screwball comedies. I was so surprised that she hadn't seen me for who I really was that I started laughing.

Emily disentangled herself and sat up, fast. "Oh," she said.

"Hold on," I said.

But she leapt to her feet and started gathering up her things. "Don't laugh at me. Don't you dare laugh at me." She threw her dress over one shoulder, clutched her moccasins to her chest, and headed for the window. I was worried she planned to take off across the yard like that, barefoot and buck naked. Instead she sat down on the sill and shoved a foot into a moccasin. "You must do this all the time," she said. "What a fool

I've been. This may not mean anything to you, cowboy, but it does to me. I promised myself I wasn't putting up with this sort of thing anymore." She pulled on her other moccasin and put a foot on the windowsill.

"Don't go yet," I said.

"Don't try to stop me," she said.

"Your dress," I said.

She looked down at it draped across her shoulder, bunched it up in her hands, buried her face in it, and burst into tears. I tried to put my arm around her but she shoved me away. "Don't touch me," she said.

"Fair enough," I said, and sat on my bunk again. "But listen to me for a minute, will you?"

She shook her head vigorously, still buried in her wadded-up dress.

"I'm laughing because that's about the last thing I expected to hear you say."

She lifted her face. "Why? Do you think *I* do this sort of thing all the time?"

"I sure hope not."

Because I saw it then, a glimpse of life's possibilities, viewed from the deck of a yacht. In San Francisco, I'd finish my undergraduate degree at Stanford. Heck, go to medical school there, too. Emily would float me financially at first, and then she'd be more than paid back after that by having her own private physician, me. Honestly, wouldn't you be more surprised if I said that idea *hadn't* occurred to me? Of course, *of course* I was in love with Emily. Why wouldn't I be? As a former guest who got her start working the necktie counter at Neiman Marcus had sagely opined over dinner once, "It's just as easy to fall in love with a rich man as a poor one."

"Let's get married," I said.

I don't know what response I expected, but it wasn't the one I got. Emily dropped the dress but didn't say anything. After what felt like an eternity, I picked the dress up and returned it to the hook it had been hanging on. Both of us stared at it on the hook until I said finally, idiotically, "We don't want that pretty thing to wrinkle."

"You don't mean that," she said. "About getting married."

After another eon or two I said, "No. Of course not. Forget I said it."

Now it was Emily's turn to laugh, although honestly it was more of a cackle. "It would be a crazy thing to do, wouldn't it? Tell you what. Why don't you see if you can convince me to come around to your way of thinking."

She kept her moccasins on.

Later, while we were catching our breath, I told Emily Margaret's story about the cleft in my chin. Emily put her thumb in it and kissed me. "It's true. You are perfect. How did I get to be so lucky? Imagine stumbling onto you, here. My diamond in the rough."

After my run-in with Portia I got jumpy, sure the kid would rat me out. But it seemed she'd chosen an option some of my patients with frightening symptoms used to go for—ignore the problem, and maybe it will go away. Sometimes that approach works. Usually it doesn't.

A couple of days later, with Margaret's permission, I was set to drive the Pierce-Arrow into town so that Nina and Emily could meet with their lawyers while the others rode in the Chevrolet with Sam. Coming back from fetching the car keys hanging on their designated hook by the back door, I almost blundered into Emily in the front hall, arguing with Portia. I hung back in the dining room. I didn't want to interfere.

"No, thank you," Portia said bitterly. "I will not go into town with you to see your divorce lawyer. How could you ask me to do such a thing?"

"I wasn't asking you to do that. I was asking if you wanted to go into Reno with us and look around some *while* I see my di—"

"I don't, I don't, I don't, I do not want to go, do you hear me? You don't need me there to tell the guy that my father is a bad man, and that you never loved him. You can tell him that yourself."

"Portia, that's not true. Your father is not a bad man."

"So my father isn't a bad man, but it's true that you never loved him? I knew it!"

"Oh, Portia, I loved your father," Emily said. "I loved him once. I promise you I did."

"So why can't you love him again?" Portia wailed. "Is that so much to ask?"

I didn't wait for Emily's answer. I didn't want to hear it. I pushed through the swinging doors into the kitchen, put my shoulder to the wall, and closed my eyes. It's not a good feeling, knowing the price of your future happiness is being paid for with someone else's pain. Of course I felt guilty about it. I am not made of stone.

When I opened my eyes again, Margaret was regarding me with some concern. "You look like somebody just ran over your dog, Ward," she said. "What's wrong?"

"That poor kid," I said, guiltier still for passing off what I was feeling as worry for Portia. "Emily's daughter just wants her parents to stay together. So they can be one big happy family again. Or one little happy family. I don't see that happening. Do you?"

Margaret wiped her hands on her apron. "I don't," she said. "Some kids would do anything to keep their parents married, but let me tell you, Ward. When a couple stays together for the children—" She shook her head. "That story usually doesn't end well for anybody. The parents are miserable and the kids don't know to hope for any better for themselves."

"My parents never fought. They were devoted to each other. Are, I mean." I hadn't told Margaret yet that they were dead.

Margaret tsked and shook her head. "That's hard in a different way, Ward. Makes your standards too high. You waste your life thinking you'll find the perfect match, but perfect matches don't exist."

"Oh, yeah? You and Max seem pretty perfect together," I said.

She laughed. "Trust me, sweetheart, we're not perfect." She leaned her elbows on the counter that ran through the middle of the kitchen and got that starry-eyed look she wore whenever she talked about Max. "We do love each other, though. I got lucky. We both did."

"It's a good thing you two happened to go to the same beach that day," I said.

"Beach? What beach?"

"The beach in Atlantic City. Where you met."

Margaret looked confused. "I didn't meet Max at the beach in Atlantic City. Who on earth told you that?"

"Nina. She says you still have the swimsuit Max was wearing when you met him."

"Ha! Max in a swimsuit. That I'd like to see. That girl has such an imagination. No, I met Max in Chicago. He was doing work for my husband. My husband introduced us, in fact. Poor guy. He never saw what was coming. None of us did."

"I didn't know you've been married more than once," I said.

"I haven't been," she said. "My husband wouldn't agree to a divorce, so—" She shrugged, then winked at me. "Don't tell the guests. I don't want to shock them."

By the time I pulled the car around for Nina and Emily, Portia had vanished. But we saw her when we reached the turnoff for the highway, astride an unbridled Dumpling, bareback. Or I surmised it was Portia, anyway, as it was someone wearing the clothes Portia had been wearing earlier, plus the papier-mâché ass's head. Instead of sitting up front with me like in the good old days before Portia came, Emily had gotten into the back seat and Nina had piled in after.

In my side mirror I saw Nina roll down her window to wave at Portia. "Cute kid," Nina said. "Looks more like her father every day."

Nobody spoke for a few miles after that. I stole a glance in my rearview at Emily, who was indulging in the kind of frowning Zep would have warned would give her wrinkles. Nina, meanwhile, rolled the window up again and sighed.

Soon after that, Emily snapped at Nina, "Will you stop making that infernal racket?"

"What?" Nina asked distractedly.

"What are you jingling in your pocket? Is it change? The sound is driving me crazy. Quit it."

"Or what?" Nina said. "You'll put me in the corner for the afternoon? Make me write on the blackboard a hundred times, 'I will not jingle the bullets in my pocket'?"

That set Emily back. "You're playing with bullets?" she asked.

"The ones that go in my revolver." Nina pulled the evidence from her pocket. I peeked in the rear-view again and saw the three small brass and copper cartridges laid across her palm.

"Why?" Emily asked.

"So I won't bite my fingernails," Nina said. "Bullets aren't dangerous unless they're coming at you from the barrel of a gun. You do know that, right?"

"I'm not an idiot," Emily said.

"Of course you aren't," Nina said, her tone softening. "I'm sorry, Emily. I'll try to leave the bullets alone if the sound is bothering you. I forgot that I'm not the only one here who might be on edge."

"I'm sorry I snapped at you," Emily said. "I'm not myself today."

I looked in the mirror again long enough to see Nina put the bullets back into her pocket. "Emily, I know you're worried you're making a mistake, leaving Archer," she said. "There's no real way of knowing, I suppose, though it seems the only way to go to me. But since when am I an expert? I never should have married Hugh. My mother told me it was a mistake, and I knew it was a mistake, but I did it anyway. I didn't love my first two husbands. I *liked* them. The first one, anyway. But Hugh—" Her sentence ended so abruptly that my eyes flicked to the mirror to see if she was crying, but her face was blank with despair. "Hugh and I weren't like the other kids, but it didn't matter because we had each other. Him I loved. And it just—" She shook her head. "There was no way."

Emily clasped Nina's hands in hers. "How about this?" she said. "How about we hold hands? That way you'll stop playing with the bullets, and you won't be able to bite your nails, either."

"Deal," Nina said.

Every time I stole a look at them in the mirror the rest of the way in they were still holding on to each other for dear life. Neither said anything else. I kept my trap shut, too.

I don't think Nina expected Hugh to be waiting for us in front of the lawyer's office, but there he was, his bike propped against a lamppost. Emily marched straight into the office building so he and Nina could have a moment together. I stayed in the car, trying to make myself invisible behind the steering wheel.

Hugh gave Nina such a hug that I heard a couple of her vertebrae pop. When they pulled apart, he said, "We did our best, didn't we? Be brave."

Nina said, "I'm the bravest person you know."

"That's true," Hugh said. "You're the bravest woman in the world."

"Bravest person," Nina said.

"Of course. The bravest. Period. No qualifications necessary." He said it lightly, though I could see that he was crying just a little.

Nina could see it, too. She palmed the tears from his cheeks and said, "Buck up. Worse things will happen to you than this."

"I hope not, but probably so," Hugh said.

Then Sam pulled up in the Chevrolet with the other ladies. Nina hurried into the office building so she wouldn't have to stay and chat. After all the womenfolk had straggled inside, we three gents were left behind on the sidewalk, sharing an awkward moment. "So, Ward," Sam said finally, "you want to split up this grocery list of Margaret's? You take dry goods? I take meats?" Though he wasn't looking at me or the list when he spoke. He was eyeing Hugh's bicycle.

Hugh saw what Sam was looking at, and asked, "Do you want to try it out?"

"We got these errands we need to see to," Sam said. "But I do appreciate the offer."

"Give me the list," I said. "I know you've been itching to ride that bicycle, Sam."

"You don't mind?"

"Not a bit." It was the least I could do. Poor Hugh was looking so hangdog and Sam was always such a tonic for what ailed you. Running the errands alone would also free me up to fall by The End of the Trail, Reno's premier pawnshop, to do a little window-shopping. I wanted to see if, by chance, they had any diamond rings for sale there as convincing of the seriousness of my matrimonial intentions as the rock Big Howard had presented to Miss Pam when he'd asked her to be his wife. When push came to shove, financially-speaking, my mother had refused to part with her engagement ring. "Over my dead body," she'd said. Well.

For the record, I didn't see any rings I liked that I could have afforded. I suppose my standards were too high.

Chapter Twenty

"The dead has arisen," Zep said to Emily when she showed up at breakfast in her pajamas toward the end of her stint with us. The Zeppelin would be gone in a day or two, but Emily's six weeks would be stretched to seven since she'd dragged her feet initially about filing her paperwork.

Emily flopped into the chair alongside Nina and nabbed a corner of uneaten toast off Nina's plate. "Am I too late for breakfast?" she asked.

That was the way things went at the Flying Leap as our lodgers' time with us wound to a close. They fell to eating off each other's plates and turning up in their nightclothes at the breakfast table. Their hair still in pin curls, the anti-wrinkle warriors among them with what remained of the gobs of cold cream they'd smeared on their faces the night before. The Zeppelin, for example, laser-focused on her imminent return to society and constricting French corsets, had taken to wearing cold cream and pajamas day and night. She eyed Emily critically and said, "You aren't looking quite yourself, my dear."

"Look who's talking," Nina said.

Emily frowned at Nina. "Be nice," she said.

"Why start now?" Nina asked.

Sam cycled into the room then, bearing a plate of eggs in one hand and a silver rack full of toast in the other. He positioned each on the sideboard carefully, adjusting their angle in relation to each other until it suited him aesthetically. As if it would stay that way for even half a minute after the ladies had descended on it.

Emily leapt to her feet, filled a plate, and came back to sit with Nina.

"Yowza," Nina said. "Is half of that for me?"

"Hands off," Emily replied. "I can't remember the last time I was this hungry."

Zep smacked the tabletop and Mary Louise steadied the coffee cup I'd just refilled for her. "There, Nina! You see?" the Zeppelin said. "I knew it. I am never wrong about these things."

Nina rolled her eyes. "Emily, will you please tell this old busybody that you aren't pregnant?"

Emily sat more upright in her chair and blinked. "Pregnant?" she asked. "Alas, no. I've been trying to get pregnant since Portia was two years old, but it seems my store closed for business early. It's the desert air, I think. It makes me ravenous."

Indiscreetly, Emily looked at me when she said this. To distract the Zeppelin from interrogating Emily about the contents of her womb, or maybe just to get a rise out of her, Nina said, poker-faced, "I can't find my nice set of lingerie I just bought at Woolworth's. Has anybody seen it? Pink and frilly. I'm horribly worried someone has run off with it."

"It's possible a thief nabbed your underthings off the clothesline," Margaret said, "but more than likely they're jumbled in with someone else's wash. The one time the lingerie hanging out to dry got stolen, that sneak took every bit of it."

"Margaret's probably right," Zep said, "None of my French lingerie is missing, and French lingerie is irresistible. Or so the gentlemen tell me."

"My underthings are made by Spanish nuns," Mary Louise said. "Have I mentioned that?"

"Yes," Nina said. She took Emily's hand under the table and gave it a little squeeze.

"That reminds me," Mary Louise said. "I woke up thinking that I'd dreamed something, but now I wonder if it might have really happened."

"What's that?" Margaret asked.

"I looked out my window in the middle of the night and saw a prowler. Over by the corral."

Sam hesitated on his way into the kitchen with the emptied egg plate and toast rack. "Over by the corral?" he asked. "Was your prowler wearing a hat?"

"Yes!" Mary Louise said. "Did you see him, too?"

"Might of been my hat. I leave it sit on a post of an evening to air out. You might of took it for a prowler."

"I brought in the laundry before dark, anyway," Margaret said. "So your prowler couldn't have snagged Nina's underwear. No, I'm sure there was just a mix-up. Ladies, please check your drawers for Nina's drawers."

"My prowler?" Mary Louise asked. "Why is he my prowler? I don't want a prowler. Now I'll never get to sleep."

"It could be a ruffian looking for somebody rich to kidnap," the Zeppelin said.

Nina and Emily exchanged glances. *Ruffian,* Nina mouthed.

"It really is such an inconvenience being wealthy sometimes," Zep continued. "People are always looking for ways to get money out of you."

Nina snorted. "You know what's even more inconvenient than having a lot of money?" she asked. "Not having any."

"As if you knew anything about that," Zep said.

"Ladies," Margaret said. "Please."

"I can make the rounds in the night now and again, if that will make the ladies rest easier, ma'am," Sam said. "Ward and I can swap out sentry duty, if need be."

"With a rifle propped up on your shoulder, like a palace guard?" Mary Louise asked. "I spent the weekend in a palace in Belgium once. That's a town in France."

"It's a country, actually. Next to France," Nina said.

"Have you been to Belgium?" Mary Louise asked.

"No," Nina said.

"Well, I have," Mary Louise said decisively. She gathered the feathered border of her robe around her neck. "I didn't care for it, or that castle, either. It was cold and the plumbing wasn't up to snuff and there wasn't a moat or a drawbridge or a palace guard armed with rifles on patrol at night or anything. It was very disappointing."

"Max don't hold with keeping firearms on the property, ma'am," Sam interjected. "He says guns make more trouble than they make go away. But he has a shovel I could prop up on my shoulder that might pass for a rifle in the dark, if what it looks like I'm toting is what matters to you."

I went back into the kitchen for a fresh coffeepot without hanging on to hear what they decided. Sam would fill me in on anything that mattered.

Hugh, Nina, and Portia roared off on the motorcycle together soon after that, having told Emily some plausible fiction about their destination—the hot springs, a ghost town, the golf links over in Reno. Off the hook once again for entertaining her daughter, Emily went upstairs to sleep and I took care of outdoor chores. As the shadows lengthened I set out to the barn with the milk pail. I tipped a little feed into the cast-iron pot inside the cattle stanchion and Katie obediently stuck her head through to get at it. Good old Katie. Always giving and not getting much in return aside from food and shelter. I wondered sometimes if she ever wished for another calf. I said as much to Sam once, and he laughed at me. "Have you ever seen a cow birth a calf, city boy?" he asked. "Don't look like much fun to me."

I was latching the slat of wood that held Katie's head in the stanchion when Emily waltzed into the barn. "I've been looking all over for you," she said.

"What exactly did you have in mind?" I asked. "I can't keep Katie waiting long for her milking."

"Oh, goodness, not that." She blushed. "I was just wondering. If Sam's patrolling tonight, maybe I shouldn't come to see you. Also I could use a good night's sleep."

"All right," I said. "Although I'm not sure how much patrolling he plans to do. I think he just said that to make Mary Louise happy. Sam sleeps with one eye open already, so if we had a prowler, he'd be the first to know."

Emily considered this for a minute. "Does he know about us?" she asked.

"Yes. He took me aside and warned me to watch my step."

"Oh, dear. Does Margaret know?"

"If Margaret knew, I wouldn't be sitting on this stool right now, milking Katie. I'd be out on my can."

"Good. That means Sam won't squeal on you before we leave. You being gone makes more work for him."

Her assessment of the situation rubbed me the wrong way. "That's not why he won't squeal on me," I said. "Sam is my friend. The only reason we've gotten away with this as long as we have is because I know I can trust Sam, and Max and Margaret think they can trust me. I don't feel good about putting Sam in an awkward position, or about how those two would react to me betraying their trust. They've been good to me. Like a second set of parents."

That angle of my duplicity hadn't struck me until I said it. If I ran off with Emily I might never talk to Max and Margaret again. Sam, either. It was crushing to consider how cavalierly I planned to sacrifice them on the altar of romance, and so soon after losing the family I'd been born to. Here I'd been feeling morally superior to Archer, though I was as much an infidel as he was when it came to betraying loved ones.

"They'll get over it," Emily said. "I can guarantee that."

"Oh?" I said, eager to hear her plan for making things right with everybody again. "How do you know?"

"I'm leaving all the staff here such a juicy tip."

I wasn't so sure that would set things straight. Sure, a juicy tip might help pay the mortgage, but it doesn't do much for the soul. That's something common to so many rich folks, though. They assume the approval of everybody they come in contact with can be bought.

Chapter Twenty-one

My stolen nights with Emily had me keeping vampire hours, so once I was given that night off I found I couldn't fall asleep. Eventually I got tired of rolling around alone in my bed. Got up and dressed, hat and all, and ambled outside to enjoy a little of what folks these days call "me time." Now, of course, I get more time to myself than I know what to do with; but in those days, between all the fetching and serving and chatting and dancing and whatnot with our guests, I didn't get many moments to call my own.

The ranch really was at its best in moonlight. All silvery light and deep shadows, like an art-house film shot in black and white. I don't know how it is for you kids who grew up with movies presented in what they used to call "living color," but in my youth it was easy to imagine yourself the star of your own picture in a landscape lit up by the earth's nocturnal gaffer, the moon.

I remember thinking I should wander the predawn hours more often, little realizing that would be my lot in life once I became a small-town doctor. When I was on emergency call I was summoned to the hospital regularly, sometimes three times a night, to deal with the bloody business of life and death. Honky-tonk stabbings, car wrecks, childbirth. The roller coaster of joy and sorrow. Delivering babies, now, I do miss that. As long as there aren't complications, nothing on this earth is more gratifying than catching a newborn as it comes down the chute. I know I've mentioned that I never did have a child of my own, but at the same time I had so many, and all without a single bill for college tuition turning up on my desk.

Yes, I did try to figure out once how many babies I've delivered. At least a thousand, I decided, give or take. So many little faces smiling out of snapshots pinned to the corkboards that ran the length of my office hallway. I have delivered the children of children I delivered, and a few times brought forth their grandchildren. Sure, sometimes I think it would be nice if a fraction of that thousand came to visit me of a Sunday, but everybody is so busy with their own lives and families. That's why it has been such a joy to have these nice long visits with you.

That night, that night, yes, that night, wandering the Flying Leap. I crossed paths with Caterwaul on the prowl for mice and members of his harem and saluted Sam's hat airing out on the post. When I reached the corral I saw Hugh's bicycle propped against the fence. He must have loaned the thing to Sam to learn on while Hugh was getting around via motorcycle.

I've always believed fragrances are richer late at night, though that's not something I know for a fact. That's why I hiked up to the ranch house porch, paused by the trellis, and closed my eyes while I took in a noseful of that rose's aroma, a little self-consciously I'll grant you, imagining myself a true poet along the lines of Keats or Shelley or Byron. I always was a sucker for the Romantics. Thought of myself in those days as some sort of sensitive genius, instead of as exactly what I appeared to be, an ignorant hick cowboy with boots that smelled like sour milk.

I hadn't been there long enough to exhale when I got beaned by something that like to have knocked my hat clean off. I was about to light out for the shed to arm myself with Max's shovel when I noticed a leather pouch with lengths of ribbon as long as my arm attached lying at my feet. What the heck?

I picked the thing up, hefted it in my palm, and peeked inside. A chunk of gravel was in there for ballast, and a folded piece of paper. The moonlight may not have been bright enough for me to see what color ink that folded note was written in, but it was bright enough to read by. *Look up,* the piece of paper said.

I looked up. Nina's head and shoulders were sticking out beyond the edge of the porch roof. I'd been working at the ranch long enough by then to be prepared to expect the unexpected, so this wasn't the surprise it might have been out in the real world. Nina held a finger to her lips, *shhh,* then motioned to the trellis. She seemed to be suggesting that I climb up and join her on the roof so we could have a confab.

I stepped back to get a better angle on her face and shook my head. Motioned for Nina to come down the trellis. She made an exasperated gesture and got to her feet, so close to the rim of the porch that it made my innards clench. I saw then that she was wearing the fairy costume, wingless, and holding a book with her thumb stuck in it to keep her place. With her other hand she gestured at what she had on and shook her head.

I saw her point. Emily would have her hide if Nina make confetti of all that gauzy fabric she'd gone to such trouble to piece together again. I held up two fingers pointed downward and made a gesture that conveyed,

I hoped, the act of two legs walking down a flight of stairs.

Nina put her book down, shuffled around a little while looking at her feet in a way that suggested she'd stuck a toe in it to hold her place, then grabbed the hem of her costume and lifted. *"No,"* I hissed, gesticulating frantically to signal *stop.* I jerked a thumb in the direction of the house and made the sign for walking down steps again. "Stairs," I stage-whispered.

Oh, she mouthed. She nodded once, pointed at me, and held up a finger.

I tiptoed up the porch steps and waited. Nina wafted wraithlike out that front door, gentled it shut behind herself so that it closed without a click, grabbed the pouch out of my hand, and used its ribbon to mark her page.

"What is that thing?" I murmured.

"Message bag," she murmured back. "My plane isn't fitted with a radio, so if I need to be in touch with someone on the ground, I can write a note, shove it in the pouch, and toss it over the side. The ribbons make it easier to track while it's falling. They also make it an excellent bookmark. When I'm on the ground, of course. I don't read novels while I'm flying." She took my hand and dragged me to the shadows at the far end of the porch where two chairs were tucked away. "I didn't want to wake Portia turning on the lamp, so I was out on the porch roof, reading. *A Tale of Two Cities.* Do you know it?"

"'It was the best of times, it was the worst of times,'" I said.

"Exactly. Then I saw you wandering around, and I was afraid they would see you, and everything would be spoiled."

I wondered if Nina was trying to suggest she'd seen me heading to what she figured was an assignation with Emily. "Who would see me?"

"Sam and Hugh."

"Sam and Hugh?"

"It's one of the better ideas I've had recently."

"I don't understand," I said. "Sam and—"

"—Hugh, yes. Shhhh. Here they come now. I don't want them to think I was spying on them. Which I wasn't." She put a hand on my arm and gestured toward the corral with her chin. In the distance beyond it, Sam's head and, shortly thereafter, Hugh's crested the near end of the wash where Emily and I had whiled away a blissful half hour on that saddle blanket. The men's bodies materialized above the lip of it top to bottom, like that children's song, head and shoulders, knees and toes, until the all of them was in sight, and walking across the uneven earth on their way to the corral.

Hugh collected the bicycle and rolled it inside after Sam opened the gate and propped it open. Sam took the handlebars and threw a leg across while Hugh held the bike steady and ran alongside, one hand on the handlebars and another on the seat. He released the handlebars first, then the saddle, and Sam was on his way. When Hugh stepped back, Nina took my hand and squeezed it. "Look at the two of them together," she said. "I knew they'd like each other."

I couldn't hear anything the men were saying when they leaned close to talk, but they did seem to be getting along. The only sound that made it all the way up to the house was hushed laughter when Sam slowed down too much, the bicycle wobbled, and he hit the dirt. Hugh helped him up and brushed him off. Like any cowboy worth his salt, Sam got right back in the saddle. He rode around the corral's perimeter where the ground was the hardest while Hugh stood in the middle, rotating to monitor his progress and applauding silently now and again.

I don't know how long the lesson lasted. Five minutes? Fifteen? It's hard to say. Eventually Hugh pulled out his pocket watch, consulted it, put it away again, and waved to his pupil. Sam climbed off the bike and propped it against the fence alongside the post where his hat hung. He picked the hat up, settled it on his head, then reconsidered and settled it on Hugh's head. Hugh said something to Sam, took the hat off and put it on Sam. It went back and forth between them like that for a few more rounds, then Hugh settled it on Sam's head one last time and hugged him. Then they kissed, briefly but vigorously enough to knock Sam's hat off his head.

"Oh," I said.

"Turns out I wasn't the only one who wished I'd been born a boy," Nina said. "Oh, well. I'm happy for them. Really I am."

Hugh swung into the bicycle saddle then, skimmed out of the corral, and bumped silently down the drive. When I looked back to see what Sam was up to, he was leaning against the closed corral gate, holding his hat and staring into the well of its crown as if it were a crystal ball. Finally he put the hat on his head again and walked into the bunkhouse. After he'd been gone a good amount of time, Nina got up and went inside the house. Soon after that I went to bed myself.

No, I never found out what kind of relationship Hugh and Sam had or didn't have. It was none of my business, really. What I do know is that I've seen too much misery brought about by people trying to force themselves into molds that were not a fit for them. Like Cinderella's stepsisters, lopping off their big toes so they could try to cram their feet into that glass slipper.

I bet those women were crippled for life if they didn't die right quick. Bled out if Cinderella didn't think fast and snatch a hot poker from that fire they always had her tending to cauterize the stumps.

The next morning Portia was at the breakfast table with Zep, Mary Louise, and a few of the other guests, Theresa, Liz, Martha from your photograph, more than likely. I seem to remember those three sticking together, playing endless games of pinochle to pass the time instead of spending it inventing fun new ways to stir up trouble.

Speaking of Nina, when she slouched into the dining room, still wearing the fairy dress, and poured herself into a chair, Zep asked, "Did you sleep in that costume?"

"It's only a costume when I'm wearing the wings," Nina said. She resettled the fabric underneath herself and fingered one of the seams Emily had stitched when she mended the tattered section. "The rest of the time it's pajamas."

"I'm surprised to see you up," Portia said.

Sam brought Nina a cup of coffee as she unfolded a napkin and spread it across her lap.

"Why's that?" Nina asked.

"I woke up in the night and your bed was empty," Portia said. "I got worried you'd been kidnapped."

"Nothing as exciting as that," Nina said. "There was a full moon and I didn't want to wake you so I sat out on the porch roof, reading. It's nice out there when the air is chilly but the roof is still a little warm from the sun the day before."

"That's funny," Portia said. "I looked out the window and I didn't see you."

"I was sitting with my back against the wall, right by the window," Nina explained, so blithely I almost believed her myself. "If you'd reached an arm out of the window, you could have tapped me on the shoulder."

"See any sign of Mary Louise's prowler, miss?" Sam asked.

"I did not," Portia said. "What's funny is that I could have sworn I heard voices coming from the front porch. It sounded like you, Nina, talking to Ward."

I pushed through the swinging doors into the kitchen and plastered myself to the wall on the other side. I intended to let Nina answer that one, then roll with whatever story she came up with.

"You must have been dreaming," Nina said. "What would I want to talk to Ward about in the middle of the night?"

"I wondered that myself," Portia said.

Chapter Twenty-two

Let me see that photograph again. Hand me my magnifying glass if you don't mind. Nope, I don't recognize the handwriting. I would if it were Margaret's. I knew Sam's handwriting, too, almost microscopic and very tidy; and Max's scrawl, very nearly indecipherable unless you were familiar with it, like a doctor's. Some of our guests' writing I can still picture, too, if I close my eyes. The *look up* note that Nina scribbled, *Ward,* block-lettered but still girlish on an envelope from Emily, and of course that bombshell from Portia that—but wait, I'm about to get ahead of my story again.

Where did we leave off last time? Ah, yes, Portia pointing the finger at me for talking to Nina late at night.

I was in the kitchen helping Sam with the breakfast dishes later that morning when I heard Hugh's motorcycle thunder up the drive. Sam, just-washed dish in one hand and a dish towel in the other, eased over to the window and looked out. By the time Hugh roared off with his passengers, that dish of Sam's was as dry as the Forty Mile Desert southeast of Reno.

If I'd been at the window, too, counting heads when the motorcycle left, I wouldn't have been as surprised to come upon Portia later on that day, halfway up the staircase with a kitten in her lap and her head tilted toward the library.

I said, "I thought you went off with Hugh and N—"

Portia held her finger to her lips and looked daggers at me. Then I heard the voices coming from the library. Emily's, and a man's. I nodded amiably at Portia—*none of my business, nothing to see here*—walked out the front door, down the porch steps, and around to the library side of the house. Luckily for me, the windows were open and I was able to position myself under one in time to hear Emily say, "You're wasting your breath, Archer. I want you out of the house by the time I get back to San Francisco."

"I will not have you take my child away from me," the voice that must have belonged to Archer said.

"*Our* child," Emily said. "Find an apartment close enough to the house and you can see *our* child every day if that's what you want. Up to you. All I know is that you aren't living in *my* house with us anymore."

"I won't have it, do you hear me? Portia needs her father under the same roof, to—"

"—to show her how she can expect to be treated by her husband? To teach her that she's supposed to look the other way when the man who says he loves her doesn't love her enough to keep his hands off other women?"

"But I didn't love any of those other women," Archer said. "Why can't you understand that? It isn't fair to Portia to—"

"Don't pretend this is about Portia, Archer. All she is to you is a bargaining chip."

The thing about Emily's voice always sounding so ragged was that it made it hard to gauge how upset she was when you couldn't see her face. She wasn't shouting, that's for sure. It sounded like she had more grace under pressure than you might expect of someone no bigger than a minute, who'd once seemed afraid of so many relatively inconsequential things.

"That's not true," Archer said. "You know it isn't."

"Isn't it? Well, how about this? Take her with you when you move out. Take her today, for all I care. See how much you like putting up with her moods. It's a pretty thankless business, raising *your* daughter."

I didn't stick around after that. All I could think of was Portia on the staircase, clutching that kitten and listening in. That's the danger of eavesdropping, isn't it? Sometimes you overhear things you wish you could unhear.

The kid wasn't on the staircase when I went back inside. The kitten was, though, mewling pitifully over the injustice of having been abandoned there. I scooped up the poor little creature and returned it to its stall down at the barn. On my way back I saw a taxi vanishing down the driveway. Then Portia came out of the house wearing the papier-mâché donkey's head. She gave me a wide berth as she passed me on her way out to the barn.

I found Emily alone in the library, curled up in Nina's armchair and staring out the window.

"Who was in the taxi?" I asked innocently.

Emily got up, put her arms around my neck, and pulled my face down to meet hers. She kissed me full on the lips, then said, "Nobody."

"Careful," I said. "We wouldn't want anybody to catch us doing that."

She pulled away from me and eyed me. "So what if they do?" she asked. "You know what? I think we should get married as soon as I'm divorced from Archer. Walk across the hall and do it right away. What do you think of that idea?"

"What about Portia?" I asked. Don't get me wrong. It tickled me to think of becoming Mr. Emily Sommer on my way to turning myself into Dr. Howard Stovall Bennett. However. "I'm not sure she's going to go for having a stepfather."

"It's about time Portia learned the world doesn't revolve around her. Anyway, she'll be gone from the house soon enough. Like Nina said."

"Keep your voice down. She might hear you."

"No, she won't. Portia's off somewhere motorcycling with her pals."

"Not today," I said. "I saw her in the hall earlier. Sitting on the stairs. I think she was looking for you." I was turning over in my mind whether I ought to mention what the kid might have overheard, but I couldn't think of a way to do it without confessing that I'd been listening in myself.

Before I'd bulldogged the horns of this dilemma and got it wrassled to the ground, Emily puckered her brow and said, "Oh? I'd better go find her."

"Maybe so," I said. "Last I saw her she was headed down to the barn."

Emily considered this for a moment. "Or. Maybe I'll wait until Nina gets back from wherever she's run off to. Portia is always nicer to me when Nina's around. It's so tiresome, always fighting with that child. There's no pleasing her. Sometimes I wonder why I bother trying."

I agree I should have told Emily all I knew right then. Everything might have ended differently if I had.

Later, while pinning laundry on the line for Margaret, I noticed that same sad, floppy-eared half-donkey, half-girl on the porch steps, waiting the way a dog will by the front door for its master to come home. Then I heard the distant rumble of the motorcycle and saw the swirl of dust as it turned off the main road and into the driveway.

After Nina climbed out of the sidecar and Hugh thundered away, she sat by the kid on the stairs and said, "We missed you today, Portia. What did your mother say about the kitten?"

A negative shake of the donkey's head.

"I don't suppose it's the sort of thing you could smuggle home inside your luggage," Nina said.

Portia dragged the ass's head off. "I don't want to go back to San Francisco," she said. "Why can't I go home with you?"

"I don't think your parents would be happy about that," Nina said.

"They wouldn't care."

"I'm pretty sure they would. Besides, I don't know where I'm going next. So I don't think it would be a good idea for you to tag along with me."

"You're as bad as they are," Portia said. "I hate people." She pulled on Bottom's head again.

Nina rested a hand between its terry cloth ears and said, "For the record, I hated people when I was your age, too. Sometimes I still do."

Portia knocked Nina's hand away, got up, and stomped off in the direction of the barn.

"Where's Portia?" Emily asked Nina, her hands kneading the back of a chair before she pulled it out to take a seat at dinner. "I haven't seen her all day."

"She's out in the barn," Nina said.

"Playing with the kittens?"

"Communing with her boyfriend Dumpling. The only being in heaven or on earth who really understands her. Says she."

"I could go out and fetch her for you, ma'am," I said.

"No, no. That's all right. No reason to poke the bear."

Throughout dinner I tried to catch Emily's eye, but she wouldn't look at me. I tried not to read any significance into that, but I confess being so willfully ignored put me on edge.

When the meal was over and Portia still hadn't straggled in, Margaret made a sandwich for the kid and asked me to take it out to her. Sam put a couple of cookies on the plate and I poured a glass of lemonade.

Portia was huddled in a corner of Dumpling's stall, still wearing that infernal donkey's head. Although by then the thing wasn't looking judgmental so much as pathetic. It hadn't been constructed to stand up to the hard use it had gotten lately.

As for Dumpling, he had on the fairy wings. Their harness wasn't designed to fit a horse, so the wings flopped against either side of the gelding's neck instead of spreading as magnificently as the wings of Pegasus.

I knocked on the closed lower half of his stall door. "May I come in?" I asked.

"No." Portia's voice sounded like it was rising from the bottom of a well.

Dumpling nickered softly. At least he was glad to see me. Or maybe he hoped I'd relieve him of those silly wings.

"Thanks, pal," I said. "Don't mind if I do." I let myself into the stall and said, "Oh, Portia, I didn't see you there. I'm glad I found you. Margaret fixed a plate for you."

"I'm not hungry," the muffled voice said. "Go away."

I put the plate down inside the feed trough. "Now, don't you eat this, Dumpling," I said. "Sugar is bad for your teeth, and anyway, it's for Portia."

"What about my teeth?" Portia asked in a faraway, woeful voice.

I decided it was better not to respond to that directly. "Portia can come in and brush her teeth after she eats that cookie, you see. Maybe I should get you a toothbrush, too, huh, pal? When I go into town to buy myself a new pair of boots, I'll pick one up for you."

I rested my forehead against Dumpling's blaze and scratched him where his jaw met his neck, the way he liked it. "Those wings look better on you than they did on me," I said, though I hoped that wasn't so. There was something so sad about the flaccid way they hung there. "Okay then. I'm leaving you in charge here, old man. See you in the morning." I patted him one last time while he lipped my shirt pocket hopefully. I didn't have a thing in there for him. I've always regretted that.

That night, Emily slipped out of the house and made it up to me and then some for missing the night before. Then she gasped, sat up and said, "Ward, I can't marry you."

"What?" I said. "Why not? Because of Portia?"

She started laughing. "Please don't look at me like that. I was kidding. It just struck me that I don't know your middle name. How could I think of marrying a man whose middle name I don't know?"

"It's Stovall," I said, trying not to seem as shaken as I felt. "Howard Stovall Bennett III, at your service. That's why I go by Ward. My father was Howard."

"Well, come here, Howard Stovall Bennett III, and service me again."

Afterward, she asked, "What'll you call your son? Quarter?"

"Quarter?"

"Because he's the fourth? As in, a fourth of a dollar?"

"I see. Ha." I thought for a minute. I had never considered what to call any progeny of mine. "'Stovall' sounds pretentious, and calling the kid 'Stove' would set the kid up for all kinds of teasing. 'Howard' is too formal for a kid. Howie, maybe?"

"How about 'Steve'?" she asked. "My grandfather's name was Steven and we called him Papa Steve. He was such a sweet old man."

I almost said, "I'll have to run that by my mother." Then I was overwhelmed with such sadness. My face crumpled, thinking about the descendants she'd always wanted but hadn't lived to see.

"Oh, no," Emily said quickly. "I didn't mean to upset you. Call him anything you want. 'Sonny.' Or 'Hey You.' Whatever. Archer always said Portia probably thought her name was 'Stop That' when she was little."

"I'm sorry," I said. "My mother was really looking forward to having grandchildren, that's all. It just hit me that she'll never get to meet little Quarter. She's gone, my father's gone, the house. My whole life. Nothing's left."

After a long pause, Emily said, "You still have their rings, don't you?"

I nodded.

"Can I see them again?"

I got up and fetched them from the bottom drawer of my bureau. I kept them knotted inside a sock there so they wouldn't fall through a crack in it or the floorboards and disappear. She slid Miss Pam's ring onto her finger and the other onto mine. They both fit pretty well, something I took as a good sign. "So you'll start over," she said. "Have a family of your own. Another house. I hope you'll be very happy with Mrs. Howard Stovall Bennett III. I hear she's a lovely woman."

Emily left dangerously late the next morning, just as the sky started going gray. I stood at the window watching until she disappeared into the house. Just before she did, she turned and blew me a kiss. Fifty years on, and I can still see her there as if it were yesterday, her face turned back to me in the halo of brightness cast by the little porch light Margaret left on all night long. I waved and blew a kiss in return, even though I was pretty sure she couldn't see me. I realized then that I still had my father's ring on, and that she'd forgotten to return my mother's to me. I took off Big Howard's and slid it into my pocket. I figured she'd notice Miss Pam's on her finger soon enough and keep it safe until it was time for me to slip it on her finger for good, in the process transforming the ex-Mrs. Archer Sommer into the lovely Mrs. Howard Stovall Bennett III.

After Emily went inside I stood at the window as the sky lightened, hoping she was right. We'd be happy together, wouldn't we? Even if we never managed to have a baby of our own, Portia would come to love me and I'd think of her as my own flesh and blood.

While I stood there mulling over the change in my fortunes I saw Hugh drop from Sam's window, collect his bike, and ride silently away.

The next morning Portia's plate and glass were empty. So was Dumpling's stall. Also Portia's bed in Coyote. She must have slipped inside the house sometime during the night while Sam and I were otherwise occupied. Bottom's head was on the mail table with an envelope propped inside his mouth and the fairy wings folded beside it. The envelope was addressed to Max and Margaret, and inside was a ten-dollar bill and a note:

Dear M&M, Here's some money to pay for Dumpling, plus one bridle and a saddle. I'll send more later, once I'm settled. I'm pretty sure I can get a job now that I know how to fly an airplane. Thanks for everything. Portia.

Chapter Twenty-three

I don't like the next part of the story much, so let's try to get through it quickly.

When Emily and Nina finally came downstairs both their faces were stiff with anger. Nina's hair was a mess and she had on the fairy costume, so I gathered Emily had shaken her awake with the news of Portia's note. "I forgive you in advance for all the rotten things you just said to me," Nina croaked, her voice still rough with sleep. "You're going to be pretty ashamed of yourself when I'm the one who finds your daughter."

"She told you where she was going?" Emily asked. "And you didn't warn me?"

"Of course Portia didn't tell me where she was going. I'll do an aerial search."

"That airplane," Emily said bitterly. "None of this would have happened if it weren't for you and it. This is your fault. I can't believe I ever trusted you. I hate you."

"Join the club," Nina said, and walked out the front door. Sam drove her to the airport in the ranch house station wagon. She didn't even take the time to change into real clothes before she left.

Meanwhile, I chauffeured Emily into town. I thought it odd at first that she chose to sit in the back, but I'd also noticed that she remembered to take off my mother's ring, so I gathered she was trying to be discreet.

"Portia didn't really run away," she said, as much to herself as to me. "Knowing her, she ran to her father. I'm sure she's having breakfast with Archer right now. They must be having a wonderful time talking about what an awful person I am."

I didn't know what to say to that, so I didn't answer.

As we pulled up to Archer's hotel, she added, "Portia always loved Archer best because he lets her get away with murder. She wants to live with him, in whatever squalid little apartment he finds? Fine. We'll see how she likes that. That girl doesn't know how lucky she is." Before she got out of the Pierce-Arrow, Emily said, "Give me the car keys, Ward. You're riding Dumpling back to the ranch. I'll drive Portia."

I handed her the keys. "It's going to be all right," I said, only half believing it.

We found Archer in the lobby of the Riverside Hotel, reading a newspaper and drinking a cup of tea. Alone. To his credit, instead of blowing up when Emily managed to choke out what had happened, he leapt to his feet and wrapped his arms around her.

For the drive back to the Flying Leap, Emily handed over the car keys without making eye contact, as if I were a valet driver at a restaurant bringing around her car. I tried to take comfort from the fact that she and Archer rode all the way there pressed against opposite doors. The only words that passed between them was Archer asking, "What made this stain here on the upholstery?" and Emily answering, "Kittens."

I pulled into the barnyard behind the Chevrolet just as Sam stepped out from behind the wheel. Cowboy boots first, then fairy costume.

"Who on earth is that?" Archer asked.

"That's Sam," I said. "He must have changed clothes with Nina before she got into her airplane."

"Why?"

"Because she asked him to, I imagine," I said. "She left in a hurry. That dress is what she sleeps in."

"How do you know what she sleeps in?" I did not like the imperious tone he took with me.

"Because I tuck all our ladies in before I read them bedtime stories," I said. "Didn't Emily tell you?"

I know it wasn't the sort of thing I would have said under normal circumstances, but it had been an upsetting morning and his supercilious attitude really put my nose out of joint. I know that was uncharitable of me since the man's daughter had gone missing and he was on his way to losing his wife. Still.

Sam was in and out of the bunkhouse in a flash. Once he was in dungarees again he set off on a buckskin mare named Honey, the fastest of our horses, to trace the various routes our afternoon trail rides followed. Max took the Chevrolet into Reno to confer with the sheriff, and Margaret disappeared into her office, calling around to neighboring ranches to put out the word. Emily and Archer spent the morning huddled in the porch chairs Nina and I had occupied not so long ago, two untouched glasses of iced lemonade I'd brought them sweating rings onto the Switzerland of wicker table that stood between them.

Somehow Margaret and I managed to get lunch on the table. As I was clearing afterward, I heard the distant drone of an airplane and clattered my tray of dirty dishes onto the mail table in the hall so I could hurry out to the porch. To the west, an orange dot on the horizon resolved itself into Nina's plane. It buzzed the barnyard and loosed a flutter of bright streamers that fell to the corral. I ran to pick it up.

The note inside the message pouch read, *Buzzards. Gopher field. Horse down. Kid up.* The plane wheeled away again. I squinted after it and saw the carrion fowl circling in the distance, a grim merry-go-round of black dots against the flat, white sky. Nina's plane circumnavigated that spiral to be sure we spotted it. I remember thinking what a blessing it was that Nina had taken to the air to look for Portia, as Sam never would have ventured into that forbidden territory on horseback. The kid had never been on one of our trail rides, I realized, and so hadn't been warned off it. Nor had she gotten very far before catastrophe struck. That makes sense to me now, of course. If there's anything I've learned from years of working in hospital emergency rooms, it's that most terrible accidents happen within a few of miles of home.

Then: Emily and Archer, eyeing me anxiously as I cleared my throat a couple of times before managing, "Good news. Looks like Portia is okay," and handing Nina's note to Emily.

Archer and Emily hugging. Him shushing her as she wept on his shoulder, stroking her hair, kissing her forehead. Emily not pushing him away.

Me, asking Archer, "Do you know how to ride, sir?"

and him answering, "Do I know how to ride? I played polo for Harvard."

Of course you did, I thought.

Archer lounging against the breezeway wall, watching me tack up three horses, never lifting a finger to help but eyeing me critically, as if he were grading my performance.

Emily vanishing, then reappearing, just as I had all three horses set to go. She looked like she'd been crying. "It's going to be all right," I repeated, believing it less and less.

Boosting Emily into her saddle and seeing Nina's unloaded revolver tucked into her waistband. We both knew what "horse down" might mean, but she was the one who thought two steps ahead and went for the gun. As I swung into my saddle I wondered how old Dumpling had gotten to be. Fifteen? Sixteen? Old, but not so old.

Riding the outer perimeter of the fenced-off gopher field. Tying our horses to the wooden posts of the barbed-wire fence. Putting one foot on the bottom strand of wire and holding another as high as I could while Emily and then Archer scooted through. Nina's plane, reduced to a child's toy by the distance, landing across that pitted minefield for the four-legged. Nina running at the farthest reaches of the wash that first

Emily and I, then Sam and Hugh had used as our lovers' lane. The V of Dumpling's ears swiveling above the ditch's bank alongside the crown of Sam's old hat perched on Portia's head. The kid leaping to her feet. The old gelding stretching out his forelegs, one grotesquely swollen, its hoof at a crazy angle. Dumpling groaning and subsiding to the ground again.

Portia, her face dirty, sweaty-headed from Sam's old hat, sobbing, "I wanted to come for help, but he kept trying to get up to come with me." Running to her father's arms, not her mother's. Archer, outside the gopher field again, lifting Portia onto the horse I'd ridden out, the two of them galloping hell for leather back to the ranch house.

Emily, pulling the revolver from her waistband and Nina rooting around in the pocket of Sam's jeans, pulling out a bullet like a magician producing a rabbit from a hat. I remember marveling at Nina, knowing Emily would think of the pistol, and at Emily for understanding Nina could be counted on to supply the ammunition. The two of them, so perfectly hand-in-glove. Emily, snapping the empty cylinder open to slip it into the chamber like a hardened movie gangster, and handing the loaded gun to me. Me kneeling in front of my old friend, realizing I'd never offed anything bigger than a horsefly, much less a horse. So blinded by tears that I had to feel around to find my buddy's face.

Nina, calm and dry-eyed, nudging me aside, taking the revolver and putting muzzle to the jagged slash of white that paved the center of the gelding's forehead. Dumpling exploring her pockets for sugar cubes. Nina coming apart then worse than I had.

In the end, Emily took the gun, pressed barrel to target, pulled the trigger. Done.

I have witnessed many deaths since then. I won't say none have hit me harder, but I do know that I've never let myself crumble like that since. Emily may have wronged me in many ways, but I'll always be glad to have witnessed her sangfroid in the face of the inevitable. If not for her example I might not have made it through the war and the forty-some-odd years of tough calls that came afterward in my work as a physician. If she could be so cool-headed when it counted most, so could I.

"I'm keeping the gun, Nina," Emily said. "You can't be trusted with anything."

Nina wiped her face on her sleeve and mumbled, "I'm all right now. Give it here."

"No, you aren't," Emily said. "You took my daughter up in that deathtrap of yours. What is wrong with you? What if you'd crashed? What if she'd died?"

"I never took her up in my plane," Nina said.

"Liar," she spat.

Emily crawled back through the barbed wire unaided, the revolver stuck in the waistband of her pants. Untied the last horse and rode away at a conservative trot, her elbows pressed against her sides. Never once looked back.

"Come on, Ward," Nina said. "We need to get this tack off before Dumpling starts to stiffen up." She dropped to her haunches and brushed away the flies that had already started to congregate around his half-closed eyes.

"You never should have let Portia fly your plane," I said.

"I didn't."

"I know you did. You told me so yourself."

Nina stood. She was as tall as I was and I thought how odd it was, being eye to eye with a woman instead of talking down to her. "I told you I let her *sit* in my airplane. Wings folded. She was never airborne. Not once." She helped herself to the bandana protruding from my pocket and wiped her face with it. "She outplayed us, Ward."

"Who did?"

"Portia. She wanted her parents to stay together."

"They're not staying together," I said. "Emily loves me. She told me so. She's divorcing Archer and marrying me."

"Oh, kid." She stuffed the bandana in the pocket of Sam's borrowed dungarees and squatted at Dumpling's head again. "Come on. Let's get this over with."

"You are a liar. Everybody knows that about you."

Nina seemed to give my accusation serious consideration before responding. "I'm more of a fibber, actually. When it counts I tell the truth. I'll take the bridle off, okay? You shouldn't have to do that. Then we'll both deal with the saddle." She reached between Dumpling's ears.

"Don't," I said. "Don't you dare touch him."

"Look, I'm sorry you got hurt, Ward," Nina said, straightening up again and pensively wiping her hands on the bandana she'd lifted from me. "I wanted things to work out between the two of you. Honestly I did."

As sometimes happens when you're young and foolish, I wanted nothing more than to lay the blame for my misfortune at somebody else's feet. I'd like to think that I've outgrown that, but of course some people never do. "I don't believe you," I said. "You don't think I'm good enough for her."

She shook her head. "Based on everything I know about him, Ward, you're twice the man that Archer is. I did my best to convince Emily, I promise you. It would have made a sweet story, too, wouldn't it, me talking her around to picking the right guy? Then maybe someday I might do the same thing for myself." Nina shaded her eyes and looked over my shoulder, in the direction of the ranch house. Both of us were tall enough to see over the edge of the wash, and I thought—I hoped—she'd seen Emily riding back to us. But what she was looking at, if she was looking at anything at all, was the afternoon sunlight glinting off the ranch house windows. "Do me a favor, Ward. Tell Max and Margaret I'm not coming back."

Of all the responses I might have come up with, what I said was, "If you leave before next Monday you won't get your divorce."

"So? I'm cashing in my chips, pal. I'm not planning on marrying again between here and the kingdom, so I don't see the point in going through with it anyway. Hugh's the best friend I've ever had. Maybe that's enough." She started savaging her fingernails.

"Stop that," I said.

She shoved her hands deep inside her pockets, cleared her throat once or twice and scuffed a toe in the dirt. "I'm sorry about everything, Ward," she managed finally. "Look, promise me you won't waste your life pining over somebody you can't have, kid. That's a fool's game. If anybody knows that, I do."

She stumbled off across the pitted gopher field then, climbed in her airplane, and took off. The little orange and silver biplane circled overhead a few times, to drive away the buzzards, I thought, until I saw the bright ribbons of a leather pouch fluttering against the white-hot sky.

The scrawled note inside read, *Maybe E's not good enough for YOU.*

I'll admit it was a struggle working Dumpling's tack off by myself. I had to squint while I removed his bridle because his eyes had already started to film over and seeing them without the light in them like to have killed me. Once I got the bridle off I covered his face with a bandana, knotting pebbles into the corners first so it wouldn't blow away.

Getting the saddle off was both easier and harder. I had to sit on the ground and push my boots against Dumpling's withers to roll his carcass up enough to drag the damned thing free. The blanket underneath and the wooly lining of the saddle were still warm and damp from his back. After I finally managed to extricate everything I lay flat in the dust with the saddle in my arms and closed my eyes. *Sic transit Dumpling.* I heard a sort of rustling sound and opened my eyes to a couple of buzzards lit on the brink of the ditch perusing the day's menu. They probably couldn't believe their luck, happening on a banquet featuring two of your fancier meats, horse and human, instead of the usual high-desert offerings of jackrabbit and lizard. I sat up fast and threw rocks at them until they flew away. I knew the carrion fowl were there to do the job nature had designed them for, but that didn't mean I had to like it.

I rested there with my back against Dumpling's until every bit of warmth had left him and it was so dark that the buzzards called it a day. Then I got up, draped the bridle around my neck, gathered the blanket and saddle in my arms, and headed back. I tripped some on the uneven ground and stepped in a hole or two without coming to any harm before I reached the barbed-wire fence. Instead of crawling through it with my burden I walked along it until I found the gate. Left open by Portia, I imagined, when she rode Dumpling through. I was careful to shut it behind me.

Chapter Twenty-four

By the time I made it back to the barn with Dumpling's tack, Archer had driven the Pierce-Arrow to Reno with Emily and Portia at his side. Nina, true to her word, never came back to the ranch at all, flying from the gopher field to the Reno airport, and from there to parts unknown. She did at least call Sam from the airport to let him know she'd send his clothes back, and to ask that her books be shipped to her parents' house in St. Louis. I don't know if either of those things came to pass because I was gone from the Flying Leap myself before the next day was out. That's the end of my story, more or less.

All right, yes. There was a little more. Not much. But some.

It was black dark by the time I got back to the barn. Dinner had long since been served and the dishes washed and put away without any help from me. I went straight to the bunkhouse and fell onto my bed, fully clothed. I felt a hard lump underneath my spine, fished around, and found Nina's revolver tucked under the spread.

I checked the chambers to make sure the gun was empty. Yes.

I slept.

The next morning I forked the last of the old straw out of Dumpling's stall and lay down fresh. Then I washed up and went into the house to help with breakfast. Margaret didn't mention my absence the night before—nobody did—and I didn't bring it up.

After the breakfast dishes had been taken care of I sat on the kitchen stoop watching buzzards' distant spiral over the gopher field. Margaret came out, sat beside me, and put an arm around my shoulder. "I know you loved him," she said. "He was such a good horse."

I didn't trust myself to answer that. "I need to borrow the ranch wagon this morning," I said at last.

"What for?"

"To go into town. I need new boots."

"Finally." Margaret hefted herself to her feet. When she returned she was holding the keys to the Chevrolet and Bottom's battered head. "While you're at it, please do something with this wretched thing. It gives me the heebie-jeebies. Its eyes have been following me around all morning."

"What do you want me to do with it?" I asked.

"Your call," she said. "I trust your judgment." Then, briefly, she rested her hand on my head in a sort of benediction and went back inside to pluck some chickens.

I pocketed the car keys and cradled that abused and abandoned noggin in my arms while I considered what to do with it. I could have taken it back to the college, but I didn't like the idea of trying to explain how I came to have it. Leaving the head on the doorstep of the drama department seemed a sad and undignified choice, particularly since it seemed likely they'd take one look at its sorry state and toss it unceremoniously.

So I decided to put it and me out of our misery. I took Bottom's top out back of the barn and dropped it in the metal barrel we burned trash in. I dug my uncle's letter out of my pocket, read it over a few more times, and then twisted it into a wick to light the funeral pyre. As I watched the papier-mâché go up in smoke I remember thinking that was the beauty of an old-school cremation, getting a visual of the spirit taking flight. I did get a little ease from that small commemoration of Dumpling's passing, and with it also, unexpectedly, my parents'.

After I was sure the fire was completely out I drove into Reno. I didn't have a solid plan laid out. All I knew was that I had to talk to Emily before she got away from me. At the very least I had to know whether Nina had been lying to me, or if I'd been lying to myself.

I lucked upon the Pierce-Arrow parked outside a casino over by the train depot. I realized it was more likely I'd find Archer inside since Emily professed to dislike gambling, but nevertheless I pulled the Chevrolet in alongside the convertible, took a seat on a bench outside the casino, and waited.

Even though it wasn't time for lunch yet, the joint was packed, its frontage of tall glass doors all thrown open to the sidewalk to let the breeze in and the cigarette smoke and noise out. It was quite the racket: shouts of victory and defeat erupting around gaming tables, bells of slot machines binging, the roulette tables whirring as they spun the little balls that bounced and rattled into slots. My patience was paid off when I saw Emily come out of the bank across the street and walk toward the convertible. She was dressed more conservatively than was usual for her, in a way we used to call "Sunday-go-to-meeting," in a peachy outfit I'd never seen before plus high-heeled pumps and a purse tucked in at her elbow.

I stood up and called out, "Ahoy, Em." The words were hardly past my lips when I noticed the envelope she carried, *Ward* written on it in block letters big enough for me to read from where I stood. I knew for certain then that we were done for.

She'd been digging in the purse for her keys. Her head snapped around when she heard my voice. "Oh. It's you," she said. "This is a surprise." She seemed about as happy to see me as she would have been to find a live scorpion curled up on her pillow. She cast a longing look at her automobile and jingled the car keys in her right hand.

"What you got there?" I asked, gesturing at the envelope, not quite ready to surrender yet.

"This?" she said. She hesitated, then held the packet out to me. "I might as well give it to you now. I was going to drop it by the ranch on our way out of town."

I didn't take it. "Where you headed?"

She took a deep breath and then let it go. "San Francisco."

Even though I knew there was no point, I said, sounding like a broken record, "You know, if you leave Nevada now you'll have to start divorce proceedings all over again."

"About that, Ward—" That was as far as she got before I interrupted. Somehow I thought it might hurt less if I came out with it first.

"Let me guess. You're going back to Archer."

She didn't answer, which was an answer.

"You don't think I'm good enough for you," I said. My voice cracking just enough to make me wish the earth under me would do the same and swallow me whole.

She pulled herself together. "I never said that."

"You didn't have to."

After a freighted pause Emily said, "We were just pretending, weren't we? Like actors do in movies."

"I wasn't pretending," I said.

"Sure you were, Ward. Don't kid yourself. You knew it couldn't work. What would happen in ten years, when Portia's your age now, you're the age I am, and I'm just—old?"

"That wouldn't matter," I said. "I'd still love you."

"If you believe that," Emily said, "maybe you are as stupid as you look."

We stared each other down after that, angry, mute, and frozen, for a good long while. We might still be standing there today if a gambler hadn't shouldered between us in his hurry to get into the casino. Emily remembered herself and the envelope then and thrust it at me. I stepped back and raised my hands over my head so I wouldn't have to take it. She reached around me and stuffed the envelope into my back pocket. After that she ran for the Pierce-Arrow, climbed into the driver's seat, and watched me through the windshield while she fumbled the key into the ignition and started the engine. The envelope fell from my pocket and I picked it up. It bulged rectangularly, in a way that could only mean it was full of money.

"Emily," I said. "I don't deserve this."

"Sure you do," she said, and threw the car into gear. "You gave good service. It's your tip." She pressed down on the gas without checking her rearview mirror and very nearly backed into a passing taxi. Then she was gone.

I slumped onto the bench and opened the envelope. A sheaf of hundred-dollar bills, a handful of twenties. Probably about the same fraction of her net worth as the buffalo nickel I'd given the gangly kid at the airport weeks earlier. At the bottom of all that I saw my mother's wedding band. I shoved the cash into my pocket to get it out of the way and shook the ring out onto my palm. There was something off about it. Miss Pam's wedding band had been more rose-gold, like the one you're wearing, whereas this one was a Goldilocks yellow. Though its surface had the tiny nicks and scratches that come with years of wear, same as my mother's, it didn't have the inscription running around its inside: *HSB to PKH, 3/12/12. I'd be lost without you.*

This wasn't Miss Pam's ring.

I'll tell you how I felt about that. I was irate, imagining Emily in such a rush to get away from me and Reno that she confused the ring she'd taken from me with the one Archer had given her.

Back at the ranch I informed Max that I'd just learned my parents were unwell and not expected to recover so I had to leave for Tennessee immediately. A believable white lie in the days before widespread vaccinations, when whole families might be wiped out over the course of a few days by some plague or another. My excuse was not exactly true but true enough. I hadn't known my parents were dead for very long and there wasn't much likelihood of them getting any less dead than they were.

Before I left that afternoon Margaret fixed a sandwich for me to eat on the train. Salami and cheese, my favorite. I must have looked more distressed than grateful when she handed me that waxed-paper bundle, because she took my chin between her thumb and finger for the last time ever. "Oh, honey," she said. "Oh, my boy, my sweetheart, my Ward, I'm so sorry. Good luck to you." Then she kissed me on the forehead and sent me packing.

Sam drove me to Reno. He was headed to Ted Baker's livery stable to engage an understudy for Dumpling until he and Max acquired the gelding's permanent replacement. No animal was in the class with the old boy, of course, but they'd find a pale imitation pretty easily and for very little money. A horse you might have gotten hung for stealing fifty years earlier was all but being given away in 1938.

At the train station Sam got out of the Chevrolet long enough to hug my neck. "I will miss you, friend," he said. "Won't be the same round here without you."

"I expect Max and Margaret will replace me right quick," I said.

"Can't be did," Sam said. "Simply cannot be did."

I never saw Sam again. That man was a prince. An oasis in the desert. Ever since, I've always tried to be as calm and philosophical and as accepting of all comers as my buddy on the ranch. Margaret told me once she and Max had hired Sam not so much for his looks as for the answer he gave when they asked him to list his skills. "Well," he said, "I can fix most anything you got that's broke." If fixing broken things isn't the very definition of doctoring, I don't know what is.

So you see what I mean about me not taking anything for the lessons I learned working at the ranch. I'm not sure I would have amounted to a hill of beans if I hadn't done my time there first.

When I'd arrived in Reno years earlier, I'd toted my few civilian clothes in an old suitcase I'd bought at a thrift store over in Ripley before setting out for my job at the Boulder Dam. The day I left I packed my cowboy duds in that same bag and ditched the thing in the men's room at the train depot. I figured whoever found it would have better use for dungarees than I did. After I left I swore I'd never wear a pair of blue jeans again. Back when everybody and his dog started wearing denim in the 1960s, the nurse who worked in my office, Hannah—yes, Hannah of Hannah and Judy, those tough little girls who rode their pony bareback all over Whistler—had tried to talk me into buying myself a pair. I would have none of that. When she asked what I had against blue jeans I drew myself upright and said, "I hate the way dungarees squeeze all the blood out of my lower half every time I sit down." Yes, yes, it was a joke of sorts. As you can see, with age I went to bone rather than to flesh. The Zeppelin was right about that, you know. Favoring five pounds of potatoes shifting around inside a rumpled ten-pound sack does make a person look older.

At the train depot that day in Reno I removed a few things from the bag before I abandoned it. Margaret's sandwich. My malodorous boots. Nina's gun. My copy of your photograph. I left the sandwich I had no stomach for on a bench in the waiting room where I hoped somebody hungry would find it. The cowboy boots I dropped into a garbage can outside the station where anybody who wanted them could help themselves but at the same time be forewarned about their sad condition. After that I wandered over to the Virginia Street Bridge and threw the revolver into the river, along with the wedding band that wasn't Miss Pam's.

I stood there on the Bridge of Sighs for what felt like a long time after that, staring at my copy of that photograph of yours and feeling like God's own fool. Finally I folded the photo in half, in a way I hoped would separate me cleanly from Emily while leaving Margaret and Sam and Max and Nina in the picture with me. But see how close Emily is snuggled up here? When I tore the thing along the fold my face came away with the wrong half of the photo. So I ripped the whole thing to shreds, tossed it over the railing and watched the pieces bob down that glittering, chuckling stream until they sank and disappeared.

Emily's tip I kept.

Chapter Twenty-five

I arrived in Whistler from Nevada rumpled, exhausted, and heartsick, but despite that I walked straight from the train depot to the cemetery.

At first I was distressed because I couldn't find a headstone with my parents' names on it. Finally it dawned on me that the fresh double mound without an inscribed slab must have belonged to them. I got the confirmation I needed from the little metal marker with a typed label stuck into the ground at its head. Also from a woman roughly Nina's age, planting a rosebush alongside a headstone a few graves away.

"Ward Bennett," she said. "That's you, isn't it? Look how grown up you are! I wouldn't have recognized you if you weren't the spitting image of your sweet father. Tell me, how is school?"

"School?" I asked.

"Aren't you in medical school?"

"Oh," I said. "No. I'm taking a break from school right now."

She brushed her hands on the seat of her britches and held one out to me. "I'm Hannah Gretz. You probably don't remember me. I think you were in the first grade when I was in the fifth. I came down from Memphis for the day—I'm a nurse at St. Joseph's over there now—to plant this bush for Mama. I rooted it from a rose at our old house. The people who bought the place were kind enough to let me take a cutting."

"Your mother died?" I asked. "I'm sorry." I could see that grass had grown over her grave and the mound of it had flattened, so it couldn't have been very recently.

"So am I," she said, her face reddening and her eyes filling a little, as if it had only just happened and she could hardly keep it together. She fanned herself and expelled a puff of breath. "I can't get used to it," she said. "She's been gone awhile now, but I still miss her every day."

I didn't press her for further details. The last thing I wanted was to get both of us tuned up to cry. "How's your sister Judy?" I asked. "Is she still in Whistler?"

Hannah laughed. “Heck, no. Judy couldn’t wait to get out. Ran off to Hollywood to be a movie star.”

“How’s that going for her?” I asked.

“Who knows?” she said. “I haven’t seen her in any movies yet. Have you?”

Somehow I managed not to come apart when Hannah offered me her condolences for my own losses as she walked me to Schaefer’s Funeral Home on her way to the depot to catch her train to Memphis. That’s one of the nice things about small towns that were laid out before the automobile: All the most important places are within shouting distance of each other. Train station to town square, church to pool hall, hospital to cemetery. Many years later, when I moved back to Whistler after my medical residency and Hannah came to work for me, she found us office space just across the street from the hospital, a handy location tucked between a grocery store and the funeral home and just down the street from Whistler’s graveyard. One-stop shopping, we used to say. If a patient died on us, we could borrow a grocery cart from the store and wheel the deceased to the mortuary, thereby saving the family the twenty bucks the ambulance would charge to transport the body half a block.

That day walking back from the cemetery to Schaefer's, Hannah explained that it was normal for a grave to be marked the way my parents' was until the headstone got delivered. It had taken something like six months for her mother's to be carved and placed after she had ordered it. "You'd think the thing was made of gold, it cost so much," she said. "I made payments on it for years. It must have been nice not to have to pay over time for your parents' headstone, like you were buying them a Frigidaire."

She thought the Bennetts were still rich, I realized. I didn't see how this could be possible. "Remind me how long ago you left Whistler?" I asked, as casually as I was able.

"I left before Mama died," she said. "That was, let me see, coming up on six years ago now, so I've been gone for seven. Judy left for California the year before. I should have realized Mama was sick, but I was pretty hot to get out of here myself. I didn't come to visit near as often as I should have. I've had such a hard time letting go of how guilty that makes me feel."

I counted back in my head and realized I'd been at the Boulder Dam by the time Hannah's mother shuffled off the coil. "I was away when your mother died," I said. "Nobody told me."

Hannah shrugged. "Mama didn't exactly run in the same circles your people did. Even though my mother and your mama were related. Third cousins twice removed. My mother's maiden name was Horn."

"I had no idea," I said.

"I bet not," Hannah said. "I believe among the relatives my father was considered a disappointment."

"I wish I'd known we were cousins," I said, even as I admired her mother for resisting the urge to gossip with her about how her snooty third cousin twice removed had fallen on hard times. "Think of all the fun we missed when we were children."

"Think of all the kids we could have kicked the stuffing out of when they were mean to you," she said. "Oh, well."

Mr. Schaefer, the funeral director, explained to me that the metal marker wasn't the placeholder for a slab that hadn't been delivered yet because my uncle hadn't ordered one. "Your parents had just about enough money left to cover either caskets, or a headstone," he said, spreading his hands apologetically. "I couldn't see my way clear to burying them in tow sacks."

I told him that I understood and was prepared to settle whatever outstanding balance remained, and ready to buy a monument. Mr. Schaefer, who knew all about my parents' misfortunes, said, "Will that be on the installment plan?"

I pulled Emily's prodigious wad of cash from my pocket and said, "I can pay in cash."

"Good lord, boy, did you rob a bank?" he asked.

"Something like that," I said.

After our business had been transacted, Mr. Schaefer escorted me out and locked up the funeral home after us. "Don't let your uncle see that bankroll of yours," he said as he pocketed the key, "or like as not he'll figure a way to come between you and it."

"That's not going to happen," I said. "We aren't in touch. If I never lay eyes on him again it will be just fine with me."

"I'm sorry to hear you say that. Judge not lest ye be judged," he said, wagging a finger at me. "That poor soul. Always so worried somebody might be getting a bigger share than he has, so he figures he better grab a double handful of whatever he can, every chance he gets. His kind of empty is a sickness. He deserves our sympathy and forgiveness."

"Not mine," I said.

"Someday maybe you'll come around to it," he said. "He's still your kin."

"Don't remind me," I said. Not out loud. I didn't want to insult Mr. Schaefer for being so good-hearted even as I wished he would keep his opinion of my duty as a nephew to himself.

Before we parted ways Mr. Schaefer asked me what my plans were. I told him I was looking for work. He said he had a friend looking for an assistant at his mortuary in Oxford, Mississippi. Maybe not the kind of work I might be interested in, but if I did happen to be interested he'd be glad to call and put in a word. Next thing you know I was on a train again, headed south. Oxford was just a handful of stops down the line from Memphis.

Mortuary work wasn't such a bad job for someone still harboring the dream of going to medical school. It cured me of any squeamishness I might have had about being around dead bodies and was a crash course in all the timely and untimely ways a person could meet his end. It was also an object lesson in empathy. Occasionally I was called on to attend the funerals of unfortunates who had no one to mourn them. On such occasions I always thought about that Nevada mining ex-millionairess, Eilly Bowers, and wondered what sort of funeral she'd had after she'd died penniless and alone in San Francisco. Who, if anybody, stood by to lament her passing.

I confess I thought about my uncle, too, and wondered what had become of him. He'd written one letter to me in Oxford, having tracked me down via Mr. Schaefer, I supposed. I tore that missive up unread, but a month or so later Uncle Daniel telephoned the funeral home. By chance I was the one who answered. I recognized his voice immediately, so I disguised mine, or tried to, saying, "Ward Bennett doesn't work here anymore," and promptly hanging up. The phone rang again almost right away, and like an idiot I answered it. Uncle Daniel said, "Ward, I—"

He was still talking as I eased the receiver back into the cradle.

While I lived in Oxford I slept in the spare room over the funeral home, a perk the assistant before me had passed on but one I accepted enthusiastically. I liked living among the dead. They didn't ask me a lot of questions about my past or try to set me up with their daughters. Matter of fact, if you ever want to see ladies scatter like cockroaches when you turn on the kitchen light, say you spend your days draining blood and whatnot out of corpses. Another perk of the job, by my way of thinking in those days. I'll tell you something else. There is nothing like cleaning under a body's fingernails to make you appreciate that there is no coming back from death.

Every cent of the prodigious wad of cash I had left when I arrived in Oxford I parked in a bank there. I didn't want to dirty myself up with touching Emily's money, but I'll admit it was a comfort knowing it was there in case I needed it. No, I didn't use the wad to pay for my medical education. After the war the G.I. Bill took care of that. By then I'd lost all interest in going back to Yale. I finished my undergraduate degree at the University of Mississippi, then went on to medical school at the University of Tennessee in Memphis. My residency I did at Charity Hospital in New Orleans.

Ah, you remembered how I said that New Orleans was the last place on earth I'd ever set foot because I did not want to run into my uncle there. Very good. Well, I'll tell you. I began to soften toward Uncle Daniel after my stint at the funeral home, plus the carnage I encountered in the course of the war, followed by my work in the emergency room during medical school. I'd witnessed a lifetime's worth of sad ends close up and had seen many a tear shed over opportunities lost for forgiveness and reconciliation. Like Max used to say about the beautifully tailored suits shot full of holes in gangster movies, it made a person think.

I hadn't heard from Daniel in more than half a dozen years when I accepted that residency in New Orleans. I didn't mean to look for my uncle, not exactly, but if we happened on each other quite by accident, well, so be it. When that didn't happen I took to casually running my finger down page after page of the H's in the telephone directory, looking for *Horn, Daniel,* then invested many dimes in calling every one I came across. I started digging through hospital records, too, on the off chance he'd come in to be treated for pneumonia, to have his appendix removed, or get sewn up after a knife fight. But nothing. Daniel Horn was a ghost.

Turns out I wasn't much of a detective after all. Eventually I started lying awake nights, feeling eaten up with guilt as a nephew and a human being. If I meant to be as good and forgiving as my mentor, Sam, well, I was doing a rotten job of it so far. Steps must be taken, I decided, so I tapped the contents of my tip jar to hire a professional. Within a week the detective had found out what I had not been able to after many months of half-hearted looking. Daniel Horn had died in 1941. His body lay unclaimed in the city morgue before landing in a pauper's grave, location unknown. Like his brother-in-law, my father, he'd taken his own life. Of course I felt bad about that. That poor soul. I'd done more to commemorate a dead horse's passing than I had my own flesh and blood.

Chapter Twenty-six

On the way over today you stopped by my house to have a look? Well, I must say I'm flattered you've taken such an interest in all things Ward Bennett. Yes, it is rather large. The biggest house in Whistler proper, until people started building those sprawling behemoths they call McMansions out on the highway between here and Ripley. Although in fairness I suppose the house Big Howard built was considered a sprawling behemoth when it was new.

You know, when I bought the old place back I stood in the yard with the keys in my hand and let myself have a moment, just a moment, of imagining living there with Emily as man and wife. Filling that place up with children, the way my parents had imagined they would but didn't manage to after having me. Pointless thinking of Emily and me there together, I know. Even if we'd married, I'm sure Emily would have insisted the threshold I carried her across would be hers, up in San Francisco. So you see there was an upside to getting ditched. I'm grateful for the life I've had here in Whistler. It makes me think of that old joke I tell the nurses when they help me get settled in my chair and then ask, "Are you comfortable?" Then I say, "I make a living." Some of them even get the joke. You do? Exactly. Good.

Too bad I didn't know you were stopping by the ancestral manse. I could have given you the keys so you could go inside and look around. Much the way I left it, I suppose. Furniture draped in the dust shrouds, as if a family of ghosts has settled in. Mine. My parents, plus all the unborn grandchildren Miss Pam wanted, babies she could play with to her heart's content but wouldn't have to housebreak. I guess Barrymore the undertaker will get his hands on the old place after all once I'm gone, as I'm the end of the line.

This wedding band I have on? It was Big Howard's. I came across it, still tied up inside an old sock, when I moved my things into my parents' house once I got it back. I never did get married, no. Bad luck, I suppose. Was never in the right place at the right time to meet the person I was meant for. I'd seen too much, was too busy with my career, too set in my ways, too selfish. Take your pick. Whenever Hannah heard one of my lame excuses she'd laugh and say the truth was that Miss Pam had raised me up to think nobody on this earth or in Whistler was good enough for me.

I hope that isn't so, despite evidence to the contrary. Without giving Hannah any particulars about my past, I'd protest I'd been in love twice, maybe three times, and that every time I'd gotten my heart stomped on. "Oh, hush," she'd say. "You've got all your own teeth and hair, you're a doctor and a man. If you wanted to be married, you'd be married. Trouble is, cousin, all you ever wanted was the Romeo-and-Juliet stuff, not the slog of living with somebody day to day. You aren't fooling anybody, claiming you wear your daddy's ring out of fondness. Ha! You wear it the way folks wear garlic necklaces to scare off vampires."

I'm not so sure about that. You see, I'd look at the ring my mother gave my father and, just like Margaret said, think how impossible it would be for me to replicate the bond my parents shared. There's a difference between being choosy, and being afraid to choose. Why risk matrimony if I wasn't sure I was in love and moreover was never lonely? During the Hannah years, my cousin was what you could call my "office wife" and the rest of my staff was my substitute family. I had a steady stream of patients to charm with my famous bedside manner, grateful souls who in return provided me with an endless supply of homemade pies, cakes, jams, and crocheted toilet paper cozies. My housekeeper cooked and cleaned and didn't complain about never seeing me because I was always at the hospital. I was a happy man. Fulfilled in my career. Hannah, meanwhile, no poster child for marital bliss, cycled through three husbands and three acrimonious divorces.

Of course, I'm lonely now.

I missed Hannah something fierce after she retired out to California to live with Judy, who finally resurfaced, not in the movies but teaching high school history at Immaculate Heart, a Catholic girls' school in Los Angeles. Hannah and I talked on the phone for years after that, every Sunday night.

That's right. Hannah had three husbands, no children. Just like Nina O'Malley. Do I know what became of our friend Nina? As a matter of fact, I do.

So. After I found out about my wastrel uncle Daniel's death, I fell to thinking more and more about the goodhearted cowboy family I'd tossed aside so casually by setting my sights on Emily. It took longer than it should have for it to dawn on me that Max and Margaret probably had no idea that I'd betrayed their trust in me. Given that, I couldn't see any downside in trying to get back in touch.

This was after the war and medical school, you understand, ten or fifteen years after I left Reno. First I called the ranch, but the number had been disconnected. I wrote a letter that came back to me marked "no such person at this address." Then I had the bright idea of calling Parker's Western Wear in Reno to ask if they knew what had become of Max and Margaret. Everybody in Reno went to Parker's, so I figured if anybody knew, they would.

"The Flying Leap?" asked the young man who answered the telephone, a person who'd identified himself as "Luke." Indeed I do still recall that fellow's name. I'll tell you why. I'd known every man jack of the staff there back in the day, and when I placed the call I remember thinking I might have a nice chinwag with whoever picked up the phone. No such luck, alas. This Luke I didn't know from Adam. Irrefutable evidence that life had gone on in Reno without me there to sign off on any changes. The little details connected to what hurts your heart are always so much easier to remember, wouldn't you agree?

"Sure, I know The Flying Leap," this Luke said. "Terry Finley raises cattle there."

"You must be confusing it with another ranch," I said. "The Flying Leap is a dude ranch. For divorcing ladies. Or at least it used to be."

"Come to think of it, I knew that," he said. "I was just a kid in those days. Terry bought the place to raise cattle for the war effort after the fellow who was running the dude ranch up and died."

"Max?" I said, suddenly wishing I hadn't called. "Maxwell Gregory died?" How old could Max have been? Fifty? Maybe sixty?

"Gregory, yeah. That sounds right. Had a heart attack. In court, testifying for one of his divorcées. Dead before he hit the floor. It was in the paper, right before the war started up. I'm surprised you didn't hear about it."

"I haven't been to Reno in a long time," I said. "What about Margaret?"

"Margaret?" he asked. "Who's Margaret?"

"His wife," I said. "His widow." As far as I knew they never married, but I didn't know what else to call her.

Luke said, "Hold on." The receiver clattered onto the counter. I heard footsteps receding, voices, and footsteps returning. "Boss thinks she moved back to Chicago." Click. Seems Luke wasn't one for settling in to shoot the breeze.

After stumbling out of that blind alley I got back in touch with the detective. Then realized I didn't know Margaret's last name. I told him to look for a Margaret Gregory, on the off chance she and Max had married at some point, or pretended to; but none of the Margaret Gregorys he found turned out to be mine.

On the upside, the detective did find Sam Vittori. He'd ended up in Southern California again, not dancing in the movies but working in a plant that manufactured airplanes in El Segundo. I called the number the detective provided and listened to his phone ring probably ten times. Just before I gave up on it, Sam answered, sounding winded. He'd been out riding his bicycle, he said, and heard the phone ringing through his door when he got back. "I like to of busted a gut to get to it in time. I would of been pretty broke up to of missed you, son. How are you?" Good old Sam.

"Riding your bicycle?" I asked, then added, as if it were the next logical question, "Are you still in touch with Hugh?"

After a protracted, painful silence he said, "Hugh?"

"Nina O'Malley's husband," I said, awkwardly, wondering if I'd put my foot in it. "Hugh O'Malley?"

"Nina was the O'Malley," Sam said. "She never once changed her name, not for no man. Always held with staying her own self, that one."

"Good for her," I said.

"Nina got me this job here," he continued, tidily sidestepping any further mention of Hugh. "She pulled some strings during the war, told some muckety-muck how I could fix near anything that's broke. Got me pulled out of the trenches and put in the Army Air Corps, rebuilding engines for her crew. God rest her soul."

"God rest her soul?" I remember thinking then, oh no, not Nina too. How could she be dead? Nobody I'd ever met had been more alive than Nina.

"Oh," Sam said. "You ain't heard."

It was as I suspected. Nina had gotten herself killed during the war, in the course of training enlisted men to fly. "That and delivering airplanes was about the only job they figured lady pilots was fit for," he explained. "She was a good teacher, Nina. That know-it-all peckerwood from Boise she was trying to train up walked away from the crash what kilt her. Always figured him at fault, on account of Nina being too good at everything she put her hand to. Except for picking husbands."

Some would call it a sad end but I believe Nina would be the first to disagree. Never had to be old and tottery, which I can tell you now firsthand is no day at the beach.

Forgive me. I got choked up there for a minute. Flashed on the three of us at the beach at Pyramid Lake that afternoon. All this talk has stirred up memories I thought I'd put away for good. Emily and Nina and I—we were so young then. In my mind those two will be, always. That's the upside of never seeing someone you knew in your youth again. They stay forever young.

Where was I? On the phone with Sam. That's right. "Yes," I said. I had to hustle Sam off the phone right quick after that. I choked up then, too, on hearing that Nina was gone. Even after so many years, Sam sounded like he might bust out crying to boot. Both of us loved Nina, yes. I can say that now. Even though we hardly knew her. Still.

Before I rang off I gave Sam my phone number and we exchanged addresses. After we got back in touch we talked now and again, sent each other Christmas cards, birthday greetings. I kept promising I'd go out to visit him in the land of milk and honey, where any old boy like Sam or I could reach out his kitchen window and pluck a lemon right off the tree. Once Hannah had moved out there to live with Judy, there was really no excuse for my not going. But I was always too busy to get away, and then it was too late. Sam went first, then Hannah, and soon afterward, her sister.

No, I never thought to ask Sam if Nina ever married again, or if she got around to sending him his clothes back. I never asked him, either, if he knew what had become of Margaret. That was on purpose. He never mentioned her in anything but the past tense, so I figured she might be dead. If that was so I didn't want to know it.

And no, I didn't ask the detective to track down Emily. I didn't have to. I knew her name, first and last. I knew where she lived. I confess I'd already gone looking for her myself. Did I find her? More or less.

It was about six months after I got home from the war. I couldn't believe I'd made it through in one piece. I might not have, if I hadn't been working as a medic behind the front lines. I was still trying to get over my disappointment with French Emilie, just starting up school again at Ole Miss, and feeling like the world's oldest college sophomore. I confess I'd had a drink or two. I started thinking about Emily Sommer and feeling sentimental. Fell to wondering if Portia, who'd outplayed both me and Nina all those years before, was grown and gone. Up and called the long-distance operator in San Francisco and asked if she had a listing for Archer Sommer. The operator found it for me. Got the exact address out of her while I was at it. What the hell, I figured. I asked the operator to put me through.

A child answered the telephone. Said in this sweet little voice, "Sommer residence." Portia's kid, how about that, I remember thinking. How the generations do roll on. It struck me that it was pretty late for a small child to be answering the telephone, until I realized San Francisco was in a different time zone. "Is Emily home?" I asked.

"Mama? No, she's out to dinner with Papa."

Yes, indeed. I was surprised. When I didn't respond the child said, "My sister is babysitting me."

"Portia?"

"You want to talk to my sister?" he asked.

"No, thank you," I said.

"Okay. You want to hear a joke?"

"Sure," I said, still struggling to process the fact that Emily'd had another baby. "But first tell me what your name is."

The kid said, "My name is Steve. Here's my joke. Do you know the difference between an elephant and an aspirin?"

I heard a rush of footsteps then, and a young woman's voice said, "There you are, Stevie! You're supposed to be in bed. Who are you talking to?"

"Some man," Stevie said.

I heard a rustling sound then, Portia wrestling the receiver from the kid. "Hello?" she said. "Hello?"

Of course I didn't say anything. I hung up. And no, I never called again, although I do believe I still have Emily's address and telephone number on a slip of paper in my wallet. I can't tell you for sure about that since I can't remember the last time I put my wallet in my pocket. I never go anyplace where I would need it, you see.

I do not harbor any resentment toward Emily. No, not anymore.

Sure, for a few years I thought I hated her for the way she let me go. Treated me like a servant she was sick of fooling with. Paid me off and sent me packing. For a good long while I brooded about it more than I should have. Kept picking apart my memories of her, replaying the snooty comments she made now and again. Her assessment, for example, of Mary Louise. "Very pretty, but really nothing special." Harsh, yes, indeed, and unfair. Mary Louise didn't have the firmest grasp on history or geography, but she was unfailingly good-natured and a hell of a dancer, which is more than you can say for lots of folks.

But so much happened after I left Nevada that my anger eventually petered out. I believe I let go of the last of it when I donated what was left in my tip jar to a scholarship program for needy premedical students at

Ole Miss. After Emily's money was gone I have never felt so free. With time I even came around to feeling grateful that woman cut me loose. If we'd married, I might not have bothered with medical school or, heck, even finished college. I might have ended up just another orangutan in a tuxedo, driving around San Francisco in a limousine my rich wife gave me for my birthday. If Emily had fallen into the habit of jettisoning husbands who didn't suit her, I could have ended up her second husband of six. A leathery fake cowboy sitting at the end of some bar in Reno, on the lookout for my next millionairess.

So that's my story. I hope some of it is useful. It has been an honor and a pleasure talking to you. Good luck with your book. No, no, I'm not trying to run you off, but I don't want to keep you. There's probably someplace else you need to be.

Sure, I'd be delighted to take a look at a couple of other interesting things you dug up. It's not like I have any pressing appointments I need to get to. I hope you don't mind me saying this, but you remind of myself when I was younger. Willing to stop and chat with all the lonely old coots living in this very nursing home. It was no trouble for me whatsoever when I was still practicing, dropping by after I'd finished my rounds. I didn't have a family to rush home to like the other doctors did. Most of the inmates here were ladies, so laying the charm on them was almost like the old days back in Reno. They loved having somebody to listen to their stories, and I never minded hearing the same ones repeated a few dozen times over. That's how fairy tales got passed down through the generations before they were written, isn't it? Also Homer's *Odyssey* and what have you. Oral tradition, they call that. If those ladies' same old stories don't get told and retold, like as not they'd be forgotten.

Let's see what you've got there. A letter? Sure, I can read it for myself, if you hand me my glass. What do you know? This looks like Emily's handwriting.

Because it is? I see.

Dearest Steve—

Oh. This Steve, is it that Steve? The Stevie I talked to as a little boy? You got the photograph from him. Ah.

Dearest Steve, If you are reading this, I am dead.

No, no, I'm fine. Like I said, I figured Emily was more than likely gone now, since she had a decade on me. Not that I really minded the difference in our ages, but she couldn't seem to let that go. Women tend to outlive men, generally speaking. That's why this nursing home, like most, is chockablock with widows. Also why I always congratulated the wisdom of my female patients who married younger husbands, although of course I was prejudiced on that count. Now, where was I?

If you are reading this, I am dead.

It's almost funny, isn't it, Emily reaching out from beyond the grave to have a final word with her son. Some women find out they don't care much for motherhood, but others seem to live for nothing else. So I'm not a bit surprised Emily would have a hard time letting go. I'm happy for her, really I am. Not for being dead, of course, but for managing to have another child. I know how she wanted that. When did she pass? Uh huh. Long enough ago for her headstone to be carved, not long enough for grass to roll a blanket over her grave.

I would have liked to see her one more time, if only from afar. In fact, the last big trip I took was to San Francisco. Oh, years ago now. I confess I sat on a bench across the way from the townhouse at the address Directory Assistance gave me for a good long while, wondering if that was the same house Emily had grown up in, curious if we'd recognize each other anymore if she happened to walk out its front door. Nope, nobody, not a soul, not while I sat there. It was a nice old place, carefully maintained, fancy neighborhood, killer views of the bay. Yes, I remember the address. Yes, that's the very one. You've seen it, have you? I agree. It's not any bigger than mine here in Whistler, but like the real estate agents say, *location location location.*

Yes, yes, I'll finish reading the letter. You're right. I am stalling. I'm not sure I'm ready yet to know how Emily's story ended. But also of course I can hardly wait.

You are a wonderful, loving, thoughtful boy and I am so lucky and so proud to be your mother. I know Archer felt the same way about you, dear, every day of his life.

Are my hands shaking? Well, I'm not surprised. You had me going there for a minute. Nothing, nothing. Forget about it. I'll keep reading. Tell me how you know Steve? All right, fine. Have it your way. I'll hold my questions to the end.

But one more before I go on. Have you met Portia, too? She must be up in her sixties now. Hard to imagine her as anything but a kid. A stockbroker, you say, in San Francisco. She must have had a hard row to hoe, breaking into that line of work as a woman. I don't doubt she's good at it. Even at thirteen she knew how to hold her cards close to her chest, that one, which I imagine is a useful talent when you're trading stocks. Did she marry? No, I don't doubt she had plenty of offers but I can see how she might not be interested after having a front-row seat to her parent's marriage. I only ask because it strikes me how much Emily would have enjoyed having grandchildren. Stevie had kids? Well, that's nice. I wouldn't have minded having grandchildren myself. Too bad I skipped that necessary intermediate step, having children.

I'd like to take all the credit for you turning out to be the sort of man you've become, but in fairness I should share credit for that with your father.

The older we get, the more good we can see in people. That is a fact. Even a cheating, patronizing mooch like Archer. He's passed, too? Please forgive me. It's impolite to speak ill of the dead, even when they deserve it.

I don't know how to say this, other than to come right out and say it. You don't look a thing like Archer, but you do look very much like a young man I loved once.

Oh.

As you grew up I saw that sweet man's face in yours more and more. His name—

No, I'm quite all right. No, don't ring the nurse. I'm fine. I have no intention of keeling over now. No, I don't want you to read the rest of it for me. Better I see this with my own eyes.

His name was Howard Stovall Bennett III. Ward. He gave me the wedding band I wore all your life.

Archer and I were on the road to divorce when I met him. Ward and I planned to marry, but in the end I decided, for your sister's sake, I had to stay with Archer. He never seemed to notice I had on a different ring. Imagine. But of course you can imagine. You know how he was. Not one for noticing much of anything that wasn't Archer.

She wore it all those years. Well, well. What do you know.

To be honest, I stole that ring from Ward. It had been his mother's, so it was selfish of me to do that. But I wanted to carry something of him with me always, little suspecting when I left that I was carrying something even more precious. You.

Yes, a glass of water would be appreciated. Thank you.

I hope you can forgive me for keeping this from you, Steve. Now that everyone this information would hurt is dead, I think it only fair you should know.

Does Portia know this? Ah, sending you to look for me was *her* idea. To find me, not just for her brother's sake, but so she could make amends. She suspected all along, you say? Steve came down the chute with that cleft in his little chin. Of course. The Bennett genes are strong.

If you decide to look for Ward and find him still alive, please return his ring. And tell him, too, how sorry I am for the way I ended things. I did what I had to, even though it broke my heart. I thought if Ward hated me it might be easier for him to get over loving me, if in fact he did.

Turns out Emily was quite the actress, after all. She sure had me fooled.

Did I in fact love her? That is the question, isn't it? The truth is, I don't know. For years, decades even, I had myself convinced I did. Probably stood in the way of my pursuing likely ladies around here, though a fair number, I'll admit, chased after me when I was younger, little suspecting I was the kind of man who sat around in my underwear eating ice cream straight from the carton. Imagine the women I might have disappointed if any one or one after another of them had caught me.

There really is no predicting whether the person you marry will be a keeper, is there? Many of the rich ladies at the ranch said they didn't see the point of husbands, anyway, aside from providing children. If you weren't adept at choosing a mate, or lucky, one infidel was probably as good as another. That cuts both ways, of course. No guaranteeing anybody, male or female, will pick the ideal person to share their lives with. So why try?

Yes, you're right, I chickened out. Chose to surround myself with people who made me happy, who I could just as easily abandon at any moment. I stumbled into an excellent ersatz family, at the Flying Leap. Did my best to recreate that back home, here in Whistler. Got comfortable. Made a living. Bought back the ancestral home. For all the good it did me. Do you know, the day before I moved into this facility I stopped by the funeral home to order my headstone and pay for my funeral in advance. Not so much that I thought I was good as dead. No. I knew I might live another twenty years. It was more a come-to-Jesus moment. If I didn't have folks to take care of me in my senescence, it made sense that there would be no one to make my final arrangements. I wouldn't end up in an unmarked grave like my poor uncle, but—

But now you're telling me that I have not just a son, but grandchildren. Descendants to pass my house and all my stories down to. I confess I'd hoped, ever since that phone call—the little boy—the elephant and the aspirin—Steve—

That Portia cooked up the idea of sending someone here armed with a tape recorder? To spare my son's feelings, in case I turned out to be some cantankerous old fool not interested in acknowledging his own flesh and blood. That way at the very least Steve would get to know me, at least a little.

So before you set out on this thrilling adventure, Portia slipped Miss Pam's ring on your finger. With your father's blessings. Steve's.

Yes, please. Oh yes. Please. Let's call your father. We have a lot of catching up to do. Let's call my son. Let's call Steve.

Acknowledgments

Though I've never lived in Nevada, my father did for some unknown amount of time during the 1930s while working as a make-believe cowboy on a dude ranch that catered to the divorce trade. I know few facts about his sojourn there—once I was old enough to be genuinely interested (as in, middle-aged), it was too late to ask him about it. There were a couple of funny stories he used to tell when I was younger, one in particular about a fancy new car given to him by a woman who had taken a particular shine to him. After my father, who wouldn't be my father for another twenty years yet, drove the car home to Tennessee to show it off, his mother told him to turn right around and return it, saying, "We are not the sort of people who accept automobiles as gifts from rich old ladies."

I grew up on a farm with horses, a few cows, and upwards of twenty cats at any one time, so I know a thing or two about what living on a farm is like. Not a ranch, I'll grant you, but I extrapolated. While researching this book, I spent a week in Reno to get a sense, however limited, of the lay of the land. Every day I went to the Nevada Historical Society to dig through their files to see if I could find any mention of my father's time there. The staff could not have been more welcoming or delighted by my project. Everybody pitched in, particularly Carole Clough and Michael Moore, to help me find any mention of my father. Alas, nothing. I did gather valuable material, though, as well as a hot tip about Newspapers.com, where I could read Reno newspapers of the era on my computer back here in Los Angeles until the cows came home. Which I did. All an enormous help to me in the shaping of my story, sprung of fact but entirely fictional. My narrator, it should be noted, too, has almost nothing in common with my father other than an overabundance of charm and good looks, and being born in a small town in West Tennessee. Whistler, like my narrator, is also entirely fictional, though in my mind located in the same neck of the woods.

I also read every book I could get my hands on about Reno that touched on the divorce industry there.

Three were particularly helpful: *The Genesis of Reno: The History of the Riverside Hotel and the Virginia Street Bridge* (University of Nevada Press) by Jack Harpster; *Reno's Big Gamble: Image and Reputation in the Biggest Little City* (University Press of Kansas) by Alicia Barber; and finally, *Is Marriage Necessary: Memoirs of a Reno Judge* (Kessinger Legacy Reprints) by George A. Bartlett. Judge Bartlett's book was the source of two things I cherish that pop up in my narrative: He relayed the story of a divorcée who wanted to shed her husband because, she said, he was "an infidel." A cheater, in other words, guilty of infidelity. Also, as Judge Bartlett finalized each divorce, he pounded his gavel and declared, "Better luck next time." I am also grateful to Daniel Rosta of Sundance Books in Reno, who I met while I was in town doing research and has since been kind enough to answer random questions about things like the quality of the sky there on a hot summer afternoon.

I should also thank my mother, a beloved small-town physician, one whose patients wept and rent their clothing when she finally retired. She was from Savannah, Tennessee, and graduated from the University of Tennessee undergraduate and then, sometime in the 1950s, their medical school, in a class that included many men who, like my father, had served in World War II.

That's why I decided my male narrator should be molded by similar experiences. Even though my mother never served in that war in any capacity—she was still in high school—everything I know about doctors and doctoring and the milk of human kindness I learned from her.

I'm indebted also to a documentary I saw just as I was setting out to write this book: *Obit. Life on Deadline*, about the obituary writers of the *New York Times.* Part of that job is anticipating what noteworthy personages might kick off in the near future and then writing a largely complete piece about them to have on hand when that life reached its end. Such guesswork sometimes resulted in pre-mixed obits languishing in their files for many years. The one on file the longest when the documentary was made had been written up for Elinor Smith, a teenaged aviatrix who in 1928 flew her airplane under all four bridges spanning the East River in Manhattan. Though she seemed a likely candidate for an early demise, Ms. Smith lived to be ninety-nine years old. So of course, *of course,* I had to read her memoir, *Aviatrix* (Thorndike Press), which led to those of many, many others and an obsession with the women who, like my mother, were some of the best in a field largely dominated by men. The books that were the most helpful to me in creating my aviatrix, Nina, were two memoirs, the terrific *West with the Night*

(Open Road Media) by Beryl Markham—one of the best books I've ever read, one I somehow hadn't gotten to before—and *The Spirit of St. Louis* (Scribner) by Charles Lindbergh. Also a much more recent work of nonfiction, *Fly Girls: How Five Daring Women Defied All Odds and Made Aviation History* (Houghton Mifflin Harcourt) by Keith O'Brien.

I'd also like to thank friend of my youth and author James Ledbetter for allowing me to co-opt something so memorably funny he said to me thirty years ago that I still think about often, vis-à-vis the need for a little sleight of hand to keep the magic of romance alive. Ditto all the booksellers and fellow novelists and nice people I knew well or hardly knew at all who put me up in their lovely homes or had parties for me when I traveled across the country in the course of promoting my first novel. Making friends this way is one of the best perks of being published that nobody thinks to tell you about before you discover it for yourself. I am deeply indebted to every one of them whose period-appropriate names I lifted for characters in this book. Once again I'd like to thank my incredibly patient friend Sara Kenney for diligently reading every page of this novel as I wrote it—all three versions. It's due to the persistence and insight of my brilliant editor Kate Nintzel that the third time proved the charm and my story finally came together. Without my delightful agent Lisa Bankoff no book of mine would have made it to publication. Finally, I'll always be thankful for my daughter for proving that the delicious little girl she always was would someday grow into an even more delightful adult once she made it past that rough patch we all went through when she was thirteen. My readers who are parents know exactly what I mean by that.